MISQUOTED & DEMOTED

AN AVERY SHAW MYSTERY BOOK SIX

AMANDA M. LEE

WINCHESTERSHAW PUBLICATIONS

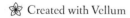 Created with Vellum

Run!

       Kelsey Cooper pumped her short legs as hard as she could, mentally urging herself on. The football field was dark and empty, the artificial turf slippery from the rain earlier in the evening. Her running shoes kept sliding and she knew that if she lost her balance and went down it would all be over.

She willed herself, begging for more speed from her legs, more air in her burning lungs.

Kelsey scanned the tree line in front of her. She knew what was on the other side: a fence. And on the other side of that fence was the highway. It was her only hope.

It wasn't that late. How could no one be outside? How could no one hear her scream? How could the school have been empty? How could she have gotten herself into this? She'd been warned, but she hadn't believed the warnings. That was on her. She believed now. Of course, it was too late now. She knew that, and yet she still ran.

She didn't have hope, yet she couldn't surrender. She knew what was coming if she fell or collapsed, out of energy.

Kelsey risked a glance over her shoulder, the sweat dripping into her eyes and burning. She didn't see anyone on the field, and risked slowing her pace to catch her breath.

Kelsey knew she wasn't alone, but had no idea where her pursuer was. He couldn't give up either. If he did, she would tell. He knew that. If he wanted to survive he had to catch her. If she wanted to survive, she had to outrun him. His odds were much better.

Still, the rules of survival were simple. So Kelsey began to run again.

She was almost at the tree line when a shadowy figure came out of the dark, cutting off her one avenue of escape. Kelsey recognized his shape before the bright moon revealed his features.

"There's nowhere else to go."

Kelsey heard footsteps behind her. She didn't have to turn to know who was there. Of course he wasn't alone. Why would he be? He wasn't the only one in danger.

"I won't tell," Kelsey said, her lie sounding hollow between her gasps for air, even to her own ears.

"Of course you will," the man said. "You all tell. You can't help yourselves."

"I promise," Kelsey said, desperate and pleading. "I'll never tell anyone ... just let me go. I swear to God I won't tell."

The man advanced. "No, you won't."

"**Y**ou have got to be kidding me!"

Ever unflappable, my editor Fred Fish regarded me with somber eyes. "Do I look like I'm kidding?"

"You never look like you're kidding," I charged. "Even when you wear more jewelry than an eighties porn star, you still look deadly serious. I'm hoping this is just some elaborate ruse to mess with me."

"Because I often do that," Fish said, his chest heaving as he braced himself for my verbal onslaught.

"Well, I don't believe you." I crossed my arms over my new Jason Voorhees T-shirt, wishing I'd opted for something a little more dignified to wear on the day of my professional disgrace. I should have worn my new "That's what she said" Darth Vader shirt. That would have made everything better. What? He's pointing at Princess Leia. It's hilarious. *Star Wars* makes everything better. I shot myself in the foot by wearing a serial killer shirt. I was just asking for it. Wait, what was I just talking about?

"That doesn't surprise me," Fish said. "You have a penchant for hearing only what you want to hear."

That's completely untrue. Okay, it's totally true. Still ... . "Well, I need you to say it again. I'm not going to believe it unless you tell me again."

"You're being transferred to sports," Fish said, not missing a beat.

"No!"

"Yes."

"No," I said, my blonde hair brushing against my shoulders as I shook my head. "I'm the best reporter you have. You don't bust your best reporter down to ... sports." I wrinkled my nose. "Only someone crazy would do that."

"I'll relay your message to the publisher," Fish said, making a show of focusing on his computer screen. "I'm sure he'll be thrilled with your ... assessment ... of the situation."

"I knew I was going to hate that guy," I mumbled, rubbing my forehead to stave off the beginnings of what was sure to be a monster headache. "You can just tell by looking at him."

"You can tell what?" Fish asked.

"He's clearly deranged," I replied. "Only a deranged individual would deprive you of the services of the best reporter in the county."

"So, you've elevated yourself from the best reporter at the newspaper to the best reporter in the county in less than five minutes? And all on your own?" Fish asked.

"I didn't elevate myself," I shot back. "That's just common knowledge." Sheesh.

"I love your sense of humility," Fish said. "It really is your greatest virtue."

I know sarcasm when I hear it – mostly because it's usually dripping from my own tongue. "My greatest virtue is my work ethic."

Fish sighed. "In the hope of saving time, and a little dignity for yourself, why don't we take this conversation into the conference room?"

"I don't care who hears us," I sniffed, shooting a challenging look across the row of desks.

"Yes, but I do," Fish said. "Give me five minutes. We have a few things to ... discuss."

I opened my mouth to argue, but Fish cut me off with the shake of his snowy head. "Five minutes."

I swiveled, my mind busy as I tried to figure a way out of this. I couldn't.

Hello, my name is Avery Shaw, and five minutes ago I went from reporting genius to sports reporter. Look out world, because I'm pissed.

"OKAY, here's the situation," Fish said, sitting in the chair next to me and patting me on the arm in a show of solace. "You're in a lot of trouble."

I wanted to rip his hand off and slap him with it. "I didn't do anything."

"Well, Jim MacDonald doesn't see it that way."

I made a face. Jim MacDonald was our new publisher at The Monitor, a mid-sized daily newspaper in Macomb County, Michigan. He was some bigwig from Chicago, and he was supposed to be able to broach the ever-tricky breech between digital and print media. He was introduced to us as our "saving grace." I wanted him to fall from his lofty perch and hit every tree branch (in his special place) on his way down. The good news is that anyone who is a publisher is in one of those high-turnover positions no one ever gets comfortable in for more than a year. The bad news is that a publisher can do a lot of damage in a short amount of time. MacDonald was in damage mode.

"What's his problem?"

Fish shrugged. "It seems that Commissioner Ludington stopped into his office for a special meeting."

I rolled my eyes. In addition to being a total douche, Tad Ludington was my former college boyfriend. He'd dumped me because I was volatile, a quality he felt less than desirable for a politician's wife. He was right on both counts, and when I found he'd been elected to a position on Macomb County's Board of Commissioners I'd made it my mission to help him at every turn. Okay, I'd really made it my mission to embarrass him at every turn, but those are basically the same goals. What? They are. "And what was Tad complaining about?"

"He says that you were eavesdropping at a commission meeting last week and you printed an article that isn't true," Fish said.

I wracked my brain and pasted my best "I'm innocent" look onto my face. "What story?"

"Oh, don't do that," Fish chided. "You know exactly what story I'm talking about. You broke it, and every other news outlet in the area picked it up. He was under siege for days ... until that cop accidentally discharged his gun while he was in the shower with his wife and his mistress at the same time."

I smirked. I'd broken that story, too. You have no idea how many premature ejaculation jokes can be generated from a simple sexual mishap involving a police officer, a gun and two hair-pulling women. I shook my head, forcing myself from my reverie. "You must be talking about how Tad wants to take all of the county funds from the black community centers and funnel them into the white community centers."

"He says that's not true."

"I heard him," I shot back. "He said those kids at the Mount Clemens center are nothing but thugs and drug dealers, while the kids out in Shelby Township are good souls who just need guidance. It's not my fault that the kids losing the money happen to be black and the kids getting the money are white."

"Well, Tad says you made that part up."

"Oh, no," I said. "I have the enrollment numbers for both centers. I checked every single kid."

"That doesn't prove it was racist," Fish said.

"I didn't say it was racist," I said. "I just had our photographer take a shot of those sad little faces at the Mount Clemens center. It's not my fault only black kids happened to be there that day."

"I don't disagree with what you did," Fish said.

"Well, then why didn't you argue against this?"

"I did," Fish said. "MacDonald has a file on you. It was hard to argue with everything in it. After the first thirty items, it started to feel fruitless."

"What's in it?"

"Well, you've made a lot of enemies," Fish hedged.

"That's because I'm good at my job."

"You also like pissing people off," Fish said, holding up his hand to still me. "Don't deny it. You like it. You enjoy getting under people's skin. While I find it mildly entertaining, others don't find it so ... cute. MacDonald is one of those people. His file is extensive."

"You still haven't told me what's in the file," I pressed.

"In addition to about twenty complaints from Ludington, there are a handful of complaints from other politicians," Fish said. "Most of those are just sour grapes. It's the complaints from Brick and Duncan that MacDonald is fixated on."

I pressed my tongue into my cheek, considering. "Brick and Duncan are tools."

"They are," Fish agreed. "They're also tools who like to file complaints."

"It's not my fault they're so sensitive."

"You like to mess with them."

"They make it so easy, though," I protested.

"You posted outtakes from Duncan's Civil War reenactment video on the NAACP's website with the caption 'war is great' and then invited comments."

"There's no proof that was me," I said.

"You signed Brick up for newsletters from the National Organization for Women and PETA."

"I thought he would be interested in the content."

"He hunts."

"Animals have feelings, too."

"He believes a woman's place is in the home," Fish said.

"Enlightenment comes in many forms."

"You like to agitate them," Fish said. "I get it. I can't encourage it, because I'm your boss, but I get it."

"That still doesn't mean I should be busted down to sports," I argued. "This is totally unfair."

"Life isn't fair, Avery."

"How long is this exile supposed to last?"

"Until you've proved you can get along with others," Fish said. "Or, until I've proved to MacDonald that we need you on news side. I'm fairly certain the former is impossible, so we're going to have to rely on the latter."

I was pretty sure I'd just been insulted. "I can get along with others."

"Since when?"

"Since ... I get along fine with Marvin," I said, reminding Fish that I was the only one who could rein in the other persnickety reporter at the newspaper. "I deserve an award for that."

"You told the pastor at St. Peter's Catholic Church that the religion reporter thought abortion was the best method of population control," Fish said.

"That priest was making me nervous," I said. "He kept trying to talk to me. He was rambling on and on about chastity."

"And you thought that was the best way to handle it?"

"At the time? Yes."

Fish pursed his lips. "When the governor came in for a meeting, you told him that the political reporter had a sticker supporting his opponent on his car."

"That was true."

"You put the sticker there."

Oh, right, I had forgotten that little tidbit. "Those are isolated incidents."

"You told the page designer that your stories were to be given top priority when laying out the front page," Fish said. "When he got in trouble, you denied saying it."

Hey, I'm not falling on a grenade for anyone. It was his fault for believing me in the first place. "That was a joke."

"Your joke just happened to push the article on Ludington giving gifts to the needy below the fold," Fish said. "He thinks that was on purpose."

"And, we're back to Tad," I grumbled.

"Tad is the one who brought your antics to MacDonald's attention," Fish said. "You have to remember, all this man knows about you is that the first day he came to work there was a contingent of sheriff's deputies in our parking lot. The sheriff had been shot – trying to protect you – and the window to his office was broken. Marvin was hiding in the photography department, and we were the subject of news reports all across the state."

"Hey, that's free publicity."

Fish ignored me. "Then, when he delved deeper, he found that you had managed to get yourself involved in no less than five big stories. You've been stalked. You've been shot at. You've been kidnapped ... twice. You've been threatened with cars and knives. Heck, you've been physically threatened by nuns."

"That wasn't my fault! I just told them that God wouldn't have invented vibrators if they weren't meant to be used."

"You've done this to yourself, Avery," Fish said. "Now you have to make the best of it."

"Well, maybe I'll just quit," I threatened.

"If you feel that's necessary, then you have to do it," Fish said. "Just be forewarned, I think that's what MacDonald wants. You have to do what's best for you."

I knew what he was doing. He was trying to force my hand. He knew I didn't like to lose. Ever. No, I'm not joking. When I played Twister as a child, I turned it into a blood sport. Fish didn't want me to quit, and he was trying to get my hackles up. Well, that wasn't going to work this time. I slammed my hands down on the table.

"Over my dead body am I going to quit and let him win!"

Fish smiled. "I think your career in sports is going to be ... the stuff of legend."

He had no idea.

"Hello, Trouble. How was your day today?"

The sight of a hot man cooking dinner in my house should have filled me with joy. Given my day, it filled me with unexplained agitation. "It sucked balls. How was your day?"

Eliot Kane had been my boyfriend for almost six months now. He was used to my moods ... and whimsy. He raised an eyebrow as he regarded me, pausing to look me up and down while he clutched the spatula. "Do you want to expound on that?"

I dropped my purse onto my small kitchen table and viciously kicked my new Vans *Star Wars* shoes into the corner of the kitchen. "Well, most men have balls. Two of them. Unless they're newspaper publishers, that is. My day was the equivalent of sucking hundreds of them."

Eliot's face was unreadable. "I understand about sucking balls – and you better not have been actually doing that. I was wondering if you wanted to explain what's wrong. If you're not there yet, continue with your ball-sucking rant. I enjoy listening to you exercise your vocabulary on vulgar topics. It's a quirk of mine."

"Great. Thanks."

"Wow," Eliot said. "Someone is in a mood."

"That's because I've been relegated to hell."

Eliot turned the flame down under the spaghetti sauce as he stirred. "I'm going to need more information."

Eliot Kane is many things. He's hot. Okay, he's unbelievably hot. His shoulder-length brown hair is sexy, without making him look like he should be collecting ride tickets at a carnival. His body looks as though it was chiseled by a Greek sculptor, and his patience is longer than the line at a *Star Trek* booth at a comic-book convention. He's perfect. I still want to pop his head like a zit sometimes, though.

"I've been transferred to sports," I announced.

"Oh, cool," Eliot said. "Do you get to cover the Red Wings?"

He was clearly missing the point. "I'm no longer a news reporter."

Eliot shrugged. "That should mean you won't be in mortal danger for the foreseeable future," he said. "That's a win for me."

Since Eliot had bailed me out of a jam or two – or ten – I understood where he was coming from. I still wanted to kick him. "I'm now a sports reporter."

"I heard you," Eliot said. "What sport are you covering? The Lions are done for the season. The Pistons suck. The Red Wings are decent, though."

How could he not be getting this? "Not professional sports," I said, gritting my teeth. "High school sports."

Eliot absorbed the information. "Oh, well, that sounds like fun, too. Who doesn't love sports? You like sports."

He was trying to kill me. I just know it. "Am I speaking English?"

"Yes."

"Do you understand English?"

"Yes."

"Then why aren't you comprehending what I'm saying?"

Eliot sighed. "Okay, why were you transferred to sports?"

I told him the story. He wasn't nearly as ticked off as he should have been.

"You were threatened by nuns?" His smile was far too broad.

"That's the part of the story you're fixated on?"

"I just hadn't heard that story before," Eliot said. "Sorry."

"You should be," I grumbled, dropping dramatically down onto one of the kitchen chairs.

Eliot rubbed his forehead. "I'm not sure what you want me to say."

"I don't want you to say anything," I said. "I thought you would be naturally outraged on my behalf."

"And why are you outraged?"

"I'm a news reporter."

"Who has managed to piss off half the state of Michigan," Eliot said. "This was bound to happen. Come on, you have to have gotten into trouble before. This can't be a new thing."

"I'm good at my job," I said.

"Which means you've gotten away with murder for years, and you just assumed that would continue," Eliot supplied.

"I have not gotten away with murder."

"I've known you for a year," he said. "I let you get away with murder. I can't be the only one."

"You don't let me get away with murder."

"I rubbed your shoulders for an hour last night because you told me that carpal tunnel syndrome can travel to your back," Eliot said. "I knew it wasn't true, but you were so cute when you were telling the lie, I couldn't resist."

"It's not a lie," I protested. "And, just for the record, I haven't been proven wrong on that."

Eliot pressed his lips together, remaining mute.

"And that massage had a happy ending – for both of us – if I remember right," I added.

"That's the other reason I rubbed you without complaint," Eliot said.

"Everyone is against me." I rested my head on the table, depression overtaking me. "No one is on my side."

"I am your side, baby," Eliot said. "I'm always on your side."

"You don't seem to be on my side."

"A little less than a month ago, you were stalked by a crazy madman and almost stabbed," Eliot said. "A few weeks before that, a crazy freeway shooter decided she wanted to kill you. A few months before that, a murderous freak who chopped his wife up and used his kids' sled to disperse her body parts in the woods kidnapped you."

"Are you just talking to hear yourself talk?"

Eliot inhaled deeply, clearly trying to keep his temper in check. "I know you feel this is a personal attack on you."

"Because it is."

"You're safer in sports."

"Maybe I don't want to be safe."

"Oh, I know that," Eliot said. "For me, though, the idea of you watching high school basketball and eating dried out hot dogs is a lot more appealing than worrying about someone trying to shoot you."

"That happened once."

Eliot arched an eyebrow.

"Okay, twice."

Eliot waited.

"Fine, it happens all the time," I conceded, irritation flooding through me. "I don't want to be a sports reporter."

Eliot turned back to the stove. "Then quit."

"No, that's what MacDonald wants," I said. "I'm not giving him what he wants."

"Who is MacDonald?"

"Our new publisher."

Eliot wrinkled his nose, clearly trying to place the name. "The guy who started at the newspaper the day after Jake was shot?"

I shifted uncomfortably. Sheriff Jake Farrell had raced to the newspaper to save me from a homicidal maniac a month before. We had a long history, one that included dating as teenagers. He and Eliot had a long history, too, one that culminated in a falling out while serving together in Special Forces. They'd made up – kind of – but they were still a little competitive where I was concerned. In the moments after the shooting, when his life was draining out through a gunshot wound, Jake had admitted he loved me. I hadn't responded, and I hadn't told Eliot everything that happened that night. I was still in denial, and I had no inclination to leave. "Yes, that guy."

"He doesn't blame you for that, does he?" Eliot was finally coming around.

"Yes."

Eliot frowned. "So, basically you're telling me that this guy believes Ludington and blames you for being stalked?"

"Yes."

"He's an ass."

"Finally," I said, jumping to my feet and throwing my arms around Eliot's neck. "You are on my side."

Eliot pressed me close as he brushed a kiss against my forehead. "I'm always on your side."

I snuggled in closer. "I'm sad."

"I know you are," Eliot said, rubbing my back. "You have a choice to make, though. Either you accept your punishment and work your way back to news, or you quit. I'm behind you either way."

"I can't quit," I said.

"Are you only saying that because you don't want to lose?"

"Does that make me a bad person?"

Eliot cupped the back of my head and tilted my face up so his brown eyes could meet my blue ones. "You're my favorite person." He kissed me. "You're also a really bad loser."

"Oh, I'm not going to lose."

Eliot smiled. "See, you're already feeling better."

I kissed his chin. "I'm going to feel a lot better when you massage me after dinner."

"I have to massage you again?"

"You don't have to," I countered. "You get to. There's a difference."

"What's the difference?"

"I'm going to need cheering up all night tonight," I said. "Since

I'm going to work nights now, you're going to have to get your money's worth."

"Wait, you didn't say you were going to have to work nights," he cried.

"That's when sports are played."

Eliot cleared his throat. "Okay. I'm going to feed you, and then I'm going to rub you. After that, though, we're going to do some brainstorming. We need to get you bumped back over to news."

"Oh, sure," I said. "Once your sex life is threatened, then you're on my team."

Eliot patted my rear affectionately. "We're going to the playoffs, baby."

"OH, RIGHT there."

I was sitting on the floor in front of my couch, Eliot's knees spread to either side of me as I leaned back against him and let him work on the tense muscles in my shoulders.

"When you moan like that it makes me think of other things," Eliot warned.

"We can get to those other things," I promised. "You need to really dig in there ... right there!"

Eliot chuckled. "I'm willing to do my part to relax you, no matter how much effort I have to expend."

"Good to know."

"I'm guessing my efforts are going to be better served in the bedroom this evening."

"Ten more minutes," I pleaded.

"Five."

"Ten."

"Fine, ten more minutes," Eliot said. "Then I'm getting a full hour in the bedroom. What are you doing?"

I pointed toward the television and hit the "mute" button on the remote control so the volume would return to normal. "That story is from Macomb Township."

"You're not a news reporter right now," Eliot said. "You remember that, right?"

"Shh."

We watched the story quietly for a few minutes. A local student from Catholic Central, a private school in northern Macomb County, had been found dead in the woods next to the high school. The report didn't offer a lot of information, and the police were on the scene, but my fingers were already itching to type.

"We should go out there," I announced. "This could be a big story."

Eliot's fingers stilled on either side of my neck. "You're not a news reporter anymore."

He was acting as though I had suddenly gone deaf and hadn't heard him the first time. What? I heard him. I just choose not to listen. "But ... ."

"Avery, even if you did go out there, it's not your story to cover," Eliot said, his voice calm and soothing. "I'm sorry. I know that ... drives you crazy ... but it's true. You have no right to be there."

I lowered my head. "I know." My voice was low and pitiful.

"I'm sure that Marvin is on it," Eliot said, trying a different tactic. "You guys won't miss it."

"I know."

Eliot pulled me back to rest his chin on the top of my head. "I'm sorry."

"Why?"

"Because you're upset."

"I'm not upset."

"You seem upset," Eliot said.

"I'm just ... thinking."

"About what?"

"Life," I said. "It's a long road of betrayal."

"Oh, good," Eliot deadpanned. "I was worried you were going to get trapped in your own head and dwell on this."

"Eliot?"

"Yeah."

"I'm sad again."

Eliot resumed kneading my back. "You've got twenty more minutes of rubbing ... and then you're going to rub me in the other room."

"I might still be sad then," I said.

"Something tells me I can cheer you up."

Something told me – probably history – that he was right.

"What are you doing?"

Eliot was still half asleep, even though my wandering hands were doing their best to tip him over into full-blown consciousness.

"I'm not doing anything," I said, pressing my body flush against his. We were facing each other, and since the previous night's activities had left us naked there was nothing standing in the way of nirvana and me.

Eliot opened his eyes and fixed me with a sleepy smile. "I feel you doing something."

"Is it something you don't like?"

"No," Eliot said, his eyes traveling to the clock on the nightstand. "I'm fairly certain ... shit, is that the time?" He bolted out of bed, leaving me with nothing but a view of his naked rear end as he moved from the bedroom and headed toward the bathroom.

"Hey!"

"Sorry, Trouble," Eliot shouted over his shoulder. "I was supposed to open the store an hour ago."

In addition to building a private investigation business, Eliot was the proprietor of a pawnshop in downtown Mount Clemens.

He didn't have a lot to do with the day-to-day operations of the shop these days, but he still had to open and close on rare occasions.

"Why did we stay here if you had to open?"

Eliot's apartment is located above the pawnshop. We generally split our time between his apartment and my house, but we've been spending more and more time at my place since my cousin Lexie moved out a few weeks ago.

"I like cooking in your kitchen," Eliot said.

I heard the shower come alive. I couldn't see him, but I could hear him brushing his teeth as he talked around his toothbrush.

"Eliot?"

"Huh?"

"You're not doing much for my ego," I admitted.

Eliot reappeared in the doorway, his nudity glorious in its simplicity. "Why?"

"I was in the middle of something," I reminded him.

Eliot's mouth tipped into a smile. "I know."

"You jumped out of bed like I had lice or something," I said.

"I ... I have to get to work." He looked conflicted.

"Fine," I sniffed, dragging the covers over my head. "I've gone from a news reporter who had to beat her boyfriend off with a stick to a sports reporter who can't entice him, even when she's got her hand on his .... My life is over."

Eliot was quiet in the other room. When I finally pulled the covers down far enough to catch sight of him, he was regarding me with a humorous look.

"What?" I was starting to feel exposed.

"If you come and get in the shower with me, I'll fix the ... problem," he said.

"I'm not sure that will make me feel better."

"What will make you feel better?"

"I was halfway there before you treated me like I had the plague," I said.

Eliot cocked his head to the side. "How long are you going to milk this depression thing?"

"How long will it work?"

Eliot raised his finger in warning. "Not long."

"Is it working now?" I asked hopefully.

Eliot sighed. "Yes. I have to turn the shower off, and you'd better not expect foreplay."

"I never do."

Eliot frowned. "What?"

"Hurry up," I ordered. "I need you to make me feel better."

"Like I can say no to that," Eliot grumbled.

STANLEY Witter has been the sports editor at The Monitor since before I started there almost seven years ago. I don't think he's ever spoken to me – except to tell me I was being too loud. When Fish walked me over to the bank of sports cubicles Wednesday morning, Stanley didn't look thrilled with his new employee. I couldn't blame him.

"What do you know about sports?"

"It depends on the sport," I said.

"What do you know about basketball?"

I didn't like his tone. "That's the one with the puck, right?"

Stanley made a face. "No."

I think Stanley missed the line when senses of humor were being handed out.

"I know about basketball."

"What about hockey?"

"I understand hockey," I said.

"What about swimming?" Stanley asked.

"You do it in a pool, right?"

Stanley rolled his eyes until they landed on Fish. "Tell me why we have to be punished with her again?"

"Because she's protected by the union," Fish said. "We can't fire her."

"She's impossible to deal with," Stanley said.

"You haven't seen anything yet," Fish said, chuckling as he disappeared around the corner.

Stanley turned back to me. "Swimming is done at meets."

"Awesome."

"There are different events."

"I figured."

"They even dive."

"Like at the Olympics?" That sounded fun.

Stanley shook his head. "It's nothing like the Olympics."

I tried to tamp my temper down. "I'm sure I can figure it out."

"Well, that remains to be seen," he said. "I've told Peter to send you a copy of our setups."

"What are setups?"

If I didn't know better, I could have sworn I'd just kicked Stanley in the balls. That's how tortured his face looked. "Setups are for sports."

"Oh, wow, I never would have guessed."

"Are you being sarcastic?"

I considered the question. "No." What? He has issues.

Stanley let loose with an exasperated sigh. "We have different setups for different sports. We cover more than one sport." The good news is I'm now being treated like the office virgin by a guy who is clearly still an actual virgin. I don't think he's even paid for it. "Each sport has a setup. Swimming is agate. Wrestling is agate. Basketball and hockey are roundup items, although basketball has an agate box, too."

"Just send them to me," I snapped. "I'm sure I can look at them and figure it out."

Stanley didn't look convinced. "Do you know the rest of the staff?"

That was a loaded question. "I know Brick."

"He's our page designer," Stanley said, clearly missing my snark.

"Huh."

"He's going through a rough time," Stanley said. "His fiancée is in the county jail awaiting trial on murder charges."

He had to be messing with me. "I know. I'm the one who put her there."

"Oh, that's right," Stanley said. "I'd forgotten about that."

"You're lucky." Quitting was starting to sound better and better. "It's hard for me to forget a woman trying to kill me."

Stanley wasn't impressed. "I heard you drove her to the act."

"Is that what Brick said?" Brick was one of those guys who needed to be smacked, and not just because he named himself "Brick." Yeah, he picked out that name for himself. Everyone mime coughing "tool" into their hands in unison right now. Better? Not for me. I was hoping sports had a baseball bat on the premises so I could be in charge of the nightly smacking.

"Brick says you entrapped her," Stanley said.

"How did I entrap her into killing her boss, and a few other people, before I ever met her?"

"He says you're a witch."

Of course he did.

"Actually, he says you're a witch, with a b," Stanley said. "I think that means he thinks you're ... ."

"Yeah, I got it," I said, rolling my eyes. "Trust me, it's not the first time I've heard that little nugget."

"It took me a little while to get it."

Somehow, that didn't surprise me. "Is there anything else?"

"You're just supposed to look over the setups tonight," Stanley cautioned. "At the end of the night, I want you to look over the roundups. That should give you an idea of what we expect."

"Great."

"Don't answer the phone tonight," Stanley said. "You're not ready."

"I'm not ready to take dictation over the phone?"

"It's a special skill."

"Like foreplay?"

"I don't know what that means," Stanley said, all guile missing from his face.

"Yeah, that doesn't surprise me," I grumbled.

"Did you say something?"

"I said you're ... ."

"Hey, Avery," Marvin said, slinging an arm over my shoulder as he rounded the corner into the sports department. "How are things?"

Marvin Potts is ... unique. He's pushing fifty and he's still single. He makes no apologies for his attitude or his drive. That's why I like him. He's always on the prowl, and his personality is like sushi – it appeals to a select few. I happen to be one of the people who like it.

"They suck balls," I said.

"I heard," Marvin said. "How is it going, Wit?"

I regarded Stanley curiously. I realized, on an intellectual level, that Stanley and Marvin had worked together for a number of years. I'd never seen enough personality from Stanley to even consider he and Marvin had anything in common. Marvin has more personality than the average ten people.

"Hey, newsroom," Wit said, brightening considerably. "What are you doing over here?"

"Newsroom?" I was confused.

"That's his nickname for me," Marvin explained.

"Why?"

"We used to work in the same area when we were in the old building," Stanley said. "He always answered the phone by saying, 'Newsroom, Potts.'"

"And that's how he got the nickname," I finished.

"Exactly."

"Awesome," I said, raising my eyebrows in Marvin's direction.

He smiled. "I heard what happened with MacDonald."

"He's a douche."

"I like him," Stanley said.

"That doesn't surprise me," I said.

"What is that supposed to mean?"

Marvin swooped in. "Nothing," he said. "You'll like Avery. I promise. She's very ... smart."

"I'll take your word for it," Stanley said. "I have no empirical knowledge to back that up."

I narrowed my eyes. "You know what?"

"What?"

"Nothing," Marvin said, dragging me away from Stanley. "Can we talk for a second?"

"No."

"Yes, we can." Marvin is stronger than he looks. His black suspenders and outdated Reeboks make him look like a total schmuck. Once he got me out of Stanley's line of sight, he relaxed his grip. "What is your deal?"

"I don't like him."

"You don't like anyone."

"The list is small, and you used to be on it ... ."

"Oh, shut it," Marvin said.

"Shut it?"

"You're pissed, I get it," Marvin said. "I don't blame you."

"I am pissed," I said. "I'm getting screwed."

"It will work out. I have faith."

"Since when?"

"Well, I've started seeing a new psychic," Marvin said.

I rolled my eyes. "You drive me crazy."

"Right back at you."

I growled at him for good measure.

"It won't last," Marvin said. "Fish won't be able to go without you for more than a few weeks."

"I know ... wait ... a few weeks?"

"That MacDonald guy is a tough nut," Marvin said. "He's going to take some convincing. You're going to have to make the best of this situation."

I considered the thought for a moment. Marvin was making sense, which meant the world had tilted on its axis. "We need to get him fired."

"How do you suggest we do that? Not that I'm not all in, because I'm definitely all in."

"We're investigative reporters," I said. "There has to be some dirt he's hiding."

"Maybe he's a pedophile," Marvin suggested, his face hopeful.

"That would be nice." I realized what I'd just said. "Not for the kids, of course."

"I get what you were saying," Marvin said. "I'll start digging as soon as I can."

"When will that be?"

"I have to finish the piece I'm working on." Marvin said.

The news story from the previous night niggled at the back of my brain. "Are you working on the girl found at Catholic North?"

Marvin nodded.

"Have they identified her yet?"

"No."

"Are they saying how she died?"

Marvin pursed his lips. "No."

"You know something," I prodded.

Marvin's shoulders slumped. "I know that she was raped to within an inch of her life and strangled."

"That's horrible. How do they know she was raped?"

"It was pretty brutal," Marvin said. "I can't use the information I got for print, but my source says she was ... used up."

"More than one person?"

"Yeah."

Sexual brutality drives me crazy on a regular day. When there's nothing I can do about it drives me to the brink of insanity. "You can't just let this go."

"I have no intention of doing that."

"Good," I said. "If I'm stuck here, then you're the warrior out there."

"I'm always a warrior," Marvin said.

"I know. I wasn't saying anything negative about you," I replied hurriedly, my esteem for the man growing. He would do what was right.

"I'm the ultimate warrior," Marvin said. "Oh, hey, did I tell you what happened on wrestling Monday night?"

That esteem ebbs and flows at the oddest of times.

"What do you mean you're in sports?"

I love my mother, I really do. I also wish I could move to a heretofore undiscovered subcontinent where the Internet and cell service don't exist.

"I got transferred to sports," I said, resting the desk phone against my shoulder as I opened Stanley's email and looked at the setups he'd sent me. It was Thursday, and though he'd insisted I study them the previous evening, online shopping was just so much more fun. Now I was cramming. "It's a punishment."

"What did you do to warrant getting punished?"

"What makes you think I've done anything?"

"I raised you."

Did she just make a point? I'm going with no. "It's a male-dominated hierarchy trying to keep me down."

I could practically hear my mother's mind working over the phone. "What did you do?"

"I didn't do anything."

"You must have done something," Mom said.

"What could I have possibly done?"

"I'm sure you did something."

"I'm your daughter," I said.

"I remember the labor."

"You're supposed to be on my side," I said.

"Avery, when you were fourteen years old you told me your teacher had it out for you," Mom said.

"Mrs. Moseley was evil."

"You said you'd turned all your homework assignments in on time and she just had it out for you," Mom said, ignoring my retort. "When I went in to talk to her, she told me that you interrupted her lessons and you were too busy reading trashy magazines to pay attention to her lectures. She said you had to be the center of attention, which is hard when the teacher is supposed to be the center of attention."

"And you believed her," I said. "Don't you feel stupid now?"

"I saw the magazines."

"Hey, *In Touch* is not a trashy magazine."

"You've always been this way," Mom said. "You think that you're above the law because you're ... well ... you. I blame myself. Oh, wait, who needs that? I blame the rest of the family. They encouraged you to be obnoxious."

"You make that sound like a bad thing," I said. "Oh, crap, these setups do look complicated."

"What does that mean?"

"Nothing," I said, focusing back on the conversation. "You know, you're my mother."

Mom waited.

"You're supposed to ... I don't know ... lift a car off of me when it falls on me," I said. "You're pressing down on the car right now."

"Has a car fallen on you?"

"Kind of."

"You still haven't told me what you've done," Mom reminded.

"I didn't do anything."

"Tell me the truth."

"Why do you think I'm lying?"

"That's what you do."

I'd argue, but I had made a profession of lying to her when I was a teenager. I'd turned it into a game. She wanted to believe me, so she did. She didn't balk until I told her that I'd mistaken the condoms in my purse for water balloons. She can only be pushed so far. "I was doing my job."

"Were you really?" Mom always thinks I'm lying. Yes, I once told her that the cooking wine in the cupboard had evaporated, but that was really her fault. She should have found a better hiding place.

"Yes."

"Well, you'll just have to live with the repercussions of your actions," Mom said.

"I didn't do anything!"

"You must have done something."

"You never take my side," I grumbled.

"And you're always the consummate victim."

My mother can piss me off like no other person in the universe. I knew the one thing that would push her over the edge to my side, though, and I whipped it out now. "I can't come to dinner Friday night."

Friday night dinners at the family restaurant in Oakland County are mandatory. The only excuse for absence is death – or arrest --both of which have been utilized, sadly. This tidbit would be enough to drive her insane.

"What? Why?"

"I have to work nights now," I said.

"Well, you can't miss dinner."

An idea formed in my head. "You'll have to take that up with my boss." I waited as I listened to her endless diatribe. "Oh, yeah, I have his number right here."

THIS is Joe Howlett," Stanley said, introducing me to another sports reporter.

I had seen Joe before. You couldn't miss him. Yes, I know that's going to sound rude – especially when I describe him to you – but I idle at rude. Joe is ... big. He's like six-hundred-pounds big. I could live with that. I've known the love of fast food myself. That steak-and-egg breakfast bagel at McDonald's is amazing. That's not why he freaks me out. He's also annoying, and he has a certain smell that he tries to mask with a bottle of cologne each day. Those are the things I can't tolerate.

"I've met Joe before."

"She's got a crush on me," Joe said, winking. "I'm a whole lot of man, and she's got a whole lot of love she wants to share with me. She's just worried I'll crush her."

Stanley was flummoxed. "Do you two date?"

"No," I said, repulsed.

"She wishes," Joe supplied.

I rolled my eyes. "Why am I over here?"

"You're going to watch Joe take calls tonight," Stanley said. "This is just another step on your path to sports greatness."

Oh, I was wrong, Stanley does have a sense of humor. I waited for the punch line – or a laugh. Neither came. "Oh, well, great."

"You just need to watch him tonight," Stanley cautioned. "You're not ready to take calls yet."

"Watch him do what?"

"Answer calls."

"Is he going to do magic tricks while he does it?"

"No."

"Then why do I have to watch him?" I was starting to lose my trademark cool. What? I'm cool.

"You need to learn how to take calls," Stanley said.

"You sent me the setups."

"That doesn't mean you know what you're doing."

The battle for my temper was tipping in the favor of Mordor. "It's not rocket science."

Stanley ran his tongue over his teeth. "I don't like your attitude."

Join the party. "I'm not watching him answer calls."

"I'm good at it," Joe said. "We can flirt between them."

That sounded ... great. "Just throw me into the deep end of the pool," I said. "It will be fine."

"I don't believe you," Stanley said. "I've heard you're a liar."

I narrowed my eyes. "Is that what Brick said?"

"Did I hear my name?" Brick poked his head out of his cubicle, fixing me with an evil look. He was clearly happy with the new arrangement.

Brick has Little Man's Syndrome. He never grew to an appropriate height – he needs at least another three inches for that – and his attitude has taken up the slack. I'm also guessing he's hung like an infant, because he won't stop overcompensating. He's like an angry little koala bear – without the cute quotient.

"I said Brick, not dick," I clarified.

Brick's smug smile faltered. "What did you just say?"

"I said you're a prick."

"What?"

"I said you're a delight and I can't wait to work with you," I corrected, the idea of another memo in my file fueling me.

Brick smiled evilly. "You're at our mercy, aren't you?"

"I'm not at anyone's mercy," I countered. "Well, I was at your girlfriend's mercy when she tried to kill my cousin and me, but we shouldn't dwell on things like that. Has she found a nice girlfriend in the county jail?" I always know when I cross the line – exactly two seconds after I do it.

"What did you just say?"

I had two choices: I could apologize or I could make things worse. I decided to play it smart. "I said you're a pain in the ass and you have shitty taste in women." Oh, wait, did I say I decided to play it smart? I meant I'm a complete and total moron.

"I'm reporting you," Brick seethed, his chest heaving.

"It won't be the first time," I grumbled.

"You're not reporting her," Fish said, rounding the corner with an exasperated look on his face. He focused on Stanley. "I told you to keep her on the other side of the room. She can't be over here."

"She needs to learn how to take calls," Stanley said.

"She can take calls," Fish said. "She's not an idiot."

Stanley balked. "Are you saying only idiots can do what we do?"

"Of course not," Fish countered.

"Then, what are you saying?"

Fish glanced at me, his expression unreadable. "She's smart," he said. "She learns on the job. She'll be fine."

"These are important details," Stanley said. "Do you have any idea how mean an angry sports mom can be?"

"I do," Fish said. "I take the calls during the day when you're not here."

Stanley faltered, brushing his thinning brown hair from the spreading bald spot on the top of his head. "Right. I forgot about that."

"Stanley, I know you're under pressure here," Fish said, playing the game to the best of his ability. "I can promise you that Avery is more than up to the challenge."

"This is a fast-paced world," Stanley said.

"And she works better when it's fast," Fish said, shooting me a pointed look. "I think you're missing her obvious worth."

"Which is?" Stanley asked.

"Yeah, which is?" I repeated. I had no idea where he was headed.

"Send her out to cover a game," Fish said calmly. "She knows how to do an interview."

"A game story is not an interview," Stanley argued.

"She still knows the basics," Fish said. "She'll figure it out. She always does."

"And what if she screws it up?" Stanley asked.

"Then we'll figure something out," Fish said.

Stanley was intrigued by Fish's half offer. "How many mistakes does she get?"

Fish scanned me worriedly. "Seven."

"Seven?"

"Five," Fish corrected. "She gets five mistakes. And they have to be genuine mistakes. Her telling the coach who calls in that he's an idiot doesn't count. She's going to do that. You just have to get used to it."

Stanley tilted his head, considering. "Agreed."

"Great," Fish said.

"She still has to watch Joe answer calls tonight," Stanley interjected.

I was immediately shaking my head.

"She'll do it," Fish said.

"No way," I said.

"You will," Fish said. "You owe me."

"What do I owe you for?" He was clearly messing with me.

"I just had a call."

"Just tell them you don't want to change your long-distance service," I suggested.

"It was from your mother," Fish said.

I paused, internally checking the rooster crowing in my chest. "Oh, really? What did she want?"

"She called to tell me that you can't work Friday nights," Fish said.

"Oh, yeah, family dinner." I pretended that I was being drowned in a sea of worry. "My grandparents are really old. It's a big deal to my mother."

"Friday nights are busy for us," Stanley said.

"Well, you've been working without Avery for Friday nights for years," Fish said, clearly not swayed by his argument.

"But ... ." Stanley was angry. The color clouding his cheeks told me that much.

"I don't care," Fish said. "Avery can't work Friday nights. Give her busy work for the afternoons, but she can't work nights on Fridays."

"And why is that?" Stanley asked.

I already knew the answer, and I had to fight to keep my face placid as I waited for Fish to explain his reasoning to Stanley.

"Her mother is the Devil."

The smile tugging at the corner of my mouth was winning the war.

"You're kowtowing to her mother?" Stanley was incensed.

Fish fixed me with a look. "I'm kowtowing to the Devil."

See, my mother is good for something. I'm not the only one she can browbeat into submission. That's good to know.

"Why am I here again?"

Dave Stewart wasn't any happier about having me in sports than Stanley was. The bad news for Dave was that Stanley was not only in charge, but irritated with him, too. So, when Dave announced he had a wrestling quad to cover, Stanley ordered him to take me as a teaching exercise.

We'd both argued ... and lost.

"Stanley hates me," Dave said.

"Why?"

"Because he thinks I try to take over too much," Dave explained.

"Well, then he's going to loathe me."

"I think he already does," Dave said.

"Why? He barely knows me. I'll have you know, many people have called me delightful."

"Anyone you've ever worked with?" Dave asked.

I shrugged. "Nope. It's mostly people I've slept with."

Dave grinned. "You're kind of funny."

"I agree."

"You should just be prepared," Dave said. "Stanley is going to purposely try to get you to make mistakes, especially now that Fish has given you a limit on how many times you can screw up. I can't believe he did that, by the way. Stanley is going to be gunning for you."

"Well, I don't mess up," I said.

"Isn't that why they shuffled you over to sports?"

"Um, no," I said. "I'm in sports because the county commissioner I slept with in college has a really small ... ."

"You probably don't want to finish that sentence in front of a bunch of parents at a Catholic school," Dave warned.

"Right," I said, scanning the gym. "I thought we were here to cover wrestling."

"We are," Dave said, pointing toward the bleachers. "Go about halfway up. We'll be able to see everything from there. Don't sit in front of those women wearing matching sweatshirts."

"Why? Are they some sort of cult?"

"They're wrestling moms," Dave said.

I had no idea what that meant, but I'm against anyone wearing matching anything. Once we were settled, I took the opportunity to really look around the gym. "There are a lot of people here."

"It's a quad."

"I don't know what that means," I admitted.

"It means that four schools will be wrestling against each other," Dave said. "You have parents from four different schools here. It's usually not as busy when it's only two teams."

"Why don't they just say that?"

"Why do you think it's called a quad?"

He had a point. Crap. I decided to show him I wasn't a complete and total idiot. "Where's the ring?"

Dave is an amiable guy, for the most part, but the look he shot me wasn't hard to read. "Ring?"

"The one with the ropes they throw each other against," I replied, nonplussed.

"It's not professional wrestling," Dave said.

"Well, I know they don't get paid," I scoffed. "That's illegal for high school sports, right?" What? I know stuff.

"Just ... watch," Dave said.

"Watch what? Nothing is happening."

"It will start in a few minutes."

"I can't wait." I leaned forward so I could see the edge of the mats clearer. "Where are the folding chairs? They're not going to be able to hit each other if there are no folding chairs."

Dave rolled his eyes. "How many times do I have to tell you that this isn't professional wrestling?"

I had no idea how I'd done it, but Dave looked as though he wanted to hit me with a chair. I have a gift. If I could bottle it, I'd be rich. It would be the best-selling perfume ever. I'd call it "Irritation."

When the wrestling finally started, things only worsened.

"What's with their little outfits?" I asked.

"Those are singlets. It's what they wear."

"Why?"

"I don't know. Why don't you travel back in time and ask the person who designed them?" Dave challenged.

"If I could go back in time, I'd travel back to my college years and push Tad Ludington in front of a bus," I grumbled.

"Is he the guy who complained about you to the new publisher?"

"Yes."

"I'd go back in time and help you," Dave said.

Oh, that was kind of sweet. He was on my side.

"That way you'd never come to sports," he added.

I'm really starting to dislike him.

Action on the mat closest to us caught my attention. "Why is the referee holding up his hand like that?"

"Because that kid was using an illegal hold."

"So, it's like a foul in basketball?"

Dave looked surprised by the question. "Kind of. Yes. You know about basketball?"

"I understand basketball," I said.

"Then why didn't Stanley send you to a game?"

"I'm guessing it's because he wants to punish us both," I said.

"Obviously."

I bit my tongue to keep from lashing out and focused back on the wrestling. "So, wait, are all these kids gay, or just some of them?"

Dave pursed his lips. "Excuse me?"

I pointed to the two boys on the floor, one of whom had his groin pressed snugly to the behind of the boy on all fours in front of him. "That's a sex position."

"No, it's not."

"Hey, I might not know a lot about wrestling," I said, "I know about sex, though, and I've seen that position a time or two, including last night. Now, granted, it's not just for gay men, but there are two men doing it right now."

"That's the defensive starting position," Dave argued. "It has nothing to do with sex."

I knew he was messing with me now. "This sport is all about the sex," I said. "It's extremely homoerotic."

"How do you figure?"

"Well, first off, they're in those little rubber outfits," I said. "Those only work in certain circles, and none of these guys look like the gimp from *Pulp Fiction*."

Dave didn't respond, but I could swear I heard him growl. I took it as a sign of encouragement.

"They've got those little helmets on," I continued. "When the straps slip up and fall into their mouths, they look like ball gags."

A pair of teenage girls sitting two rows down from us started giggling.

"And ball gags make sense, because the faces these kids are making suggest that they're being cornholed when no one is looking," I said, opting to play to my audience. What? This was the most fun I'd had since joining sports. "So, we have the doggie position, ball gags, rubber outfits and cornholing. How is that not homoerotic?"

Dave's mouth dropped open. I have no idea what he was about to say, because one of the women wearing matching sweatshirts from a few rows over decided to get involved in our conversation. "How dare you say that? My son is not gay."

"Which one is he?" I asked.

"He's ... what does that matter?"

"I just want to see him for myself," I said. "Sometimes the mother is the last to know – not that there's anything wrong with that."

"I ... who are you?"

Uh-oh. I sensed danger. "I'm with the *Detroit Free Press*."

"I'm calling your boss tomorrow," the woman said.

"Go for it," I said. "My name is Amber Williams."

"I'm not going to forget that," the woman said.

"I certainly hope not." Once she was gone, I turned to Dave. "Amber Williams once tried to sleep with a police officer to beat me on a story. She'll think twice about doing that again."

Dave shook his head. "This is going to be a long night."

"Well, in that case, where's the food?"

DAVE had been more than happy to direct me to the concession area, even telling me to take my time – and stuff my mouth – with as many hot dogs as possible. When I pointed out that hot dogs were a funny thing to serve at a sausagefest, he'd stopped talking to me completely. Oh well, it was his loss. I could do a whole standup routine on high school wrestling. It would definitely be better with folding chairs, though.

I took the opportunity to watch some of the students milling about the tables. When I'd found out the wrestling meet was going to be at Catholic North, I'd been secretly pleased. I'd kept arguing in front of Stanley, because I knew he'd change his mind about sending me if he thought I wanted to come, but I wanted to talk to some of the students. They would have more information about the dead girl than school officials were willing to give to the media.

I munched on my hot dog as I listened to two girls chat.

"Well, we all knew it was going to happen."

"That's not nice, Ashley," the other girl said.

"I didn't say she deserved it, Allison."

Ashley and Allison? Why didn't that surprise me?

"Of course she didn't deserve it," Allison said. "What happened to her was a tragedy. Or was it a travesty? Which is worse? I want to get it right for when the television reporters come back tomorrow."

I made a face. Television reporters are the scourge of news reporting. They're lazy glory hounds, and not in a fun way like professional athletes and Hollywood actors. Still, I didn't think that was the right way to approach these girls.

"Were the news crews here all day today?" I asked.

Allison pushed her bottle-blond hair out of her face and arched a brown eyebrow. "Of course they were. We're in the middle of a tragedy."

"I think travesty is more poignant," Ashley said.

"I think you're right," Allison said.

My eyes rolled so hard I almost tipped over. "What can you tell me about the dead girl?"

"Kelsey," Ashley supplied. "She was an angel."

Allison nodded shrewdly. "A total angel."

"Do you think that's too much?" Ashley asked.

"I have no idea," I said, fighting to keep my temper in check. I hate teenage girls. Some of them are okay, but most of them are heinous little beasts who can be diagnosed as rampant sociopaths with narcissistic personality disorders. See, I told you I know things. "What kind of rumors are going around about Kelsey?"

Ashley and Allison exchanged a look. "What do you mean?" Ashley asked, averting her gaze.

I was a teenage girl once, and not all that long ago. Sure, I made it my job to torture girls like Ashley and Allison then, but they didn't need to know that. "Well, there are rumors going around about Kelsey."

Allison's eyes widened. "What kind of rumors?"

I wrinkled my nose, considering. "I heard she wasn't very popular." That could be taken a multitude of ways.

"Oh, she was popular," Ashley said, snickering.

Ah, jealousy. That meant Kelsey had stolen a boyfriend from at least one of them. "I meant with other girls," I said. "I know she was popular with the boys."

"She was a slut," Allison said. "The boys loved her."

"I knew girls like that when I was in high school," I said. Okay, I'd been one of those girls in high school. Just because Allison and Ashley were casting aspersions on Kelsey, though, that didn't mean she was actually a slut. Bitterness makes teenage girls ugly.

"Everyone knew Kelsey," Ashley said. "She was a regular fixture at wrestling parties every Friday night."

I faltered. "They have wrestling parties?"

"The wrestling team here is state ranked," Allison said. "They're the school heroes."

That made absolutely no sense. "I thought the popular boys were usually football players?"

"Our football team sucks," Allison said.

"But I thought the wrestlers were gay?"

"Oh, no," Ashley said. "Rolling around on the floor with other sweaty men doesn't make you gay. I asked the priest, just to be sure."

I was starting to like her. "So, they have parties every Friday night? The whole team?"

"Yes," Allison said. "It's a big deal to get invited."

"How many girls get invited?"

Allison shrugged. "I'm not the kind of girl who gets invited. I'm virtuous."

"She only gives hand jobs," Ashley said.

"Oh, nice," I said. "Have you heard anything about these parties through the grapevine?"

"Like what?"

"I don't know, like any weird sexual stuff?"

"I told you they're not gay," Ashley said.

"I didn't mean ... ." I shook my head, trying to regroup. "How many of these parties have they had this year? And where are they held?"

"The location changes from house to house," Ashley said. "Wrestling just started last week, so there have only been two parties."

Well, that was interesting. "Where was the party last Friday?"

Ashley shrugged. "I can't remember."

"Where is it this Friday?"

"We're not the type of girls who get invited," Allison said. "I already told you that."

I forced a tight smile onto my face as I got to my feet. "Well, thanks for the information." I couldn't talk to these girls one more second without knocking their heads together.

"No problem," Ashley said.

As I started to move away, I heard them giggle. "What kind of girl wears Converse and *Star Wars* shirts?"

"A desperate one," Allison said. "She must being trying to pick up a wrestling dad."

"Eww."

Eww indeed. I found Dave where I'd left him on the bleachers. "Did I miss anything exciting?"

"Catholic North and George Washington High are tied, and there are only two matches left," Dave replied.

Huh. "Let me rephrase that," I said. "Did I miss anything I would find exciting?"

"This is a big deal," Dave said. "Catholic North is state ranked."

"In what, crotch grabbing?"

"That's some low-hanging fruit you keep trying to pick," Dave said. "It's not funny."

I pointed to the two boys on the mat. "No, that's some low-hanging fruit he's trying to pick while he tries to wrestle that boy into submission," I said. "And I'm totally funny."

"So, Dave Stewart sent Stanley an email about your conduct at the wrestling meet last night," Fish said, not bothering with pleasantries as he greeted me Friday morning.

"You're welcome," I said, refusing to rise to the bait.

Fish stilled. "For what?"

"Someone had to tell those mothers that their sons were destined for flashier weddings," I said.

Fish rubbed the heel of his palm against his forehead. "You do realize that high school wrestling isn't code for homosexuality, right?"

"Not a very good one, that's for sure."

Fish frowned. "You're just being ... you ... aren't you?"

"I have no idea what you mean by that," I said.

"Stanley wanted to count your excursion last night as one of your five fails," Fish said. "I explained that, since you were just there to observe, it was impossible for you to fail."

"Oh, well, way to have my back," I said.

Fish shook his head. "I'm glad to see that your precarious work situation hasn't left you bereft or depressed."

"No, I've been using my raging sadness to get nonstop back rubs and ... other stuff," I said.

"What other stuff?"

"Oh, I can't tell you that," I said. "I wouldn't want to be accused of sexual harassment again."

"I never accused you of that."

"No, that would be the office tool," I said. "And, oh look, here he comes now."

Duncan Marlow has been the bane of my existence since I started at The Monitor. He's certifiable and full of himself. He thinks he looks like Tom Cruise, when he really looks like Sheldon Cooper. He's obsessed with what everyone else eats, and if he feels he's being maligned in any way he'll force you into a conference room to talk until you agree that he's the greatest man in the world. I neither encourage nor play his games. I do often rig the games to amuse myself, though.

"Well, well, well," Duncan said, slinking up behind Fish. "If it isn't our newest sports reporter."

"Well, well, well," I said. "If it isn't the in-house douche." What? I can't stand him. Plus, he keeps saying he has a high IQ – one point off from being a genius, if you believe him (which I don't). He already knows he's a douche.

"Fish, I have told you repeatedly that if she doesn't stop calling me a douche ... ."

"Then don't act like a douche," Fish snapped. "You're the one who came over here to poke her."

"He wishes," I muttered.

Duncan narrowed his eyes to brown slits. "What did you say?"

"I said that you're ... ."

"Supposed to be working," Fish interjected.

"That's not what I was going to say," I said.

"Yes, it is."

I shot a winning smile in Duncan's direction. "Did you need something?"

"I was just on my way to the coffee machine," he said.

"That's in the opposite direction from here."

"Well, why are you here during the day?" Duncan asked. "You're a sports reporter now. You're supposed to work nights."

"Not on Fridays," I said.

"And why is that?" Duncan asked. He thinks everything that happens at the office is his business. I think the same thing, but I go about it in a much sneakier way.

"Ask Fish," I said.

Duncan shifted his attention to our put-upon boss. "Well?"

"Her mother is terrifying," Fish said.

I smirked.

"Her mother?" Duncan was incensed. "You're saying that her mother got you to change her schedule?"

"She's very convincing," Fish explained.

"Well, maybe I should call my mother and have her explain how I'm allergic to Avery," Duncan suggested.

"Unless your mother can shrivel my balls with the mere threat of dropping by I don't think it will work," Fish said.

Ah, yes, my mother does have a rare super power. You should see her super-hero uniform. Maybe I should take her to a wrestling meet? She'd fit right in.

"I'm offended by that statement," Duncan said.

"Why?" Fish asked.

"I don't think he knows what it means," I explained. "He doesn't have the proper equipment for comparison's sake."

It took a moment for my words to sink in, but when they did, Duncan was off and running. Unfortunately, he was running straight toward human resources.

"You realize he's going to file another sexual harassment claim about you, right?"

"Hey, I still maintain that Civil War reenactments are gay," I said. "I didn't say that was a bad thing."

"This is going to come down on me," Fish said.

I patted his shoulder. "Thanks for having my back."

. . .

"SO, I talked to some girls at Catholic North last night," I informed Marvin when he arrived for his afternoon shift after lunch.

"What were you doing there?"

I told him about the evening's sport activities, leaving nothing out. When I was done, he was laughing so hard he was almost crying. "That sounds awesome."

"Then I'm telling the story wrong," I said. "Wrestling is homoerotic."

"I wrestled in high school," Marvin said.

Since Marvin often whines like a woman, that didn't surprise me. "Were you the bottom or the top?"

"Wrestling is a manly sport," he shot back.

"For two people who are in love, absolutely," I said.

Marvin shot me a scorching look. "Tell me what the girls said."

"They mentioned something about wrestling parties at Catholic North," I said. "Apparently, only certain girls are invited, and the parties jump locations from week to week."

"And why does this interest us?"

"They treat the wrestlers like gods at that school. This Kelsey girl was apparently popular with the wrestlers. That can't be a coincidence. I mean ... they're wrestlers, for crying out loud."

"So?"

"They don't even hit each other with chairs," I said.

Marvin chortled. "I think we should make a television show out of you watching wrestling," he said. "That would be a hit sitcom for sure."

"I'd prefer a reality television show," I said. "I want to vote wrestlers off if they do it wrong."

"Just wait until you cover a meet where the girls are allowed to wrestle," Marvin said.

Well, wrestling just got more interesting. "Wait, there are girl wrestlers on the high school level? Do they wear bikinis and walk around with those little cards?"

"That's boxing."

"It's the same thing."

"No, it's not," Marvin said.

"Let me guess, you used to box, too?"

He nodded. "Of course you did. Anyway, why is girls' wrestling such a big deal?"

"The boys don't like to wrestle them," Marvin said.

"That's because they don't have the right parts to make the corn-holing sexually arousing."

"First off, that's gross," Marvin said. "Secondly, the guys don't like wrestling with the girls because it's a no-win situation for them."

"Go on."

"If they beat them, they've only beaten a girl."

I pinched Marvin's forearm viciously.

"Ow!"

"I'm tougher than you," I said.

"You're just mean," Marvin said. "Anyway, if they lose to a girl, then they've lost to a girl … even if she's as mean as you."

"How many teams have female wrestlers?"

Marvin shrugged. "You'll have to ask Stanley."

"I'll pass."

"He's really a good guy. You should give him a chance."

"He's a tool," I said. "How come Catholic North doesn't have girl wrestlers?"

"Probably because it's a Catholic school," Marvin said. "Girls are supposed to do girlie things in that circle."

"Like giving birth while still a virgin?"

"That's definitely girlie," Marvin agreed.

"Are you saying that girls at Catholic schools can't wrestle, but girls at public schools can?" I smelled blood in the water, and I was starting to circle.

"I think it depends on the individual school," Marvin said. "I don't know enough to comment."

I filed the discussion away to revisit later and then shifted gears. "What did the autopsy on Kelsey Cooper say?"

"It wasn't good," Marvin said, lowering his voice. "There was no semen present, but vaginal tearing and bruising around her ... girl region ... says that she was a virgin before the assault, and the assault was brutal. The cause of death is strangulation, although there were no usable fingerprints."

I felt sick to my stomach. "Girl region?"

"You know. Down there."

"If you can't use the right words for the parts, no one is ever going to let you see them," I said.

"That shows what you know," Marvin said. "Sweaty Back is going to let me see her parts tomorrow night."

Marvin has taken to naming the waitresses at his favorite watering hole before he tries to get them into bed. Sweaty Back has, well, a sweaty back. The Mole has a beauty mark on her lip. And Easy Bake Oven is ... self-explanatory. If you don't get it, I'm not explaining it to you.

"So, wait, you're seeing Sweaty Back again?" I was under the impression that they'd broken up when he couldn't flip her switch. He has issues, and he shares too much. I still find him hilarious.

"She just called me out of the blue the other day," Marvin said.

Marvin is also a walking doormat when it comes to women. "Has it occurred to you that Christmas is three weeks away?"

"So?"

"She probably wants to see you again so you'll have to buy her a Christmas gift," I said.

"That's a horrible thing to say," Marvin said. "Our love is pure."

I arched a dubious eyebrow. "Did she drop any hints on gifts?"

"Of course not," Marvin said. "She just said her wrist was the perfect size for a tennis bracelet, and they happen to be on sale at the mall right now."

"Huh."

"I know what you're thinking," Marvin said. "She's not like that."

"I didn't say anything," I said. Hey, I was thinking it. I didn't say it.

"This is the reason women don't like you," Marvin said. "You're judgmental and mean."

He's not wrong. "I'm sorry," I said. "You're right. She likes you for your mind."

"Thank you," Marvin said.

He also doesn't always catch on to sarcasm. "So, are you going to get her the tennis bracelet?"

"Of course," he said. "It's on sale, and my boy parts are lonely."

I think I need to shower.

Weekly dinners in my family are not only mandatory, they are an exercise in mass hysteria and delusion. Still, they had gotten me out of working Friday nights. I couldn't help but be excited for this one.

My family's restaurant is in northern Oakland County, and it's a throwback to an older time. The booths are vinyl, the waitresses wear polyester uniforms, and my grandfather holds court on a counter stool for the bulk of his daily shift. Technically, he still owns the restaurant. My uncle Tim is the one who handles day-to-day operations, though, so my grandfather is usually there just as entertainment.

Since Eliot had to leave from a job in Detroit, we'd agreed to meet at the restaurant. Even though I'd told him his attendance wasn't mandatory, he got a kick out of my family. It didn't hurt that my mother had decided he was her only chance to marry me off, so she doted on him as though he was royalty. He'd be practically perfect in her eyes if he would just cut his hair. I told him I'd dump him if he did. That's shallow, I know, but his hair is sexy. Sue me. Plus, and I know this makes me look bad, I love irritating my mother. I could have majored in it in college.

When I got to the restaurant, I found half of the family already there. My cousin Derrick, who is also a Macomb County sheriff's deputy, was sitting at the adjoined tables that made up the Friday family table with our cousin Mario. They appeared deep in discussion.

"What's up?" I asked, kicking Derrick's leg so he would slide over.

"What was that for?"

"Move over."

"You sit over there," Derrick said, pointing to the middle table.

"No. I want to sit there."

"Why?"

"Because Eliot is coming, and I don't like to put him in the corner," I said. "He feels trapped."

"That's because your mom keeps trying to trick him into proposing to you," Derrick said, reluctantly sliding over.

"I noticed."

"Eliot's holding strong, though," Derrick said. "He's smart. Why buy the cow?"

I narrowed my eyes. "Speaking of cows and free milk, where is Devon?" Devon is Derrick's television-reporter girlfriend. She's full of herself, and my own mother thinks her job is more important than mine because she's on television. I can't stand her. Huh. Maybe Marvin is right about my problems with other women. Oh, wait, no he's not. I'm always right and they're always wrong.

"She's working on the Kelsey Cooper story," Derrick said, an evil grin flitting across his face. "She's a news reporter."

I was wondering if he'd heard about my demotion. I guess I didn't have to worry about how I was going to tell him.

"Yeah, I hear you're in sports now, Avery," Mario said. "How is that?"

"Don't ask," Eliot said, swooping in and dropping a kiss on the top of my head. "It makes her grumpy."

"Where did you come from?" How did I miss his arrival? He's so handsome he sucks the air out of the room – and horny females – whenever he enters. That's hard to miss when it happens.

"Heaven?"

"Nice," Mario said, winking at Eliot. Mario is a lovable guy, but his Charlie Brown head makes sex appeal elusive in his world. He has to charm women first. He still tries to emulate Eliot every chance he gets.

"Have you ordered yet?" Eliot asked.

"No, I just got here."

"How was work?"

I told him about my day.

"Do you want me to beat Duncan up?" Eliot asked. "It wouldn't be much of a fight, but I think he's earned it."

"That guy is a piece of work," Derrick agreed.

"I want to meet him," Mario said. "He sounds hilarious."

"If you think mental impairment is hilarious, then you'd love him," I said.

Mario rolled his eyes. "I think you just rub people the wrong way. I'm actually surprised you managed to find a guy who can put up with you."

That was rich coming from him. He'd started taking interpretive dance at school just to irritate his father – and to pick up women.

"How do you put up with her, dude?" Mario asked Eliot.

Eliot's smile was lazy as he slung an arm over my shoulders. "I happen to like the way she rubs me."

Derrick shot him an irritated look. "You know she's like a sister to me, right?"

"So."

"So, don't talk about my ... sister-cousin rubbing you at family dinner," Derrick said. "I'll have to arrest you."

"On what charges?" Eliot asked.

"Grossing me out," Derrick said.

"I'll risk it."

Derrick considered his response. "I'll tell her mom."

Eliot faltered. "Fine. I won't talk about her rubbing me."

"Good." Derrick turned back to me. "So, I heard Ludington is behind this whole sports thing."

"Yeah, I haven't figured out how I'm going to get him back yet, but it's going to be epic and mean," I said.

"Revenge usually is with you."

"Are you still whining about the time I told all the cheerleaders you were dying? I was trying to help you. I thought they would give you pity sex. It wasn't revenge for you telling Mom I was making out with Jake under the bleachers, no matter what you think." Because Derrick and I were in high school together – a very small high school, at that – we'd often stepped all over each other during our teenage years. He still held a grudge.

"You told them he was dying?" Eliot asked, interested.

"Of a resistant strain of herpes," Derrick said, his expression dark.

Eliot barked out a laugh. "Nice."

"Don't encourage her," Derrick said. "She's the Devil when she wants to be. If she had just left Ludington alone she wouldn't be in the predicament she's in now."

"And what predicament is that?" Grandpa asked, sliding into his spot at the far end of the table.

"Avery got busted down to sports," Mario supplied.

"Why?" Grandpa asked.

"Because Tad Ludington has a small penis," I said.

"Is he the moron you dated in college?"

I nodded.

"You should have let me hit him with the car when I wanted to," Grandpa said. "We could have lied and said the brakes locked up. It was totally plausible."

"I can't listen to you talk about stuff like this," Derrick warned.

"Then plug your ears," Grandpa suggested. "How long do you have to be in sports?"

"Until Fish can talk the publisher into changing his mind," I said. "Apparently the guy has some huge file of my alleged misdeeds."

Grandpa raised an eyebrow. "Alleged?"

"I'm being framed," I said.

Grandpa chuckled. "Sometimes I think you're my favorite."

"Hey, what about me?" Mario asked.

"You're never my favorite," Grandpa said. "You're in line to inherit this restaurant and you're taking interpretive dance. How do you think that reflects on me?"

"I would think news of my dating prowess would reflect well on you," Mario said.

Grandpa wrinkled his nose. "Fine. You're one of my favorites, too."

"What about me?" Derrick asked.

"You can't be one of my favorites," Grandpa said. "You keep threatening to arrest me."

"Then maybe you should stop breaking the law," Derrick suggested.

"I only break laws that are stupid."

"Oh, well, that's a nice distinction," Derrick said.

"See, that's why you're not one of my favorites."

Eliot glanced down at me. "I love these dinners."

I scanned the restaurant. "Where is Mom? I figured she'd be here to grill me on the sad state of my life."

Eliot narrowed his eyes. "Are you laying the groundwork for another massage?"

"Don't pretend that ever ends poorly for you," I warned, waving my finger in his face.

"Yeah, I especially liked how excited you were by the wrestling last night," Eliot teased.

"I was just showing you some of the moves. Don't pretend you didn't like them."

"I'm going to be sick," Derrick said.

"That's because you're a cop," Grandpa said. "You should

consider changing your profession. Then you wouldn't feel sick."

"Yeah, that's it," Derrick said.

"I'm thinking of changing my profession," Mario announced.

"From what?" I asked. "Professional student?"

"Oh, you're so funny," Mario deadpanned. "I didn't realize sports reporters were so funny."

"Shut it."

The bell over the front door jangled, causing us all to turn. As much as I didn't want to listen to my mother go on and on (and on and on and on) about my job situation, I also wanted to get it over with. My mother wasn't the one standing at the door, though.

"Oh, good grief," Derrick said, his eyes lingering on his sister, Lexie, and the behemoth of a man standing behind her.

"Is Lexie dating a linebacker now?" Mario asked.

"I thought he was a car thief," Grandpa said.

I shot him a look. "Why do you think that?" I was trying to embarrass him. I knew exactly why he thought that, but I hoped he would come up with an appropriate lie.

"He's black," Grandpa said.

So much for lying.

Eliot's shoulders were shaking with silent laughter, and I couldn't risk a look in his direction out of fear I would start laughing, too. Racism is not funny. My grandfather always is, though.

Lexie is short, not even crossing the five-foot mark. The guy standing behind her easily topped six feet. They were an odd, and yet attractive, couple. Lexie only liked black guys, and she seemed to have a knack for picking them up. Unfortunately, she often picked them up when she was out scoring pot. I hoped that wasn't the case with this guy. Since opening her own yoga studio a few months ago, Lexie seemed to have gotten her life on track – and moved out of my house. I only hoped she wasn't regressing.

Lexie dragged the man over to the table. He looked frightened. I didn't blame him. We're terrifying.

"Hi," she said, her breath ragged with excitement. "I'm sorry I'm late."

Derrick ran his tongue over his teeth as he regarded his sister's new friend. "And who did you bring with you?"

"Oh, this is Desperado," Lexie said.

"Desperado?" I asked, fighting to keep my laughter from bubbling up. "Like the song?"

"Do you have a problem with that?" Desperado asked.

I shook my head and pressed my body closer to Eliot's. "Nope."

"Is that your real name?" Derrick asked.

"Well, it's not fake," Desperado said.

"Is it an alias?"

"I don't know what that means," Desperado said.

"Well, great," Derrick said.

Desperado fixed his attention on Eliot. "Hey, I know you."

Eliot didn't bother standing up. "You're one of the fighters down at Harry's Gym, aren't you? I saw you when I was working out the other day."

"That's me," Desperado said, puffing his chest out.

Lexie slipped into a seat behind the middle table and patted the spot next to her. "Sit here, honey."

"Honey?" Mario asked.

"Do you have a problem with that?" Desperado asked.

"No," Mario said hurriedly. "You look like a honey to me."

"Are you trying to be funny?"

"No," Mario said. "Not at all." He slid closer to Derrick. "Not at all."

An uncomfortable silence settled over the table. I tried to alleviate the tension. "So, how did you two meet?"

"He took a class at the studio," Lexie said. "We hit it off right away."

"You take yoga?" Derrick asked, not bothering to hide the look of derision.

"Yeah. My trainer thought it would help my movement,"

Desperado said. "I didn't believe him, but he was right. My flexibility is amazing now."

"It is," Lexie said, her eyes sparkling. "You should see how far he can bend over."

That was a terrifying visual. "Speaking of bending over," I said. "Has anyone ever seen high school wrestling? Because let me tell you about my night last night."

"I was a wrestler in high school," Desperado said. "It's a righteous sport."

I stilled. "Oh, well, then I'm done talking."

Eliot smirked. "That has to be a first."

"Shut up," I muttered.

The swinging doors that separated the dining room from the kitchen opened, revealing my mother and her two sisters. Because one of my aunts had left her husband and now lived in the upstairs apartment, I should have figured Mom was up there. She's never late.

All three women pulled up short when they saw Desperado.

"Who is this?" Mom asked.

I saw my opening. "This is Desperado," I said. "He's Lexie's new boyfriend."

"I see."

"He's a boxer," Mario said.

"And he takes yoga," Derrick said.

"And he used to wrestle in high school," I said. "And that's not a bad thing, no matter how homoerotic it is."

"What did you say?" Desperado asked.

"Oh, look, here comes the waitress." I was starting to feel reasonably good about getting out of dinner without having to talk about my work demotion. Desperado was going to be the best thing that ever happened to me.

Mom settled into the booth next to Grandpa. "What kind of name is Desperado?"

"He's black," Grandpa said.

"I noticed."

"That's a black name."

"What's a black name?" Desperado asked.

"It's a name black people give their children," Grandpa said, either missing the menace in Desperado's voice or purposely ignoring it. It was hard to be certain.

"That's racist, Grandpa," Lexie chided.

Grandpa ignored her. "What do you do for a living, Dusty?"

"It's Desperado."

"I'm going to call you Dusty," Grandpa said.

"I'm a fighter," Desperado said.

"And you make money from that?"

"I also work part time at the gym to pay my rent," Desperado conceded.

"So, you're a janitor?"

"Hey, old man, what are you saying?"

Eliot cleared his throat, causing Desperado to focus on him. "Don't insult him," Eliot warned.

"And what are you going to do about it?" Desperado challenged.

"He's going to kick your ass," Mario announced.

Eliot appeared calm, but I could feel his body tense. "Mario?"

"Yeah."

"Sit there and stare at your plate," Eliot instructed.

"Got it."

"Do you want to take this outside?" Desperado asked.

"If you feel that's necessary," Eliot said.

"If you take it outside, I'm going to arrest you," Derrick warned.

Desperado considered Derrick's statement. "I guess we don't need to take it outside," he said. "I'm not saying that because I'm scared, though. I'm saying it because my probation officer will be ticked if I get arrested again."

"Good to know," Derrick said.

I glanced at Eliot, mildly turned on by his show of protectiveness toward my grandfather. I leaned in closer to him. "I'll wrestle with you later."

Eliot smiled. "I'll kick your ass, too."

"You two are sick," Derrick grumbled.

"So, Avery, tell me what you did wrong at work," Mom said, turning from Desperado and focusing on me. "I want to know exactly what you did, because I know you did something."

Ah, the best laid plans.

After my disastrous turn at wrestling, Stanley decided my next outing would be to a sport I understood (although he was doubtful that the nuances of basketball were something I could grasp). Let me tell you something, high school basketball is not like what you see on television.

"I think they miss it more than they hit it," I grumbled to Jared Jackson. He was a photographer for the newspaper, and he'd been assigned to the game, too. Instead of taking photographs tonight, he was more interested in grilling me for information. He loves gossip.

"That's what she said," Jared teased.

I'm also fairly certain he's gay. He talks gratuitously about sex, but he's always checking out dudes. Right now, he had his eye on one of the assistant coaches across the parquet floor.

"So, do you have any other gossip?" I asked.

"I heard Duncan reported you for sexually harassing him," Jared said. "He told the Human Resources lady that you insinuated he didn't have any balls."

"What did she say?"

"I think she told him that she knows he doesn't have any balls, and that's why he's always in her office," Jared said.

I swiveled. "What?"

"Robin is sick of him," Jared said. "He's down in her office at least once a week. She told him that he's going to have a complaint put in his file if he comes down to her office one more time."

I liked this story. "What did Duncan say?"

"He made an appointment with the publisher to complain about Robin emasculating him."

"Why doesn't that surprise me?"

"Because you're an astute observer of the human condition," Jared said.

That's another reason I think he's probably gay. He talks like a woman – one who reads those cheesy, bodice-ripping romance novels and then tries to model his life after them. "Has anyone ever told you that you're weird?"

"You run around in *Star Wars* clothes," Jared pointed out.

"That's why I'm cool."

"Only in your own mind," Jared said.

"At least I have a boyfriend."

Jared tilted his head to the side, considering. "He's hot, too."

"He is hot," I agreed.

"How are things between the two of you?"

"Fine," I said, briefly wondering if he was asking because he was genuinely curious or trying to ascertain whether Eliot would be on the market anytime soon. "We're pretty happy right now."

"That's cool," Jared said. "What did you get him for Christmas?"

I shifted uncomfortably. Jared touched on a topic I wasn't entirely comfortable with. This was my first Christmas with Eliot, and I wanted to get him something special. I didn't think he would find the same joy in shark slippers that I did. "I'm still weighing my options."

Jared smirked. "You have no idea what to get him, do you?"

"Nope," I said. "He's not a very materialistic guy. He doesn't collect anything. Clothes seem too ... impersonal. He doesn't wear jewelry. I have absolutely no idea."

"What about a watch?" Jared suggested. "It's not really jewelry, but it's still classy."

"I considered that," I said. "I just don't know what I'm going to do. I'm hoping to be able to sneak around his apartment and find what he got me so I can buy something of equal value."

"That's so ... romantic."

I shot him a look. "Romance comes after the gifts," I said. "I can't get him something lame. It's our first Christmas together."

"You're nervous," Jared said.

"I am not."

"You are," Jared said. "I've never seen you nervous. It's cute."

"Whatever," I grumbled. The sound of the horn blaring signified that it was halftime, so I got to my feet.

"Where are you going?"

"I'm hungry," I said. "I need food, and to get away from you."

"Avery is nervous," Jared sang.

I ignored him as I followed the trail of people to the cafeteria area outside of the gym. After ordering a hot dog and Diet Coke, I leaned against a wall and studied the assembled students and parents. The game was being hosted at a Clinton Township high school, but the visiting team was Catholic North. That's why I hadn't put up a fight when Stanley gave me the assignment.

Kelsey Cooper's death wasn't my story, but that didn't mean I couldn't ask a few questions if the opportunity arose.

"So, you're the new sports reporter with The Monitor, aren't you?"

I shifted my attention from the crowd and focused on the man who had sidled up to me. He looked vaguely familiar, his polyester pants notwithstanding. It took me a second to recognize him. "You're the Catholic North coach."

"Fred Springer." He extended his hand.

Since both my hands were full, I shrugged in greeting. "Nice to meet you."

"You're Avery Shaw, right?"

"I see my reputation precedes me."

"You're in the news a lot," Fred said.

I fought the urge to scowl. "I am."

"Well, I can say that that the newsroom's loss is my incredible gain." Fred had "creeper" written all over him. His eyes were predatory as he looked me up and down. "Has anyone ever told you how attractive you are?"

"My boyfriend does every night."

Fred wasn't dissuaded. "I love a woman who isn't afraid to wear *Star Wars* shoes."

"Do you know a lot of women like that?"

"Not yet," Fred said. "You'll be my first."

He was grossing me out. "Shouldn't you be in the locker room with your players?"

"I let the assistant coaches handle the menial tasks," Fred said. "I'm the head coach."

Now that he mentioned it, he did have a resemblance to a certain type of head. "Well, that's nice." I looked over his shoulder for someone else – anyone else – to talk to.

"So, how are you liking sports?" Fred obviously wasn't going anywhere.

"I like it," I said, an idea forming. "It's much easier than reporting news. If I was still in news, I'd probably be on that Kelsey Cooper story. That's just depressing."

"Yeah, that's horrible," Fred said, averting his gaze.

"She was a student at your school, right?"

"She was a sophomore," Fred said. "The whole school is reeling."

"I bet," I said. "A sophomore, huh? What was a sophomore doing out alone on the school grounds at night?"

"I have no idea."

"Did she have any ties to the wrestling team?" I have no idea why I asked the question, but Allison and Ashley's tidbit about the wrestling parties was stuck in my head. I just needed to figure out why.

"Not that I know of," Fred said. "Why would you ask that?"

"Aren't you guys known for having one of the best wrestling teams in the state?"

"So?"

"I'm just flexing my sports-knowledge muscles," I said.

"Ah, good for you," Fred said. "Beautiful and smart."

He made my skin crawl. "Are they questioning the students at the school?"

"About what?"

"Kelsey Cooper's rape and murder." I don't know whom he's trying to fool, but I'm not your typical sports reporter.

"Oh, will you look at the time," Fred said, gesturing to his bare wrist. "I need to get back to the team. It was nice to meet you. If you need an ... introduction ... to the sports scene, don't hesitate to give me a call."

"I'll keep that in mind."

"WHO won the game?" Stanley asked when I walked into the newsroom.

"Catholic North."

"Are you sure?" Stanley asked. "The higher score wins."

"I'm sure."

"Did you interview the coach?"

"Unfortunately, yes."

"Unfortunately?" Stanley shot me a look. "Fred Springer is a well-known coach. You'd better not have been rude to him."

I narrowed my eyes. "I wasn't rude to him."

"I don't believe you."

"You know what?"

Marvin chose that moment to breeze into the newsroom, and he wasn't alone. Eliot was a few steps behind him, and he was carrying a small brown bag.

"Look who I found in the parking lot," Marvin said.

"What are you doing here?" I asked, confused.

"I was in the area," Eliot said, giving me a quick kiss on the cheek. "I figured you might need some cheering up." He handed me the bag. It was from Dairy Queen.

"You brought me ice cream?"

"I brought you a hot fudge sundae," Eliot said. "I figured you could use the sugar."

"Oh, he brought something sweet for his sweetie," Brick said, poking his head around the corner and focusing on Eliot.

"Brick," Eliot said, forcing his face to remain neutral. "How are you?"

"Are you asking how I am since you and your girlfriend got my fiancée arrested?"

"I think that was implied," Eliot replied, his tone dry.

"Well, I'm just great," Brick said. "I love going to see my fiancée and not being able to touch her through the bulletproof glass."

"Well, maybe she should have thought about that before she started killing people on the freeways," Eliot suggested.

"Maybe you two should have kept your noses out of other people's business," Brick shot back.

"Maybe you should have kept your girlfriend from trying to kill mine," Eliot said.

"Let's keep it civil, guys," Stanley said, clearly nervous.

Eliot ignored him. "Your girlfriend is certifiable."

"She's my fiancée," Brick said.

"Which just shows how desperate you are," Eliot said.

Brick took a step forward. "Do you want to take this outside?"

"Why do people keep asking me that?" Eliot asked, turning to me.

"I think it has a little something to do with your attitude," I teased, grabbing his hand. "Come over to my desk."

"No sex is allowed in the building," Stanley said.

For a second I thought he'd developed a sense of humor. One look at his face told me he was deathly serious. "Don't worry, if we're going to do it we'll do it in the parking lot, like Brick."

Brick shot me the middle finger.

"Oh, good," Stanley said. "Just get your article done first."

"You got it." Once we were near my desk, I opened the ice cream and took a big bite. I offered the next to Eliot. "Thanks for this. I needed it."

"I wish I could say it was for selfless reasons, but I kind of miss seeing you every night," Eliot said.

"Hey, I wake you up for sex when I come home."

Eliot smirked. "I miss just being able to sit around and watch television with you," he said. "I miss your running diatribes about the state of the horror movie industry."

"I miss it, too."

Eliot pressed a light kiss to my forehead. "I can't stay. I just wanted to see you."

"Are you staying at your apartment tonight?"

Eliot looked conflicted. "I have to be up early."

"Okay," I said, sighing.

"I already grabbed stuff from your house for you," he said. "Just let yourself into the apartment when you get there."

I smiled. He really had been missing me. "Do you want me to wake you up for sex or do you need your sleep?"

"Wake me up," Eliot said, giving me a quick kiss. "And, just for future reference, you never have to ask that question. Always wake me up."

"Good to know."

"**B**asketball again?"
Stanley pinched the bridge of his nose as he regarded me. "It's the winter sports season."

"So?"

"That means it's basketball season," Stanley said. "That's our biggest sport in the winter. That and wrestling."

"What about hockey? I was bored at basketball last night," I argued. "I bet they have hot chocolate at hockey."

"You're not ready for hockey."

"How am I not ready?"

"It's a complicated game."

"Don't you just put the puck in the net?"

"Omigod," Stanley said, rolling his eyes. "It's like you're a child."

This child was about to throw a fit. "Basketball bores me," I said. "Plus, their food is not good. I liked the food at wrestling better."

"You're here to do a job," Stanley said.

"Who says I can't do my job with better food?"

"You're going to a basketball game," Stanley said. "It's an important basketball game. Jim Hoffman is retiring."

"Who is Jim Hoffman?"

"Is that a joke?" Stanley asked.

"Nope."

"He's only been the coach at Sterling Heights for thirty years," Stanley said.

"Does he get a prize for that?"

"It's his final season," Stanley said. "This is their first home game of the season. They're having a big ceremony for him."

"So I just have to cover the ceremony?" That didn't sound so bad.

"No, you have to cover the ceremony and the game," Stanley said. "You have to do two articles."

This just kept getting worse. "One on the game and one on the ceremony?"

"Yes."

"Great," I said, rummaging through the mess on my desk to find a notebook. "What a great way to spend an evening."

"That means you have to interview Hoffman," Stanley said.

"Really? I need to interview the guy who I'm writing an article about? I'm shocked."

"No one needs your sarcasm," Stanley said.

"I need my sarcasm," I said. "I do. That's how I'm surviving this ... debacle."

"Oh, like we're glad to have to absorb you," Stanley shot back. "You're bringing us down. It's like driving a Volkswagen Beetle when you have a Cadillac in the garage."

I know absolutely nothing about cars, but I'm fairly certain that was an insult. I whipped my phone out and texted Eliot to be sure. Stanley watched me curiously. When Eliot texted back, I stuck my tongue out at Stanley in triumph. "I'll have you know, a Beetle is much cuter than a Cadillac. Eliot texted photos."

Stanley rolled his eyes. "You're unbelievable."

My phone dinged again. "Oh, and Eliot says I'm the equivalent of a Jaguar, so suck on that."

"You must be really good in bed," Stanley said as he turned and stalked away. "There can be no other explanation."

Now that was a compliment.

"SO, where is this ceremony supposed to happen?"

The woman collecting money at the table in front of the gym looked me up and down. "And you are?"

I flashed my press pass.

"I don't know what that means."

I hate sports. I don't even want to watch them anymore. Eliot is banned. "I'm Avery Shaw," I said. "I'm here to cover the game for The Monitor. I need to cover the ceremony, too, and I was told that would be happening before the game."

"Oh, right," the woman said. "They're both happening in the gym."

"Great," I said, moving toward the door. "Oh, by the way, do you guys have chicken strips here?"

"We don't have fried foods," she said. "They're not good for the kids' health. We have apples."

"Yum."

I strode into the gym, pushing my way past milling parents and excited teenagers as I made my way toward the bleachers. I opted for a spot high enough that errant balls wouldn't hit me in the face if I wasn't paying attention – there's a sentence I never thought would cross my brain – and yet low enough that I wouldn't have to sit next to flirting teenagers. No one wants that.

I pulled my phone out of my pocket and called Eliot.

"What's up, Buttercup?"

"I'm thinking of quitting," I said.

"No, you're not," Eliot replied. "You're just depressed."

"I don't get depressed," I said. "I depress others."

"You don't depress me," he said.

"Give it time."

Eliot sighed. "I know you're upset," he said. "I get it. You're good at your job, and you're being punished for it."

"I'm being punished because I'm mouthy," I said. "Let's not embellish. I'm well aware of how annoying I am."

"That's one of the things I like most about you," Eliot said. "You don't have an inflated sense of ego."

"The fact that I'm the best reporter at The Monitor and I'm stuck at a basketball game just pisses me off."

Eliot chuckled throatily. "You make me laugh."

"Maybe I should try to see if I can get a job at one of the Detroit papers?"

Eliot was quiet on the other end of the phone.

"You don't think I can, do you?"

"I think you absolutely can," Eliot said. "I don't want you to, though."

"Why not?"

"You find terrible trouble in the suburbs," he said. "I would hate to think of the kind of trouble you'd get yourself into in the city. It's a lot more dangerous there."

"That's not your problem," I said.

"Your safety is my concern," Eliot said. "I don't want you hurt. I don't think I could take that."

"You're kind of sweet," I said.

"Don't tell anyone," Eliot warned. "It will ruin my street cred."

"Your secret is safe with me."

Eliot paused, and I could practically hear his mind working over the phone. "You don't have to stay in newspapers," he said finally.

The words hit me like a punch in the gut. "What?"

"Sweetie, you have a lot of talents," he said. "You could go into public relations or something."

"I don't get along with people."

"You have a point," Eliot said. "You could write news releases."

"That sounds delightful."

"Or, you could suck it up and get your job back at The Monitor," Eliot said.

"How am I going to do that?"

"You're going to bring Ludington down," Eliot said.

"How am I going to do that?"

"Oh, please," Eliot scoffed. "That dude has corruption written all over him. You just need to find out what he's got his sticky fingers in."

"That's true," I said. "I know he's got ties to some nefarious people."

"We'll find it," Eliot said.

"We'll?"

"You don't think I'm going to let you do this alone, do you?"

"You really must miss me," I teased.

"It baffles me, too," Eliot said. "We'll put our heads together this weekend."

"I thought you wanted to put other stuff together on the weekends?"

"You have a filthy mind," Eliot said. "I happen to like it."

People were jumping to their feet and applauding. "I have to go," I said. "I'll see you in a few hours."

"Okay," Eliot said. "I'll be naked."

"See, something to look forward to ... oh, shit."

"What's wrong?"

"Shit, shit, shit."

"What's wrong?" Eliot was alarmed.

"Nothing," I said, hiding my face with my hand as a familiar figure walked to the center of the court toward the microphone. "There's just a ceremony for a retiring coach."

"And that's cause for profanity ... and scaring me to death?"

"I'm at a basketball game," I said. "What could happen?"

"It's you."

He had a point. "No, it's just ... ."

"Welcome everyone. This is a big night for Sterling Heights, and a sad one. Not only are we starting the goodbye tour for our beloved coach Jim Hoffman, we also have an actual hero here to wish him well. Everyone, give a warm welcome to Sheriff Jake Farrell."

Shit.

. . .

I HAD been hiding from Jake for more than a month. After I was assured that he would survive the gunshot wound he incurred while trying to protect me I'd left a bouquet of flowers next to his bed and disappeared from his life.

Every crime story that crossed my desk was checked extensively to make sure it wouldn't cross over into the sheriff's department's jurisdiction. If there was any risk of that, I handed it off to another reporter. I just couldn't face him.

What are the odds that I would run into him on a sports story?

The universe hates me.

I blame Tad Ludington. He's going down.

Jake walked to the microphone, and I was happy to see that his cheeks were flush with color and he seemed to be in fine physical form. I took the opportunity to look him over. His dark hair was pushed up into its usual messy bird's nest, and his smile was broad and welcoming. His uniform seemed a little loose, which would seem to indicate that he'd lost weight. Since he worked out like a fiend I had a feeling that his workout schedule had been limited due to his recovery.

I felt a pang in my chest. One of the worst things I'd ever done – and that list is long and sundry – was to break up with him via email when he was overseas. I'd been in college at the time, and we'd spent years together up until that point. I'd just decided I wanted to be adventuresome in college. Everyone kept telling me that your high school boyfriend wasn't forever, and I'd believed them. I couldn't help but wonder how different both of our lives might have been if I'd made a different decision.

Don't get me wrong; I'm happy with Eliot. He gets me in a way that Jake can't. He's just not capable of it. Despite a few wild years in his youth, Jake is a rule follower. I've never met a rule I didn't want to break. Eliot is like that, and that's why we mesh. That doesn't mean there aren't weird residual feelings for Jake that rear their ugly head at inopportune times – like this one.

"How is everyone tonight?" Jake asked, playing to the crowd. "I've known Jim Hoffman for about five years now, but it feels like I've known him forever." Jake scanned the crowd, and when his eyes landed on me I inhaled sharply.

The crowd died away as our eyes met.

Jake recovered. "Jim is one of those coaches who not only teaches kids about a game, he also teaches them about life."

Jake's eyes never moved from mine for his entire speech. I felt as if I was being swallowed whole.

THE SECOND Jake left the podium, he started edging along the far wall of the gym – right in my direction. His intention was obvious.

I started to panic. We were due for a conversation, but we couldn't have it here. I got to my feet and headed toward the door that led to the concession stand. I could only hope he wouldn't follow me.

I walked up to the woman behind the counter and ordered a Diet Coke.

"We don't have pop," she said. "It's not good for the kids."

"You've got to be kidding me."

"We have water."

"Give me a water," I snapped.

"That will be three dollars."

"For a bottle of water?" These high school concession stands are a racket.

"Yup."

"Give it to me," I grumbled.

"You got it. Oh, Sheriff Farrell, it's so good to see you on your feet."

I froze.

"Thank you," Jake said. "I'm feeling much better."

"That's good," the woman said. "We were all pulling for you. I can't believe you risked your life to save a newspaper reporter, of all things."

I pressed my lips together. I still couldn't make my body move. I was frozen in time and space.

"It was a bad situation," Jake said. "I don't regret what I did."

I knew his comments were aimed at me.

"You're such a hero," the woman said, pressing a hand to the spot above her heart. "Such a hero."

"I was just doing my job," Jake said.

"That will be three dollars," the woman said.

I realized I'd left my purse sitting on the bleachers. "I ... ."

"I've got it," Jake said, moving up next to me and handing the woman a five-dollar bill.

"Oh, we can't take your money," she said.

"Take it," Jake said. "Ms. Shaw is going to pay me back."

"Ms. Shaw? Avery Shaw?"

"See, you're famous," Jake said, handing me the bottle of water.

"Great," I said, taking it from him.

"Can we talk?" Jake's voice was unsure.

"I ... I have to cover the game," I said lamely.

"I heard," he said. "I'm sorry."

"It's not your fault," I said. "I did it to myself."

"You usually do."

I forced a tight smile as I finally mustered the courage to meet his steady gaze. "How are you?"

"You're the woman he got shot protecting," the woman said.

"Thanks for the news update," I snapped.

Jake grabbed my arm. "Let's go over here and talk."

"I can't," I said, jerking away from him. "I ... ."

"Avery," Jake warned. "You've been avoiding me for weeks."

"I've been busy."

"Avery ... ."

"I have to go and cover the game," I said, moving back toward the gym. "I'll ... I'll send you the money for the water in the mail."

"I don't care about the money," Jake growled.

"I ... I'm glad you're feeling better."

"Avery, don't you dare ... dammit!"

I didn't turn around. What? I'm a total idiot sometimes. I can acknowledge my faults.

"What are you doing here?"

Lexie was standing behind the counter at Yoga One That I Want, her new studio, and she seemed surprised to see me.

After a night spent tossing and turning, and that was after I'd woken Eliot up twice to work off my excess energy, I needed to focus on something that wasn't associated with my extreme cowardice. I'd handled the Jake situation wrong, and I couldn't get it out of my mind.

"I'm here for a class," I said.

"You hate yoga," Lexie said.

"I do," I said. "Carly is already on her Christmas break, though, and we needed something to do in the middle of the afternoon on a Wednesday. Going to a bar seems like a bad idea."

"Oh, and you came here," Lexie said. "I'm touched."

"We don't have to pay here," I said. "I gave you the seed money. We get free classes."

"I haven't forgotten," Lexie said. "I don't have a class this afternoon, though."

"That's fine," I said, perching on one of the stools at the juice bar.

"I just need a smoothie. You don't happen to have alcohol, do you? I can't drink at a bar in the middle of the day, but I think I can get away with it here."

"Up in my apartment," Lexie said. "Don't you have to work tonight?"

"I can do it drunk," I said. "They won't even notice. They already think I'm an idiot."

Lexie furrowed her brow. "You seem upset."

"It's been a long week."

"It's been a long life for me," she said. "I've washed out of two rehabs, and I only got to start a business because you got a reward and gave me the money."

"You're doing well," I said brightly. "I'm proud of you."

Lexie smiled. "Why don't you tell me what's wrong?"

I wasn't sure how to broach the subject, so it was a relief when my best friend Carly entered the studio, taking the onus of keeping the conversation going off of me.

"I hate men," she announced.

"Then why did you marry one?"

"He confused me with a big ring," Carly said, hopping up onto the stool next to me. "You know that I can't say no to diamonds."

"What did he do today?"

"Nothing specific," Carly said. "He just tried to wake me up by taking my underwear off."

"That's always a bonus in my world," I said.

"I don't bother wearing underwear," Lexie added.

"Not once you're married," Carly said. "When you're married, you want to wring every second of sleep out of your weekday mornings that you possibly can."

"That's depressing," I said.

"Aren't you already depressed?" Carly asked.

"Who told you that?"

Carly pointed at Lexie. "She texted me."

"Nice."

"Hey, I know how important your job is to you," Lexie said. "This has to be killing you."

"You have no idea," I said. "I have to get out of sports."

"You could quit," Carly said.

"I can't let the man win," I said.

"Who is the man?"

"Jim MacDonald."

"He's your new publisher?" Lexie asked.

"He's the Devil."

"I think you're focusing on the wrong person," Carly said. "You're only in this mess because of Tad."

I made a face. "I hate him."

"Hey, I'm the one who told you he was bad news when you started dating him in college," Carly said. "He brought a briefcase to a kegger, for crying out loud."

"What a tool," Lexie said, giggling.

"I should have listened to you," I said. "We could have spiked his drink with tainted acid back then and he'd be a problem for mental health services now."

"I offered to do that, too!"

"I hate him," I muttered.

"We need to find a way to go after him," Lexie said. "He has to have a weakness."

"Maybe he's having an affair with someone," Carly suggested.

"His wife has had five kids in six years," I replied. "I've slept with him. He doesn't have the energy."

"That doesn't mean anything," Lexie said. "He could have a prescription for Viagra, for all we know."

"What's up, bitches?"

We all swiveled at the same time, fixing our attention on Mario as he barreled through the door of the yoga studio.

"What are you doing here?" I asked.

"I'm moving in with Lexie," he announced.

"You're doing no such thing," Lexie said.

"Oh, come on! I'm your favorite cousin," Mario pleaded.

"You're not even in the top five," Lexie scoffed.

I patted the empty stool on the other side of me. "What's going on?"

"My dad said I either had to get serious about school or start working at the restaurant full time," Mario said, settling next to me. "I want a strawberry smoothie."

"How old are you again?"

"Twenty."

"That's too young to get serious," Carly said. "You should be having fun at your age."

I held up my hand to still her. "Mario has been going to college for two years," I said. "Last time I checked, he had exactly fifteen usable credits toward a degree."

"I don't know what I want to do," Mario complained.

"Fifteen credits in two years?" Carly was incensed. "I'd cut you off financially." She's pragmatic when it comes to money.

"Thanks," Mario said. He blew a raspberry in her direction. "It's a good thing you're hot, because you're a total bitch."

Carly stuck her tongue out.

"You can't stay here, Mario," Lexie said. "I have one bedroom, and Desperado is ... enthusiastic."

Mario blanched. "Does he stay here every night?"

"Pretty much."

Mario turned to me. "I'm staying with you."

"No, you're not," I said. "Eliot will have a fit. We just got Lexie out. He's enthusiastic, too."

"Yeah, but he's white," Mario said. "He can't be as enthusiastic as Desperado. It's physically impossible."

It took me a second to realize what he was insinuating. I slapped him on the thigh roughly. "You're sick."

"I'm less afraid of Eliot than I am of Desperado."

"You still can't stay," I said. "My life is a mess right now."

"Yes, but I'm about to venture into an unknown world," Mario said. "I need my family to help."

"Are you coming out?" Lexie asked.

"No!"

"What does this unknown world entail?" I asked.

"I bought a food truck." Mario seemed thrilled. I wasn't sure why.

"What kind of food truck?"

"The kind you park at an event," Mario said. "You cook right on the truck. I'm going to serve my world-famous hamburgers. I'm going to be rich."

"And sell them where?"

"Wherever the wind takes me," Mario said.

"How did you afford a food truck?" Lexie asked.

"Grandpa bought it," Mario said. "Dad told Grandpa he had to stop hanging around the restaurant so much because it was pissing off the customers."

"How was he pissing off the customers?"

"I don't know," Mario replied, shrugging. "There was some incident with old Millie and a flyswatter."

That sounded dirty. "You need to be more specific."

"Apparently he was killing flies; you know how he likes to do that."

My grandfather was one of the most feared fly killers in the Midwest. I'd seen it firsthand. "I still don't understand."

"Apparently he kept killing them over Millie's table," Mario said. "They were dropping in her coffee, and eggs, oh, and once in her pancakes. Have you ever tried to get a fly out of syrup? It isn't pretty. Once he told her to open her mouth and say ah."

"Nice," Carly said. "I love your family."

"Try living with them," I grumbled.

"My mom gets drunk and talks to the ceramic goose on her front porch," Carly pointed out.

I'd seen that first hand. She also dressed him up. "It's not as fun as it sounds."

"It sounds great," Carly enthused.

"Our family sucks," Mario said. "My dad said I either had to take real classes or pay my own way. Since Grandpa was mad at him already, I told him my business idea. He thought it was great. We're going to open the truck right in the parking lot of the restaurant."

I snickered. "That's going to give your dad an aneurism."

"That's the point."

I turned his business idea over in my mind. "Do you want to know what you should do?"

"Not particularly," Mario said. "I already know what I should do."

I ignored him. "You should go to high school games," I said. "There are schools that are serving nothing but apple slices and bottled water because kids are supposed to be eating healthy items."

"That's depressing," Mario said.

"It is," I agreed. "You could make a killing by selling decent food in the parking lots. Sure, it's winter, but if you get a foothold now, you could be swimming in money in the spring."

"I like it," Mario said. "You have access to the high school sports schedule, right?"

I nodded.

"Sold," Mario crowed. "I'm going to make my dad cry I'm going to be so successful."

"I get free food, right?"

Mario narrowed his eyes. "Can I stay with you?"

I shook my head. "I'm sorry, I can't. Eliot and I are already struggling for time together."

Lexie tapped her chin thoughtfully. "I know who you can stay with."

We all turned to her expectantly.

"Derrick has a guestroom," Lexie said, arching an eyebrow.

"Oh, cool, I forgot about Derrick," Mario said. "I'm going to his house right now."

Lexie held up a finger. "I have a key to his house. You can move right in, even if he's at work."

"Good idea," Mario said. "He can't kick me out if I've already moved in."

"I agree," Lexie said, handing the key over. "You know where he lives, right?"

"I've been there."

After Mario left, Lexie turned an evil smile in my direction. "That will teach Derrick to mess with my boyfriend."

"He's going to be pissed," I warned.

"I don't care," Lexie said. "He's got it coming. He's a total pain."

"I can't wait until Devon finds out."

"That's just an added bonus," Lexie said. After a few moments of silence, she turned back to the situation at hand. "So, how are we going to take Ludington down?"

"You want to go after him, too?"

"You're one of the only people who always stands by me no matter what," Lexie said. "Of course I'm on your side."

Carly smiled evilly. "So, what's our first move?"

Loyalty is underrated. Here I was feeling sorry for myself, and I had two people willing to throw their hats into the ring to take Tad down. I'm lucky, at least when it comes to friends and family. Yes, I said it.

"Okay, let's think," I said. "What's his greatest weakness?"

"His ego," Carly said. "All men can be brought to their knees through their ego."

Well, you can't argue with that.

"I cannot believe they made me come to wrestling again," I grumbled.

"I can't believe they made me bring you," Dave said, slouching on the bleachers. "Don't sit next to me. I don't want people to think we're together."

I narrowed my eyes. "You should be so lucky."

"If you were mute, I'd say you have a point," Dave said. "You're not hard to look at."

I waited.

"It's just that ... well ... when you open your mouth, I want to cut your tongue out," Dave said.

"Oh, don't do that. I might miss it."

I glanced up when I heard the voice. "What are you doing here?"

Eliot handed me a tray of chicken strips. "I figured you might need some support."

I smiled. "Admit it; you're just bored without me."

"I might miss you a little," Eliot admitted.

"How much is a little?"

Eliot spaced his index finger and thumb. "Just a smidge."

I took the chicken strips from him. "That's how much I miss you, too."

Eliot made a face. "Was that a pointed joke?"

"Nope," I said, sitting on the bleachers and digging into the food. "I have so few people on my team right now that I can't afford to alienate any of them."

Eliot settled next to me. "Don't worry about that," he said. "Apparently I've forgotten how to entertain myself when you're otherwise engaged."

"Oh, you're so cute," I said, waving a piece of chicken in his face.

Eliot grabbed my hand, stilling the food so he could take a bite. "Those are pretty good."

"The food is much better at wrestling, for some reason."

"You two are so sweet I just might throw up," Dave said.

"If you don't shut up I'm going to hit you so hard that's not going to be an option," Eliot warned.

Dave met Eliot's serious face, and I could tell he was sizing him up. He must not have liked what he saw. "I was just joking, man."

"Funny," Eliot said. He turned back to me. "So, what's the deal with wrestling tonight? Why are there so many buses in the parking lot?"

"I think they're organizing this year's county gay pride parade."

"Stop saying things like that," Dave snapped.

"Don't take that tone with her," Eliot said, extending a finger.

I stuck my tongue out at Dave behind Eliot's back.

"And don't be all ... you," Eliot said. "I'll have you know, wrestling happens to be a really great sport. It teaches you about discipline."

"Is that because they want to spank each other?"

Eliot flicked my nose. "It's a cool sport."

"Let me guess, you wrestled in high school, didn't you?"

"No, I won a state championship in wrestling when I was in high school," Eliot said.

Huh. That was ... depressing. "And you're sure you like girls, right?"

"Don't be cute."

"I wouldn't worry about that," Dave said.

"Hey, I thought you didn't want people to think you were with me," I said. "Or are you okay with it now because I have a big wrestling stud on my side?"

"Let's just say that he's scarier than you," Dave shot back. "I didn't know that was possible."

I ignored him. "Are you going to stay for the whole meet?"

"I don't know," Eliot said. "It depends on what teams are here."

"Most of the teams in the county are here," Dave said. "It's a county meet."

"Cool," Eliot said. "What schools are the best this year?"

"It's too early to tell," Dave said, warming to Eliot. "Catholic North has solid wrestlers. They're the ones to watch this year."

Speaking of Catholic North ... . "Hey, do you know anything about the wrestling parties the Catholic North kids throw every Friday?"

Dave arched an eyebrow. "How do you know about those parties?"

"Yeah, how do you know about those parties?" Eliot asked, suspicious.

"I heard two girls talking at the meet last week," I said. "They said that Kelsey Cooper went to one of the parties."

"Who is Kelsey Cooper?"

Eliot scowled. "She's the girl who was found dead in the woods at Catholic North last week."

"Why are you asking about her?" Dave asked.

"Yeah, why are you asking about her?" Eliot echoed.

"I ... hey, don't look at me that way," I said. "I heard them talking and just happened to ... ."

"What? Eavesdrop?"

"That's a horrible thing to say about your girlfriend," I grumbled.

"Not if it's true."

"Watch the boys in their little rubber outfits," I said, pointing for emphasis. "Maybe it will get you in the mood to wrestle later."

"I know what you're up to," Eliot said.

"What's she up to now?"

I froze. Tonight was the night for surprise guests at wrestling apparently, because when I shifted my gaze to the figure standing on the gym floor in front of us I wanted to set the welcome mat in front of the school on fire.

"Hey, Jake," Eliot said. "What are you doing here?"

"I have to give the medals out at the end of the meet," Jake said, climbing up the bleachers and settling next to me. I was now uncomfortably pressed between my past and present, and there was no way out. "I thought I would watch the wrestling."

"You like wrestling?" Eliot asked.

"I won a state championship in high school," Jake said, squaring his shoulders.

"Me, too."

Well, I could see where this conversation was going. As long as it didn't involve me, though, I didn't care. After chatting about their wrestling achievements for what seemed like forever – hey, sixty seconds can be daunting when the subject is stupid – Jake focused on me.

"So, what's new in your life?"

I shrugged.

Jake arched an eyebrow in Eliot's direction.

"Well, per usual, she's ticked off half of the county," Eliot said. "That's the bad news. The good news is that she can still be cheered up with fried foods."

"It's always good to go to the classics," Jake said, snagging a chicken strip from my tray. "Hey, these are good."

I've often wondered if black holes can open up and swallow people when no one is looking. I think that's what happened to me tonight.

"How are you feeling?" Eliot asked.

"Better," Jake said. "I can start full workouts again in a week."

"That must be a relief."

"Yeah," Jake said. "It's been a long recuperation."

"Well, you survived," Eliot said. "That's all that matters, especially given who you were trying to save when it happened."

I swallowed hard.

"Speaking of that," Jake said, shifting uncomfortably. "I never got a chance to thank you for saving me that night."

"I didn't save you," Eliot said. "I sat with you until the ambulance arrived. You saved her."

"I didn't save her," Jake replied, keeping his gaze focused on the gym floor. "She saved herself. I didn't see him coming. If she hadn't played things so smart we'd both be dead."

"You still risked yourself for her," Eliot said. "You're the one who deserves the thanks."

Each man avoided looking the other in the eyes.

"Oh, good grief," I said. "Do you want me to leave you two alone so you can kiss? This is the place for it, after all. Maybe you can go down on the mats and grope each other."

Eliot poked me in the side. "I'm starting to think Dave is right about cutting out your tongue."

Jake barked out a laugh. "You just make friends wherever you go, don't you?"

"I have a gift."

"Not that I don't like the chicken strips," Jake said, stealing another from my tray. "But why aren't you eating food from your grandfather's truck out in the parking lot?"

I jerked my head up. "What?"

"You didn't know?" Eliot asked. "I figured you were the one who told them to come here."

"Is Mario with him?"

"Yup," Eliot said. "It looks like they're doing good business, too."

"Oh, look at that move," Jake said, pointing to the floor as one of the sweaty boys rolled over on top of the other.

"That was nice," Eliot said.

I got to my feet. "I'm going to check out this truck."

"Bring me back a hamburger," Eliot said.

"Me, too," Jake added.

I'd just been thrown over for teenage boys in rubber suits. My ego was taking a beating tonight. "You're not coming with me?"

"I'm good," Eliot said.

"I thought you came here because you missed me?"

"We can spend time together when you get back," Eliot said, engrossed in the action on the floor. "That kid is a monster."

"He's state ranked," Jake said.

I shot a look in Dave's direction, not missing the mirth on his face as he enjoyed my predicament. "Do you care if I go to the food truck?"

"I only care if you come back."

I stomped down the bleachers.

"Don't forget our hamburgers," Eliot called after me.

I hate men sometimes. I swear.

THE line to the food truck was long. It was December, and even though snow hadn't fallen yet, it was still cold. I was impressed that Mario and Grandpa had managed to get this many people to wait in line, especially in 40 degrees and the dark. Of course, I wasn't going to wait in line. Hey, when you're family, you get special treatment.

I cut to the front of the line.

"Hey, the line starts back there," a pretty brunette said.

"Then you should get back there."

"That doesn't make any sense," she said. "I'm at the front of the line."

"I get my own line."

"How do you figure?"

"Hey, Avery," Mario said when he caught sight of me. "You were totally right about this."

"I'm always right."

"That's my motto," Grandpa said, handing a hamburger to a student. "Do you want something to eat?"

"I need two hamburgers," I said. "If you spit on them, I'll look the other way."

Mario raised an eyebrow. "Who are they for?"

"Eliot and Jake."

"You want me to spit on the sheriff's food?"

"No, I just said if it happened I wouldn't tell anyone," I corrected.

"You're a great girlfriend," Mario deadpanned.

"I know."

"So, what's going on in there?" Grandpa asked.

"They're wrestling."

"Why?"

"Because they know it bugs me," I said.

Grandpa smiled. He was used to my theatrics. Since he was the most dramatic man I'd ever met, I realized I'd probably gotten that little genetic gem from him. "It will all work out, kid. You're too good at what you do for this to keep you down."

"I hope so," I said. "I can't take much more of this."

"Hey, I'm next in line." The brunette was whining again. "Why are you ignoring me and focusing on her?"

"Because she's family," Grandpa said.

"I don't care," the girl said. "I'm the one who waited in this line for twenty minutes. I want some service."

I exchanged a look with Mario. "What do you want?" he asked her.

"I want a salad with ranch dressing on the side."

"We have hamburgers and hot dogs," Mario said.

"What kind of a food truck is this?"

Mario pointed to the menu on the side of the truck. It listed only two items.

"Oh, fine, I want a hamburger," the girl said.

"Make sure you lick that one," I told Mario, my gaze landing on the streaking form of a high school girl as she raced across the parking lot. I wasn't sure, but I could swear she'd been crying. I made my decision quickly. "I'll be back in a minute. Don't give anyone my hamburgers."

Mario saluted.

I have no idea why I did it. I didn't like crying teenage girls when I was one of them. Something about the brief glance I'd gotten of the girl bothered me, though. I couldn't just let it go. I moved in the direction she'd fled. What? I care about people.

12 / TWELVE

The parking lot was poorly lit, forcing me to follow the unmistakable sound of sobs to find my target. She was hiding between two big sports utility vehicles, bent over at the waist.

I glanced around nervously. "Are you okay?"

The girl jerked when she heard my voice. "I ... is this your car?"

I shook my head. "I just heard you. I thought I would check to see that you're okay."

I took the opportunity to look the girl over. She was small and slim. I think she could have fit both of her thighs into one leg of my jeans. Her hair was long and dark, and it cascaded past her shoulders in a series of thick waves. Her heart-shaped face was devoid of makeup. She was cute, even if her brown eyes were ringed with red.

"I'm fine."

"You don't look fine."

"Well, I am."

I knew a little about being bothered by the presence of others, so I decided not to press. "Okay. I was just checking."

She sniffled. "I'm fine."

I turned, chastising myself for worrying about the emotional state of others as I started moving back through the dark parking lot. Don't worry, it was a momentary lapse. I won't make that mistake again. The sight of four boys standing a few feet away caused me to pull up short.

"Hey, Jen," one of the boys said, ignoring my presence. "We were looking for you."

"W-w-why?"

"What do you mean why? We want to spend some time with you."

I immediately didn't like the kid. He looked like a little hairless weasel, just not as cute.

"I'm busy now," Jen said.

"Doing what?"

"She's hanging out with me," I interjected, fixing the kid with a harsh look.

"Are you her mom?"

What? Now I knew I hated this kid. "I'm Avery Shaw."

"Is that supposed to mean something?" The kid was mouthy and clearly full of himself. His three cohorts seemed less aggressive, but they weren't backing down.

"It means you should probably go," I said. "Jen clearly doesn't want to hang out with you."

"Do you want to hang out with me?"

"Not if you were the last ferret on Earth."

The boy stepped closer, puffing out his chest in what I'm sure was a terrifying stance in his mind. "You're kind of hot, for an old lady."

"Kid, have you had a date with anything other than your own hand yet?"

His friends snickered.

"What is that supposed to mean?"

"Alex, I think she was just ... ." Jen looked conflicted.

"It means that you've got a lot to learn about women, Alex," I said.

"Are you going to teach me?" Alex suggested. "I think I could get behind that."

"Oh, I don't have the three seconds you'd last to spare," I said.

The boys laughed again.

Alex's facade was crumbling. "Maybe you should go back inside with the rest of the fossils and leave us to our ... games."

I glanced at Jen. She was practically shaking. There was no way I was leaving her with the obvious date-rapist-in-training. "I'm good."

"I told you to go."

"No."

"What's your name again?"

"Avery."

"Well, Avery, why don't you pull your nose out of other people's business and leave us to our games?" Alex suggested.

"Why don't you pull your head out of your ass and try to use it for something else than giving yourself a rim job."

Alex's face contorted. "Did you just tell me to ... what did you say?"

High school boys are so easy. "I said to go screw yourself." I reached for Jen. "Come on. I'll buy you a hamburger."

Jen gripped my arm. "Thank you."

Yup. She was terrified. Alex moved to block my angle of escape. "Where are you going, blondie?"

"Get out of my way."

"What are you going to do if I don't?"

"I'm going to kick you in the nuts," I replied honestly. "You'd better hope you're wearing a cup, because if you're not, the ball in New York City isn't going to be the only one you'll be waiting to watch drop on New Year's Eve."

Alex curved his waist slightly inward. "You can't do that. I'm a minor."

"I guess we'll just have to agree to disagree," I said.

Alex squared his shoulders. "You can go, you old hag," he said. "Jen is staying with us."

"No, she's not."

"Listen, you bitch ... ."

"Is something going on here?" I recognized Eliot's voice before I saw his figure materialize out of the darkness. He wasn't alone.

"Should you boys be screwing around out here?" Jake asked.

"What is it to you?" Alex sneered.

Jake stepped forward, the light at the center of the lot illuminating his features. "Well, I'm the sheriff," Jake said. "I'm interested in all of the activities going on in my county."

"Are you all right?" Eliot asked.

Jen gripped my arm tighter. "I'm fine," I said. "These ... gentlemen ... were just leaving."

"Is she all right?" Jake asked.

"She's fine," Alex said. "She's dramatic. We were just coming to make sure she was okay."

Jake arched an eyebrow. "Is that true?"

I shook my head. I still wasn't entirely sure what was going on, but I knew Alex and his friends weren't here to deflate Jen's emotional state. "He's lying."

"I figured," Jake said.

"Oh, what, you're going to believe her?" Alex was incensed.

"Over you? Yeah."

"She threatened to kick me in the balls," Alex said.

"Narc," I muttered.

Jake kept his face even. "Why did she do that?"

"Because I told her that old ladies creep me out."

"He called me a ... mom," I said, wrinkling my nose.

Eliot snickered.

"Then he told me he wanted to have sex with me, even though I was old."

Eliot's smile dissipated. "He what?"

"Then he tried to stop us from leaving," I said.

"I did not," Alex argued.

"Not so much fun when someone tattles on you, is it?"

"Why did you try to stop them from leaving?" Jake asked.

"Hey, can we go back to the part where she threatened to kick me in the balls?" Alex asked. "I want to file a report. I want her arrested."

Jake rolled his eyes. "What else did she say?"

"Something about having to wait until New Year's Eve for the ball to drop."

Jake lost his battle to keep a straight face. "Well, I'm sure you're traumatized."

"She's a very bad woman," Alex said.

"You have no idea," Eliot said, holding his hand out and gesturing to me. "Why don't you bring your friend," he said. "I'll buy you guys some hamburgers."

I pushed Jen in front of me, fixing Alex with a challenging look as we moved past him.

"This isn't over," Alex warned.

Jake snapped his fingers in Alex's face. "You'd better hope it is," he said.

"Why, are you and the other guy going to beat me up otherwise?"

Jake shook his head. "Oh, no," he said. "I'm going to let her do whatever she wants to you. Trust me. She's a lot meaner than I could ever be."

"**DO** you want something to eat?" I asked Jen once we were back by the food truck.

"I'm okay," Jen said.

"You're not okay," I said, tapping the counter. "Get her a hamburger."

"You're so bossy," Mario said, turning to Eliot. "How do you put up with her?"

"She's kind of cute," Eliot said.

"You're so whipped," Mario teased. He inclined his head in Jen's direction. "What's her story?"

"I'm not sure yet," I said. "Do you want to tell me what's wrong now?"

"I ... nothing is wrong," Jen said. "I'm just overreacting. My dad says I do it all the time."

"All men say that," I replied. "They're stupid. Don't listen to them."

"In your case it's true," Eliot said. He looked Jen up and down. "Did those boys hurt you?"

"No," Jen said, shaking her head. "They're just ... not nice."

"They're assholes," I agreed. "Why were they after you?"

"They just like messing with me," Jen said.

"About what?"

"Nothing really," Jen said. "I go to Catholic North on an academic scholarship, and I don't have as much money as they do. They call me trailer trash and stuff. You know, saying I have to help my parents pay the rent by turning tricks on the corner. It's not a big deal."

"I knew I should have kicked that kid in the balls when I had the chance," I grumbled.

Eliot rubbed my neck soothingly. "Rein it in, killer. That kid was still a minor."

"He was a major pain," I countered.

"He has some issues," Jake said, joining us by the truck.

"What did he say?" I asked.

"He said you're mean and scary," Jake said. "I told him all women get that way eventually, so he should get used to it now."

"Who were you mean to?" Grandpa asked.

"Some little tool who called me a mom," I said. "I told him I was going to kick him in the balls."

Grandpa chuckled. "You really are one of my favorites."

"Don't encourage her," Jake said. "You're one of the reasons she's such a pain in the first place."

"Weren't you shot a few weeks ago?" Grandpa asked.

"Yes."

"If she's such a pain, how come you were the one who was shot?"

Jake made a face. "Where is my hamburger?"

Grandpa slapped one into his hand. "It's on the house."

"Why?"

"Because you got shot trying to save my family," Grandpa said. "And, even though I find all cops useless, you're also a good man. I can tolerate you."

"Well, that's the nicest thing you've ever said to me."

"Don't get used to it."

Eliot and Jake exchanged small smiles.

"Do you want a hamburger, too, long hair?"

Eliot scowled. "Do you have to call me that?"

"Get a haircut and we'll find out."

"Don't get a haircut," I said. "I like your hair long. You might lose your sex appeal if you cut your hair."

Jake patted him on the back. "You could always hide it under a hat."

"You're hilarious," Eliot said.

"Well, it looks like everyone is having a good time here."

I froze when I heard the voice, and Eliot's fingers tightening on the back of my neck told me he recognized it, too.

"Tad," I said. "What are you doing here?"

"It's the county meet," he said. "I thought I should put in an appearance. I heard the kids talking about a food truck outside, and I thought I'd check it out. I didn't realize it was your family, Avery."

I ignored him.

"I'm assuming you have a permit to operate this truck here?" Tad turned to Grandpa.

"I'm sure you've got a permit to pull my foot out of your ass."

"Excuse me?"

"He was just leaving," Jake said.

"I was not," Grandpa said.

"You were, too."

"I was not."

"If you don't leave, I'm going to have to arrest you," Jake said. "I'd really rather not."

"You know when I called you a good man?" Grandpa asked.

"Yes."

"I take it back."

"Just go," I said. "You've already made a fortune tonight."

"You're no longer my favorite," Grandpa said.

"Oh, poor Avery," Tad said. "Life just isn't going your way, is it? First you get busted down to sports because you're such a bad reporter, and now your own grandfather doesn't even like you."

I opened my mouth to argue, but the retort died on my lips when I saw a pot of water fly out of the truck and land on Tad.

"Oh, sorry," Grandpa said. "Since we have to leave I had to throw the water from the hot dogs out so it doesn't spill. Don't worry, it's only lukewarm, and you'll probably be able to get that smell out of your suit ... in a couple months."

Tad wiped the water from his face and fixed Grandpa with a scorching look. "I thought you didn't like her anymore?"

"I like her better than you."

I rolled my eyes, and turned back to tell Jen that I would take her out to buy her a sandwich. "Jen ... ." She was gone.

Eliot straightened and looked around. "Where did she go?"

"I don't know."

"I'm sure she's fine," Jake said. "She was probably having a teenage moment. We've all had them, and we all survived."

I hoped he was right, but part of me wasn't so sure. One thing was certain: Wrestling certainly brings out the assholes – and not just because everyone and their brother keeps getting in the doggie position.

What? I'm worried. That doesn't mean I've forgotten how stupid wrestling is.

"You look tired," Fish said, looking me up and down Friday morning.

"My new schedule sucks," I said. "I worked until midnight last night, and then I had to turn around and be here at nine this morning."

"That's your fault," Fish said. "If you hadn't made me talk to your mother ... ."

"If you hadn't made me go to sports, I wouldn't have had to tattle on you to my mom," I shot back. "This is really all your fault."

"You have an interesting way of looking at life," Fish said.

"I'm a joy," I said, leaning over the edge of his cubicle so I could read the daily news budget he was compiling. "What's the status of the Kelsey Cooper story?"

Fish narrowed his eyes. "Why do you care?"

"Because it's a tragedy," I said. "I hate tragedies."

"Why do you really care?"

"Because I think there's something weird going on with the Catholic North kids," I admitted.

"And you've come to this conclusion how?"

"I've talked to some of them at the wrestling meets," I said. "Most of them are real jackasses."

Fish furrowed his brow. "Would you like to expound on that?"

I told him about the previous evening's events. When I was done, he tapped his chin thoughtfully. "Where did you hear about the wrestling parties?"

"Who told you about that? I didn't tell you about that."

"Who do you think?"

"Marvin has a huge mouth," I grumbled.

"He only told me to make sure you wouldn't get in any further trouble," Fish said. "I told him to let you be. You're actually in a very interesting position right now."

"How do you figure?"

"You're a news reporter masquerading as a sports reporter," Fish said. "As long as the kids think you're in sports, they're more likely to trust you."

He had a point. Still, I didn't want to be a sports reporter. It was undignified, and I'm nothing if not dignified. I smoothed my Chewbacca "I did it all for the wookie" shirt. "I don't want to stay in sports. Have you talked to MacDonald yet?"

"I've done nothing but talk to MacDonald," Fish said. "He won't even consider moving you back to news until he's sure that you won't do anything embarrassing."

"I never do anything embarrassing."

"You idle at embarrassing," Fish said. "MacDonald says you haven't learned your lesson yet."

"I've totally learned my lesson," I said.

"Do you promise to leave Ludington alone?"

I bit the inside of my lip.

"That's what I thought," Fish said. "You're stuck ... unless you can somehow break the Kelsey Cooper story wide open. Then he's going to have no choice but to move you back to news."

His words sank in. "You want me to keep pursuing the story under the guise of covering sports, don't you?"

"I didn't say that," Fish said.

"You just said ... ."

"I said nothing," Fish clarified. "I just noted you were in an interesting position, and that the Kelsey Cooper story is a tragedy."

"You're sneaky," I said.

"Coming from you, I'll take that as a compliment," he said. "Just be sure to keep what you find to yourself. Don't tell the sports staff what you're doing, and you can't tell Marvin either. He's a great reporter, but he's got looser lips than a prostitute at fleet week."

"Nice."

"Thank you."

I moved away from his desk. "Do you want emails?"

"Send them to my home email address," he said. "I don't want anything on my computer here that could get either of us in trouble."

"Got it."

"Good."

MacDonald chose that moment to barrel into the newsroom. He scanned the area and when his eyes landed on me they lit up – and not with happiness. "You!"

I pasted a fake smile on my face. "What's up? You look especially smart in that suit today, sir."

"What did you do?" Fish muttered under his breath.

MacDonald stalked across the room. "Did you have some sort of altercation with Tad Ludington at the wrestling meet last night?"

"Absolutely not," I said.

"He says you did."

"He's lying."

"He said he got a pot of hot dog water thrown on him," MacDonald said, his gray eyes flashing. "I don't know what that is, but it doesn't sound good."

"Where would I get a pot of hot dog water? Do you think I carry stuff like that around in my purse?"

MacDonald stilled. "Why would he say it?"

"He's prone to lying," I said. "He always has been. When he told me in college that it was only that small because it was cold I believed him."

MacDonald furrowed his brow. "What?"

"Nothing," Fish broke in. "How did Ludington end up doused in hot dog water?"

"Well, I can't be sure, but I heard some kids talking," I said. "They said he happened to be walking by the window of a food truck when the guy inside tossed a pot of water out. It was an accident. He was just in the wrong place at the wrong time."

"That can't possibly be her fault," Fish said, shooting me an irritated look. He definitely knew there was more to the story.

MacDonald didn't look convinced. "Why would he say you did it?"

"Maybe the untreated syphilis has driven him insane," I offered.

"What?"

"She said she has no idea," Fish said. "Listen, I warned you when you decided to believe Ludington in the first place that he was a loose cannon. He's got a personal vendetta against Avery. It's from a long time ago."

"And this is all because the two of you dated in college?"

"I leave a lasting impression on men," I said.

"Yes, it's called Cyclical Derangement Syndrome," Fish said, his face impassive.

"Cyclical?"

"Yes, every time he circles around and runs into Avery again he goes insane," Fish said. "It appears to be temporary, but the bouts get longer each time they pop up."

"And you didn't do anything to him last night?" MacDonald prodded.

"I only said five words to him."

"What were those five words?"

"What are you doing here?"

"And then what happened?"

"Then he had a discussion with Jake," I said.

MacDonald narrowed his eyes. "Sheriff Farrell?"

"Yes."

"What was he doing there?"

"Handing out medals or something."

"What were you doing with him?" MacDonald asked. "You didn't get him shot again, did you?"

"No, but I thought about giving him a wedgie for good measure."

"What?"

"She said nothing happened," Fish said.

"I still cannot figure out why Ludington would blame you for the hot dog water thing," MacDonald said, rubbing his jaw. "He's usually so calm and put together. He was going on and on about his dry cleaner and some stray dog on the street in front of his house trying to hump his leg when he got home last night."

I pursed my lips to keep from laughing.

"He's a tool," Fish said. "The longer you're here, the more you'll realize it."

"He's an elected official," MacDonald said.

"Not for long," I said. "He lost in the November election, and the number of commission seats are being cut in half. He's only in office for another month."

"He's still going to be an important figure in the county," MacDonald said.

"How? Is he going to join the library board? Is he going to chase housewives around and threaten them with fines for overdue books?"

"Let's just say I've heard he's going to move to another position at the start of the new year and leave it at that," MacDonald said.

I narrowed my eyes. This was the first I was hearing about that possibility. "What position?" The all-too-frequent doggie position was wafting through my mind for some reason. I had no idea who was going to be on all fours, though. I was hoping it would be Tad, but somehow I doubted I'd be that lucky.

"It's still a rumor," MacDonald said. "We don't print rumors."

We certainly didn't. That didn't mean I couldn't confirm it elsewhere and somehow blow him out of the water. "Right."

"I guess I'll go back to my office," MacDonald said. "You keep your nose out of trouble, young lady."

I waited until he rounded the corner and was out of sight before I shot a one-fingered salute to his back. "I really hate that guy." I turned to find Fish watching me with curious eyes. "What?"

"Who was in the food truck?"

"What food truck?"

"The one where Ludington was doused with hot dog water."

"Oh, that," I said, taking a step away from his desk. "I have no idea."

"Was it someone who shares genes with you?"

"I have no idea how sturdy the limbs on our family tree are," I said. "I think there might be some weak links."

Fish waited.

"It was my grandfather," I admitted.

Fish glowered at me. "Don't let MacDonald find out."

"Who is going to tell him?"

"Does Ludington know he's your grandfather?"

Crap. I hadn't thought of that. "It will be fine," I said.

"Just ... go and do something," Fish said, waving me away. "I've spent only twenty minutes with you so far today and I'm already exhausted."

"If you think I'm bad, you should meet my mom," I said, swaying my hips saucily as I moved toward my desk. "They say evil skips a generation. I'm the good one in my family."

"That's a terrifying thought," Fish muttered.

He had no idea.

"What's going on in that busy mind of yours?"

I was in the passenger seat of Eliot's truck, and we were on our way to family dinner. I'd been quiet for the bulk of the ride, a dead giveaway that I was up to something. I told him about my conversation with Fish.

Eliot focused on the road ahead, and the traffic was thick, but I could see his jaw working under the dim illumination of the dash board. "I see."

"Oh, go ahead and yell," I said. "I know you want to."

"I don't want to yell."

"You want to yell."

"Yelling is counterproductive where you're concerned," Eliot said. "All it does is get your hackles up. If I do that, we're going to fight. We finally have three nights in a row together, and I'm not going to fight."

"If we fight now we can make up later," I offered. "I know you're angry. I'd rather have you yell at me and get it out of the way."

"Are you sure?"

"I'm sure."

"Well then ... you're pissing me off," he said.

"I know."

"I thought you were going to be doing easy stuff in sports," he said. "That's why I haven't been complaining about your schedule. Now Fish has you going undercover to track a killer. I don't like it."

"Um, technically that's the sheriff's department's job," I said. "He just wants me to get some dirt from high school kids. That's not exactly dangerous."

"Why don't you tell that to the douche from the parking lot last night."

"He wasn't dangerous to me," I said. "I'm not so sure he wasn't dangerous to Jen, though. There was something off about her."

"What would have happened if he'd physically touched you and Jake and I weren't there?"

"I would have kicked him in the balls."

"And then what?"

"Then I probably would have kicked him in the face for good measure," I said. "With a face like that, it could only be an improvement."

"And what about his three friends?" Eliot pressed.

"They wouldn't have done anything," I said. "They didn't say a word. They let him do all the talking. They're followers, not leaders."

"You're putting a lot of faith into your powers of observation."

"Do you doubt me?"

"No," Eliot said. "You're the most capable person I've ever met."

"Thank you."

"You're also frustrating and mouthy, and while I may love those things about you, other people don't," he said.

"I'll be careful," I said. "I promise. I have a very heightened sense of self-preservation."

"You'd better," Eliot said, reaching over so he could capture my hand. "I'd be a little lost without you."

My heart rolled. Eliot wasn't one for grand pronouncements, but that one was enough to make my face burn. "I'm kind of fond of you, too," I admitted.

Eliot smirked. "You're kind of fond of me?"

I met his steady gaze. "I'm really fond of you."

"I guess I'll take it," he said, pressing a quick kiss to my hand. "You're still frustrating."

"I know."

"I need you to be careful of one thing," he said.

I waited.

"Someone killed Kelsey Cooper," Eliot said. "It might have been a student."

"It might have been more than one student," I corrected.

"Which means, if they attack, it will be in numbers," Eliot said. "I can't follow you everywhere."

"Would you want to?"

"Woman, I've considered having you fitted with a tether just so I know you're safe."

"You're kind of cute."

"I'm totally cute," Eliot said. "And, since I'm fond of you, too, I'd like it if you didn't die on me."

"I'll do my best."

"Don't put yourself in a situation where you might get hurt, Avery," he said. "Promise me that you won't."

"I promise."

"I mean *really* promise."

"I promise."

"Okay," Eliot said, exhaling heavily. "I officially declare this fight over."

"It wasn't much of a fight."

"I'm growing, baby."

"Do we still get to make up?"

"You bet your sweet ass we do."

I THINK we're late," Eliot said, his gaze landing on the packed family table upon entering the restaurant.

"This is good for us," I said. "We can sit at a booth alone. It will be romantic."

"Yeah, nights with your family are always romantic," Eliot said. "I never feel like I'm being emasculated or talked down to."

I faltered. "You didn't have to come."

"Yes, I did," he said. "You're my woman. I like to have dinner with my woman."

"I'm your woman?"

"That's what I said."

"You're such a caveman sometimes," I said.

"It's a good thing you like it when I'm bossy," Eliot said.

"Is this part of that wrestling stuff? Do you want to put me on all fours and dominate me?"

Eliot's eyes sparkled. "That sounds fun."

"What sounds fun?"

My mother is sneaky like a cat sometimes. I have no idea how she got behind us, but she was there now. A glance at Eliot told me she'd taken him by surprise, too.

"Hi," he said, his voice unnaturally high.

"Hello, Eliot," Mom said. "How are you tonight?"

"I'm great," he said, fixing her with a bright smile. "How long were you standing there?"

"Why?"

"I ... no reason."

"Good," Mom said. "I was worried you were embarrassed because I overheard you planning to sexually dominate my daughter later this evening."

Eliot's mouth dropped open.

Mom patted him on the arm. "Don't worry. I get flirting."

I saw my opening. "That wasn't flirting, Mom. He really does like to toss me around the bedroom."

Mom narrowed her eyes as she regarded me. "Do you think you're funny?"

"Most of the time."

"That's not funny."

"You thought it was funny when Eliot said it," I protested.

"Eliot is a saint for putting up with you," Mom said. "If he needs certain ... enticements ... to stay around, then I don't blame him."

Mom headed toward the salad bar without another word or a backward glance.

"Your mother says I can get whatever enticements I want," Eliot said, grinning widely.

"You know she's picturing us doing weird stuff right now, right?"

Eliot's smile faded. "You have a sick family."

"They're always amusing, though." I led Eliot to a booth across from the crowded family table and slid into the open side across from Derrick and Devon. "What's up?"

"If it isn't our resident sports expert," Derrick teased. "How is life in the wrestling world?"

"It sucks," I said. "I hate teenagers."

"You didn't like teenagers when you were a teenager," Derrick said.

I forced a fake smile as I regarded Devon. "How are you, Devon?"

"I'm good," she said. "Now that you're not on the Macomb County cop beat no one is getting special treatment. It's a joy."

I rolled my eyes. "I didn't get special treatment."

"The sheriff gave you exclusives all the time," Devon said. "Rumor had it he was giving you other exclusives, too."

Eliot frowned. "Really?"

Devon shrank down in the booth. "I didn't believe them."

Derrick smirked. "Jake wasn't giving Avery special favors," he said. "Avery just kept getting in trouble and stumbling onto stuff. It's not like Jake could help that. She's inept, but she somehow kept falling upward due to ineptness. No one can counter that."

"Thanks."

"So, I heard there was an incident with Ludington last night," Derrick said.

Eliot made a low growling sound in the back of his throat.

"I see you like him as much as I do," Derrick said.

"I want him dead."

"You can't say that in front of a cop," Derrick said.

"I just did."

Derrick sighed. "He really is a douche. What happened?"

"He was just being Tad," I said. "He threatened to have Grandpa arrested."

Derrick made a face. "Grandpa? What was he doing there?"

Uh-oh. I was definitely going to be off Grandpa's favorite list now. "How did you know about Ludington and not know about Grandpa?"

"Jake just said Tad showed up and was being a douche to you," Derrick said.

"That's all he said?"

"Oh, God, what else is there?" Derrick rubbed his forehead worriedly.

"Do you know about the food truck?"

"What food truck?"

I told him about Mario and Grandpa's new moneymaking endeavor, culminating with Grandpa's altercation with Tad.

"Why would Grandpa want to run a food truck when he owns a restaurant?" Derrick was frustrated.

"Apparently Uncle Tim is trying to crack down on him," I said. "It's not going over well."

"That's because he's a menace."

"If it's any consolation, the burgers are really good," Eliot offered.

"It's still weird," Derrick said. "Did he really throw a pot of water on Ludington?"

"Yup."

"Well, that's kind of funny," he said. "Still ... we're going to have to put him in a home."

"No way," I said. "He's funny."

"He's a menace to society," Derrick said.

"Only from your perspective. I think he's great."

"Oh, whatever," Derrick grumbled. "You're only saying that because he thinks it's funny when you act up."

Devon was bored with the conversation. "I'm going to the salad bar. Do you want to come with me?"

"I'm getting a bacon burger," Derrick said.

"That's not very healthy," Devon said.

Derrick looked conflicted. I knew just how to fix the situation. "Yeah, Derrick, you should be healthy for your snuggle bear."

Devon shot me a look. "Do you have to be so obnoxious?"

"Sometimes I just like it," I said.

"How do you put up with her?" Devon asked Eliot.

Eliot smiled indulgently. "She's usually much more annoying to other people than she is to me."

"Don't you worry that will change some day?"

Eliot slung an arm over my shoulders. "Nope. I think I'm always going to find her funny."

"You're a sick man," Devon said before marching off to the salad bar.

Once she was gone, I fixed my attention on Derrick. "When are you going to break up with her?"

"When are you going to break up with him?" Derrick challenged, inclining his chin in Eliot's direction.

"Hey, what did I do?" Eliot asked.

"You encourage her to be obnoxious," Derrick replied. "She doesn't need encouragement. You should be cracking the whip."

"I'm doing that later tonight."

"Don't talk about having sex with my cousin," Derrick said. "It grosses me out."

"Thanks," I said.

"You know what I mean." Derrick rubbed the back of his neck. "I didn't want to say anything in front of Devon, but Jake also told me you had a run-in with a couple of Catholic North kids last night."

"Just a few of the stupid ones."

"You want to be careful around those kids," Derrick said.

Something about his words struck a chord. "Why?"

"You're in sports now, so I guess it can't hurt to tell you," Derrick said. "There are rumors that a bunch of those kids are on steroids."

Well, that was interesting. Eliot shifting on the seat next to me told me he thought the same. "Where are these rumors coming from?"

"Kids from other schools."

"Are you sure it's not just disgruntled athletes from other schools being jealous?" Eliot asked.

"At first that's what we all thought," Derrick said. "Now? I'm not so sure. When you hear something one time, it's easy to dismiss. When you hear it ten times you start wondering if there's truth to the rumors."

"Aren't high school athletes tested for steroids?" I asked.

"You're such a rube," Derrick replied. "Professional athletes are tested, not high school athletes."

"What could the sheriff's department do in this situation?" I asked.

"Steroids are illegal," Derrick said. "If we get a decent tip we can act on we'll investigate."

"Where would these kids get steroids?"

"Where do they get pot?"

"Their parents' underwear drawer."

Derrick stuck his tongue out. "You're a freak."

"Seriously, though, where would they go to get steroids?"

Derrick shrugged. "I don't know. That's what we need to find out. Just be careful, Avery. Teenagers are already irrational. Kids on steroids? They can be downright dangerous."

I was afraid to meet Eliot's eyes, but did anyway.

"You'd better be really careful," he said. "And I'm going to make you wear a dog collar tonight."

"Don't make me cuff you," Derrick said.

"**W**ake up!"

"Your tones are so dulcet, especially on a Saturday morning when I could be sleeping in," Eliot muttered, dragging the blankets over his head and turning his face away from me.

It was the next morning and I was invigorated. There's something about getting a tip on a news story that fires me up. True, I couldn't do anything about it until Monday, but that didn't mean Eliot and I couldn't celebrate. In fact, I'd woken him up to celebrate twice during the night.

"You're sleeping your life away," I said.

Eliot yanked the blanket down and looked at me from under his crooked elbow. "It's not even ten yet."

"So?"

"So? So I can't get you out of bed before noon on a regular week-end," he said.

"You're a morning person," I pointed out.

"I'm a morning person on weekdays."

"Fine," I grumbled, nestling back in the crook of his arm.

Eliot sighed. "Can I ask you a question?"

"Yes."

"Why are you up so early? You hate mornings. You're the one who instituted naked Sundays when it's cold outside."

"You could get naked now," I suggested.

"I am naked."

"Me too," I said. "What a coincidence!"

"I'm too worn out to have sex with you," Eliot said. "You've woken me up – numerous times, mind you – for five days straight."

"I thought you were a stud."

"I have my limits," Eliot said. "I'm not a superhero."

"That's not what you told me last night," I said.

"You're wearing me out, woman," Eliot growled, pressing a quick kiss to my forehead. "You're so bored with work you're fixating on ... other stuff."

"You're really killing my ego these days. Maybe you don't find me attractive anymore."

"I find you attractive," Eliot said. "I just can't keep up with you."

"Maybe I should find someone to ease your burden," I teased.

"Just make sure he's uglier than I am," Eliot replied. "I'll have to kill him otherwise."

"You're so funny."

Eliot sighed. "If you want to do all the work, I guess I can be convinced."

"Let's have breakfast instead," I said.

Eliot stilled. "Now you're hurting my ego."

"I didn't wake you up for sex," I said. "I woke you up to talk."

"Oh, good," Eliot deadpanned. "That's just what a guy wants to hear when he's in bed with a woman."

"We can talk while we do it," I offered.

"No, it's too late now," Eliot said. "You're cut off."

"You're funny."

"I do my best." Eliot rubbed the back of my head, his hands

getting caught in my tousled blond mane. "What do you want to talk about?"

"I want to know what you think about what Derrick told us last night," I said.

Eliot sighed. "I knew this was coming."

"What?"

"You're obsessed with the idea of the steroids," he said.

"Don't you find it interesting?"

"I find it troubling," Eliot said. "Steroids are dangerous."

"Because of 'roid rage?"

"You watch too much television."

"If you're not worried about 'roid rage, what are you worried about?"

"Steroids are illegal," Eliot said. "I'm worried that someone would kill anyone who uncovered a big secret, like trafficking illegal drugs."

"Do you think that's what happened to Kelsey Cooper?"

Eliot shrugged. "She was brutally raped," he said. "That has to be about something more than steroids."

"Unless they did it to throw off the cops," I suggested.

Eliot considered. "Are you saying you think that whoever killed Kelsey Cooper also raped her because they were trying to cast doubt on the motive?"

"I don't know," I said. "It's interesting to think about, though."

"Is that what we're going to do all day? Think about steroids and dead girls?"

"Did you want to do something else?"

Eliot grabbed me around the waist and rolled on top of me. "Maybe." He gave me a sweet kiss.

"I thought you were tired?"

"I got my second wind," he said. "I figure I'll feed your need, and then I'll feed you, and then maybe we can go to a movie?"

I planted my hands on the side of his face. "Sold. Now get to work."

"You're such a slave driver."

. . .

"WHAT movie do you want to see?" Eliot was staring up at the marquee with a dubious expression on his face.

"You can pick."

He shot me a curious look. "Since when do I get to pick the movie? You always want to pick the movie."

"You make me sound like some evil despot," I said. "I'm not the Hitler of movies."

"You're not?"

I rolled my eyes. "Pick a movie."

"Let's see the new horror movie," he said. "It's supposed to be scary."

I made a face.

"Fine, let's see some chick-flick thing," he said resignedly.

"No, no" I said hurriedly. "Let's see the horror movie."

"You don't want to see the horror movie."

"Yes, I do."

"No, you don't."

"Don't tell me what I want to see," I snapped. "You're pissing me off."

"Welcome to my world."

"I was so happy five minutes ago," I grumbled.

Eliot sighed. "How about this: You pick the movie and I'll pick the snacks?"

I considered his offer. "Fine."

"Great," Eliot said. "What do you want to see?"

"Let's see the horror movie."

Eliot scorched me with a look. "Are you trying to kill me?"

"No," I said. "We can cuddle in a horror movie. When you're scared, I'll keep you safe."

Eliot's face softened. "You're unbelievable."

"I'll buy the tickets," I said. "Go get the food."

"Listen, Little Miss Bossy, I'll get the food when I want to get the food," Eliot said.

I waited.

"It just so happens that I want to get the food," he said. "This does not mean I'm doing what you want me to do."

I crossed my arms over my chest.

Eliot kissed my pouty mouth. "Do you want Red Vines and popcorn?"

"I thought you were picking the food?"

"So, you want Sour Patch Kids, too?"

"And an Icee."

"You're going to put me in the poor house," Eliot said, ambling to the concession counter.

After I bought the tickets I joined Eliot at the counter. "What's wrong?"

"The Icee machine is broken."

I frowned. "Make him fix it."

"Yeah, I'll pull out my wand and magically make him get you an Icee."

"Fine," I said. "I'll have a Diet Coke."

The clerk smiled blankly. "That will be twenty-seven dollars."

"Shit," Eliot said, digging into his wallet. "We could just buy this thing when it comes out on Blu-Ray in two months for that much money."

"Do you want me to pay?"

"I can pay," Eliot said. "It's my job to pay."

"Because you're the man?"

"Because ... you're baiting me," Eliot said.

"I'm not baiting you," I argued. "I'm getting your blood pressure up. There's a difference."

"How?"

I shrugged. "I just like it when your face turns all red."

"Oh yeah?"

"Yeah."

"How's this?" Eliot grabbed the back of my head and gave me a deep kiss. When he was done, I checked to make sure I was still dressed and then shot him a happy grin.

"That was pretty good."

The sound of someone clearing their throat in line behind us drew our attention. I balked when I saw Jake standing there -- and he wasn't alone. The woman standing next to him looked appalled at our show of affection.

"Hey," Eliot said, running a hand through his hair uncomfortably.

"Hi," Jake said.

"I ... we ... um ... are you seeing a movie?" I asked, flummoxed.

"It is a theater," Jake said.

I looked his date up and down. She was thin – like really thin – and tall. She was only about two inches shorter than Jake. It didn't miss my attention that she looked like a model. I hated her instantly.

"What are you seeing?" Eliot asked.

"The new Sandra Bullock movie," the woman said, fixing me with an odd look. "Aren't you Avery Shaw?"

"Last time I checked," I said.

"Isn't this the woman you were shot trying to protect?"

Jake ran his tongue over his teeth. "She's an old friend," he said. "We went to high school together. This is Celeste, by the way."

Celeste? Who names their kid Celeste? Crazy people name their kid Celeste. "Nice to meet you," I said, forcing a faux smile as I extended my hand.

Celeste reluctantly shook it. "So, you two are old friends?"

"We are," I said.

"Do you get shot protecting all of your old friends?" Celeste asked, shaking her brown hair dubiously. The red highlights told me every color variation was fake.

Jake rolled his neck. "I wasn't shot protecting her," he said. "I was shot ... ."

Celeste crossed her arms over her model's chest and tapped her foot impatiently.

"Fine, I was shot protecting her," Jake said. "To be fair, I was shot while I was looking for her. I wasn't technically protecting her."

"Nice save, man," Eliot said.

"What are you guys seeing?" Jake asked.

"Oh, that horror movie with the Ouija board," Eliot said.

"That looks stupid," Celeste said.

I wrinkled my nose. "And the Sandra Bullock movie doesn't?"

"It's supposed to be romantic," Celeste countered. "We're going to be able to hold hands all through the movie."

Jake smiled tightly. "I'm really looking forward to it."

"Avery wants to protect me from the monsters," Eliot said. "That's her idea of romance."

Jake pursed his lips. "I remember her fondness for horror movies."

"You do?" Celeste asked, pouting.

"She made me see 28 *Days Later* five times in the theater," Jake said.

"Hey, that was a great movie," I said.

"It was pretty good."

"That's when there was some good horror out there," I complained. "Now we just get crap."

"We haven't seen a good horror movie in months," Eliot explained. "She's crabby. It doesn't help that her work situation is driving her crazy."

"I'll bet," Jake said, smiling. "Was there any fallout from the Ludington incident?"

"MacDonald doesn't know it was Grandpa who threw the water," I said. "I'm safe for now."

"That's good," Jake said.

"Jake, we're going to miss the trailers," Celeste said, her voice just short of a whine.

"We should be going, too," Eliot said, stacking our food and drinks and moving out of the way. "It's good to see you."

"You, too," Jake said, fixing his eyes on me briefly. "Both of you."

"Enjoy your movie," I said.

Jake nodded. "You, too." He turned his attention back to Celeste. "What do you want to eat?"

"You know I can't eat this junk," Celeste said. "I have to watch my figure."

I glanced at the pile of food in Eliot's arms. Yeah, I definitely hated her.

"So, how is the wide world of sports treating you?"

I was leaning back in my desk chair, counting the ceiling tiles, when Marvin returned to the office from a Monday night city council meeting. Sometimes his powers of observation are lacking for a world-class reporter.

"It sucks."

"What are you doing?" He tilted his head to stare at the ceiling with me.

"I'm debating the meaning of life."

"Cool," Marvin said. "How is it going?"

"I'm just waiting for the apocalypse."

"Plague?"

"Zombie."

"That one is better," Marvin said, dropping his notebook on his desk as he studied me. "I'm pretty sure I could survive that one. You know how easily I get sick. I'd go in the first wave of a plague."

Marvin is a hypochondriac. I once had to convince him there was no way he was going through early-onset menopause and his hot flashes were only because it was ninety degrees outside. He definitely wouldn't survive a plague, mostly because I would have to kill him to shut him up. That didn't mean he'd survive a zombie apocalypse either. "I hate to break it to you, but you wouldn't last a week in a zombie apocalypse."

"I would so."

"You would not," I said. "You've got fodder written all over you."

"That's just mean."

"I'm not saying I want you to die," I said. "I'm just saying you would die."

Marvin flapped his arms. "Well, great," he said. "I was really looking forward to the zombie apocalypse."

I arched an eyebrow as I dragged my gaze from the ceiling tiles.

"What? You don't have to shower in the zombie apocalypse and women still fall all over you," Marvin said. "Look at Daryl on *The Walking Dead*."

"Do you think you look like Daryl?"

"No. What does that matter?"

"Oh, trust me, it matters," I said. I decided to change the subject. "Anything fun happen at your city council meeting tonight?"

"Not really," Marvin said. "They're talking about bringing in a new city manager in Mount Clemens."

"Didn't they just get a new city manager?"

"Yeah, but one of the women on the council claims he pinched her butt."

"What does he say?"

"He says he thought he was pinching his secretary's butt."

"Well, that's better," I said. "Kind of."

"No, his secretary is married to another council member."

"Ah."

"I was just starting to like him, too," Marvin said.

I didn't bother to hide my eye roll. "What's going on with the Kelsey Cooper story?"

Marvin pressed a finger to his lips and looked around.

"What's your deal?"

"You're supposed to be in sports," he hissed.

"I am in sports. Why do you think I'm so depressed?"

"I think your face naturally looks like that," Marvin said. "You just look mean. You can't help it. I blame your mother."

I blamed her, too. I wondered briefly what else I could blame her for today.

"Fish told me not to talk to you about any news stories," Marvin said.

I made a face. "Why did he tell you that?"

"He says you can't help yourself. He says you're a great reporter so you have to find the story. He says you're driven, and he's never seen anyone better at snooping out a big scoop."

My head started to swell.

"He also says you're a baby and a poor loser," Marvin added. "He says you can't stop yourself from getting in everyone's business. And he says if there was a line for handing out stupid you would take the first ten spots yourself."

My ego deflated. "I am not stupid."

"Hey, I stood up for you," Marvin said. "I told him you probably just had PMS."

"Do you ever wonder why you can't keep a girlfriend?"

"It's not that I can't keep a girlfriend, it's that they can't keep me," Marvin countered. "I'm too much man for one woman to love."

"That's the word on the street."

"Wait, who told you I can't keep a girlfriend? Has someone here been talking about me?"

Marvin is also paranoid. "You told me." And he has a big mouth.

"Oh, well, on that front, who do you think I should invite as a date to my Christmas party?"

He also can't make his own decisions.

"What are your options?"

"I was thinking of asking Sweaty Back."

"You can't do that," I said. "I'll get drunk and start calling her Sweaty Back. I can't even remember her real name."

"It's Candy."

"Yeah, Sweaty Back is better."

"You're still coming, right? If you don't come, I might as well not even throw the party."

He also needs constant reinforcement.

"I'm coming," I said. "I've already marked it down on the calendar."

"Is Eliot coming with you?"

"Yeah. He's looking forward to it." Eliot's actual words had been "over my dead body." We're still negotiating. He likes Marvin, as long as he's not in a room with him. He doesn't believe men and women can be friends without wanting to sleep with one another, even though he's met Marvin and knows the competition is nonexistent. What? I'm not hung up on looks. Marvin, with his shirt off, looks like a beached manatee.

"Hey, guess what I accidentally did?"

"The secretary at the city council meeting?"

Marvin made a face. "No. I told you she's married."

That hadn't stopped him in the past.

"I was sending out invitations on Facebook to the party," Marvin said. "I wasn't paying attention. I meant to invite Steve Barton."

"From the copy desk?"

"Yeah."

"Go on."

"Well, you know how my memory plays tricks on me, right?"

"I believe you said that years of pot smoking have tilted you into early-onset Alzheimer's."

"Well, I accidentally invited Steve Barker instead."

I stilled. "The state senator?"

"Yup."

I fought the urge to snicker. "Did he answer?"

"He said he was coming," Marvin said.

"There's no way he's coming. He just said that to be nice."

"Well, I got to thinking," Marvin said. "No one is going to have a good time with a senator at the party ... and that's definitely going to cut down on pot smoking."

Uh-oh. "What did you do?"

"I messaged him back and told him I didn't mean to invite him," Marvin replied. "What? He's going to be a total downer. No one wants to talk about his plan to fix the roads."

"So let me get this straight," I said. "You invited a state senator to your Christmas party and then uninvited him?"

"Yeah."

"You never cease to amaze me," I said, shaking my head. "Did he reply?"

"He said he understood how I could make the mistake."

"He's lying."

"Do you think? Oh, man, you don't think this means he's going to try to raise my taxes, do you?"

And we're back to paranoia. "Something tells me you're safe."

"So, what are you working on tonight?" Marvin asked.

"Trying not to kill the guys in sports."

"It's not any better?"

"No, it's better. Today when he saw me, Stanley actually made eye contact before he shook his head and started hiding in his cubicle."

"I think you two just got off on the wrong foot."

"The only thing wrong with the foot we got off on is that it wasn't in his ass."

"You're really bitchy today," Marvin said. "Are you sure it's not PMS?"

"You know, every time a woman is in a bad mood it doesn't mean she has PMS."

"I know," Marvin said. "Sometimes it just means she's hungry for sex. Why do you think I like so many mean women?"

"I think you like to be dominated."

"Speaking of being dominated, can you remind me how to post my links to the official Facebook page again?"

I pursed my lips. In addition to all of his other fine traits, Marvin is also computer illiterate. I've shown him how to use iTunes more than fifty times. We were closing in on that number when it came to Facebook. "It's not rocket science," I said. "And what does that have to do with domination?"

"You're mean and bossy when you show me," Marvin said. "You would have made a terrible teacher, by the way."

"Why do you think I'm not a teacher?"

"Because small children are afraid of you."

He had a point. I pointed to his computer. "Bring up the page. You'd better take notes this time."

"See. Bossy."

"See. Stupid."

"Hey!"

"Bring up the page," I ordered. I watched as Marvin did as instructed, and I only cleared my throat twice when he forgot his password. When he finally had the page up, I started directing him. "What do you want to put up?"

"Oh, nothing," Marvin said. "One of the women at the council meeting said she sent me a tip through the private messages on the paper's account. She said she couldn't talk about it in public."

I furrowed my brow. "Why would she send it to the newspaper's message account?"

Marvin shrugged. "I have no idea. She just told me to look."

I scanned the page and then pointed to the top. "Click on that."

"Holy crap," Marvin said. "Did you know we had so many messages in here?"

"I've never looked in here before," I admitted. "It's nice to see how good our customer service is, though. How many of these people complaining about not getting their newspapers do you think cancelled their subscriptions?"

"We should probably have someone in circulation check this out every couple of days," Marvin said.

"There are tons of tips in here," I said, leaning down so I could see better over Marvin's shoulder. "Look. This guy claims that Jake is an alien."

"It's a good thing he never got you pregnant in high school," Marvin said. "If he's an alien, you could have given birth to something with eight arms."

"Yeah, I really dodged that bullet." I scanned down a few more messages until something caught my eye. "Hey, pull that one up."

Marvin did as he was told and we both read it together. "What do you think?"

"I think this isn't the first time I've heard this rumor," I said.

"Really?"

"Yeah. Derrick mentioned it at dinner the other night," I said. "He said they've gotten a few tips about steroids at Catholic North."

"Do you think this has something to do with Kelsey Cooper?"

I shrugged. "I have no idea. I definitely think it's something to look into, though."

"Maybe Kelsey Cooper stumbled on the steroids or something."

"Maybe."

"Maybe Kelsey was selling the steroids," Marvin suggested.

"Maybe."

"Maybe the steroids have nothing to do with Kelsey."

"That's also a possibility."

Unfortunately, they were all viable possibilities.

17 / SEVENTEEN

W hen I got home, I found Eliot asleep on the couch. The television was still on, but muted, and the rest of the house was dark. His face was peaceful in sleep, his features relaxed and welcoming. I wanted to be near him. It felt like the scant time we'd been able to share with each other on weeknights over the past week and a half was wedged into a limited calendar. I didn't like it.

I dropped my purse on the table, stripped out of my clothes and then lifted his arm to squeeze in next to him. He looked too beautiful to wake.

He stirred as I snuggled against him.

"Hey," he murmured.

"I'm sorry I woke you," I said. "I was trying to be stealthy."

"It's hard to be stealthy when you rub your naked body against me."

"I'm not naked."

"Close enough." He spooned behind me and rested his head in the crook of my neck. "How was your day?"

"Stupid. How was your day?"

"Normal."

"Did you have dinner?"

"Most people eat before midnight."

"Oh, right." I hated my new schedule. It was ruining my life.

"Are you hungry?"

"No. Marvin got us Chicken Shack."

"Your eating habits were bad before you started working nights," Eliot said. "They're horrible now."

"I know."

"You should try to eat a salad."

"I know."

"You should get out of these underwear, too," Eliot said.

"I thought you were sleeping?"

"I'm getting a second wind."

I rolled over to face him. "This can't go on," I said.

"You can just lay there," Eliot said. "I'll be quick."

I pinched him. "That's not what I'm talking about."

Eliot opened his eyes. "What are you talking about?"

"We can't stay on this schedule," I said. "It's bad for us. We barely get any time to spend together. I'm going to have to quit."

"You're considering quitting for me?"

His question took me by surprise. "I'm considering quitting for us. Is that ... is that a problem?" I suddenly felt exposed.

Eliot tightened his arm around me. "No. I'm just surprised. You never really show a lot of forethought when it comes to stuff like this."

"What does that mean?"

"Nothing bad," Eliot said. "You're usually just kind of focused on your work. Sometimes I wonder if you actually consider our future at all."

"You do?"

"You're a pain in the ass, Avery, but I've grown rather fond of you," he teased. "It's just nice to know that you're worried, too."

"We can't keep doing this."

"It's only been a week and a half," Eliot said. "Let's not go all ... *General Hospital*."

"Don't worry. I have no intention of getting pregnant with your brother's baby."

Eliot pinched my rear. "Cute."

"I try."

"It's going to be okay," he said. "You're just going through a rough patch right now. I'm actually impressed that you're admitting it – and are trying to make things better. That shows real growth on your part."

"Is that an insult?"

"No," Eliot said. "It's the truth."

"Hey, I'm still self-absorbed."

"That's just the way I like you," Eliot said, resting his chin on top of my head. "You're too good at what you do for this to go on. You might not be able to stay at The Monitor. I have a hard time believing, if push comes to shove, that they'll let you go, though. We just need to figure out a way to force MacDonald's hand."

"And how are we going to do that?"

"I can beat him up."

I wasn't ruling it out. "He'll have you arrested. He has narc written all over him."

"I'll wear a mask."

"I'll consider it," I said. "I want to take Tad out first."

Eliot chuckled. "I figured. I've started doing some digging on him myself."

"You have?"

"Don't sound so surprised," Eliot said. "I want you back on days ... and happy. Your schedule is screwing with my love life, and your job is screwing with your smile. I'm not happy with either of those things."

"You're kind of sweet."

"Don't tell anyone," Eliot said.

"Have you found anything?"

"I just started looking," Eliot said, rubbing lazy circles over the small of my back. "I'll find something. If all else fails, I'll beat him up."

"He's definitely a narc."

"I don't care," Eliot said. "Beating his ass is worth thirty days in jail. I'm sure Jake will give us conjugal visits."

"That sounds fun."

"Speaking of Jake, I noticed that you were a little ... weirded out ... when we saw him at the movies the other day." Eliot's body had tensed slightly.

"I wasn't weirded out."

"You acted like you had ants in your pants."

"I did not, and that's a completely lame saying."

Eliot sighed. "Well, you definitely didn't like his date," he said.

"Eliot ... ."

"I'm not jealous," he said. "Okay, I'm not massively jealous. I still noticed that you looked like you wanted to rip Celeste's hair out."

"It's not for the reason you think," I said, moving to shift out of his arms.

He stopped me. "What's the reason?"

"Jake is always going to be important to me," I said. "He's not important to me in the same way you are, but he's still ... ,"

"The first guy you ever loved," Eliot finished.

"I just want him to be happy."

"And you don't think he'll be happy with Celeste?"

"No one could be happy with Celeste," I said. "She's whiny, and not in a fun way like me. She's also untrustworthy. And she has terrible taste in movies."

"What makes you think that she's untrustworthy?"

"You saw how she was looking at me," I said. "She sees me as competition."

"You are competition."

I stilled. "W-what?"

"You are competition," Eliot repeated. "Jake has feelings for you."

"What makes you say that?"

"I see the way he looks at you."

"And what way is that?"

"The same way I do," Eliot said. "Listen, I know you two have a long history. You were kids together, and you had a lot of ... firsts ... together. I don't like it, but it's not like I thought you were a virgin when I met you."

"Are you saying I looked like a slut?"

"I'm saying you looked like fun," Eliot said. "And I was right. You are fun. I think Jake remembers that fun."

"I think you're seeing things that aren't there," I said.

"I think Jake is a man who is caught between his future and the one part of his past he's having a really hard time letting go of," Eliot said. "He knows you don't fit in his life, but he hasn't entirely let go of trying to fit into your life."

"Oh, please," I scoffed. "Jake does not want to fit into my life."

"Maybe not," Eliot conceded. "That doesn't mean he wants to let you go. That's why he dates women like Celeste. He doesn't want to risk actually forming a bond with someone who might erase you entirely."

I didn't know what to say.

"It's okay," he said. "I'm getting used to it. Jake saved you that night at the newspaper. I know he says that you saved him, but I hate to think what would have happened if he hadn't shown up. It was his gun you used to protect yourself. Without it ... I think you might have died on me."

"I could have stayed hidden back there for days," I said. "I'm stealthy."

Eliot chuckled. "You're safe. That's all I care about."

"I'm not jealous of Celeste," I said after a moment. "I just don't want Jake to be unhappy."

"I know." Eliot pressed a kiss to my forehead. "I don't want him to be unhappy either. You seem to forget, before I even knew you existed I was friends with him, too."

"And then you weren't friends."

"But we're getting back to a friendly place," Eliot said. "I'd like to think that there will be a day when things are good between us. It's not going to happen while he still has feelings for you, though. It's a work in progress."

"I still think you're exaggerating on that front." Actually, the opposite was true, but there was no way I could tell him that.

"I've come to the realization that it doesn't matter," Eliot said. "You're not the type of person who'll do anything you don't want to do." He rolled on top of me. "And, thankfully for me, I'm what you like to do these days."

"Smooth."

"I try."

I met his eyes. "I really have been missing you."

"It won't be long," Eliot promised. "If I have to beat up everyone standing between the two of us, I'll do it."

"What if I'm unemployed?"

Eliot smirked. "Then I'm going to put you in an apron and force you to cook."

"That's never going to happen," I said. "Plus, anything I cook you're going to have to eat. I hope you like botulism."

"Don't argue with me, woman," Eliot said. "I like the visual, and I'm never eating anything you cook."

I gave him his fantasy for the night – without the food.

"I want to thank Avery for coming to her first sports meeting," Stanley said, sitting down at the head of the conference room table and fixing me with a grimace that was his version of a smile. "I know it was hard to fit into her tight schedule."

"Well, I got you in between my afternoon wax and my evening bar visit. It was tough, but I somehow managed."

Stanley sneered at me. "Is that supposed to be funny?"

I arched a challenging eyebrow. "What are we meeting about?"

"The schedule for the rest of the week," Stanley replied.

"Isn't it full of games?"

Stanley stilled. "Yes."

"So, what are we scheduling again?"

"You're feisty," Joe said, winking in my direction.

"I also bite."

"I can deal with that."

"Don't gross me out," I said.

Stanley sighed. "Can you please not interrupt the meeting?"

"Only if you stop inviting me to them," I suggested.

"You're a part of the sports staff."

"Barely," Dave said.

"I agree with Dave," I said. "Can't you just ignore me?"

Stanley shot me a look. "Listen, we need someone to cover the Catholic North wrestling meet tonight. Dave has another interview with the new basketball coach in Mount Clemens."

My heart jumped.

"I can't do it," Joe said. "I have indigestion. I'll be farting all night."

"That's because you ate a whole cow for dinner," I said.

"Hey, I only ate half a cow," Joe said, smiling widely.

I wrinkled my nose. I knew what he was doing. He was uncomfortable with his size, so he was making jokes to put everyone else at ease. It was a little sad. The dude seriously smells, though. Remind me not to sit next to him at a meeting again.

"I'll go," I offered.

Stanley faltered. "You will?"

"I love wrestling."

Dave cleared his throat. "I don't think that's a good idea."

"Why not?" Stanley asked.

"She keeps making gay jokes," Dave said.

"I'm not making gay jokes," I argued. "I'm not homophobic. I love gay people. If I could find a gay person who wanted to hang out with me I'd totally make him my best friend. Unfortunately, they find me obnoxious."

"That's not limited to gay people," Dave said.

I blew a raspberry in his direction. "Seriously, I love wrestling. I understand it now. I'll turn in a great article."

Stanley didn't look convinced.

"Hey, it's either me or the farting wonder here," I said, gesturing to Joe.

Stanley sighed. "You'd better not screw this up."

"I love the supportive environment in sports," I said.

WRESTLING sucks. It's that simple. You may think I have a bias against the sport, and you'd be right. Everyone keeps telling me it's dignified. It's not. The only thing that could liven up a wrestling match is a strobe light, the Village People and folding chairs.

"Who are you with?"

The woman looking at me had wide eyes and her skin was flushed. All I could figure was that two underage boys grappling together on the floor turned her on. What? Some people are sick.

"The Monitor," I said.

"Do you have a photographer here?"

I pointed to the far end of the floor. "Jared Jackson. He's doing a photo gallery, if you're interested."

"Why would I be interested?"

I shrugged. "I just figured that some of those photos would be like porn to you."

The woman's smile slipped. "What does that mean?"

I stood up. "I need something to eat."

"The concession stand is that way."

For some reason, the thought of chicken strips didn't appeal tonight. "Hey, when you came in, was there a food truck in the parking lot?"

The woman was surprised at the question. "As a matter of fact, there was. I don't think it's supposed to be there."

"I'm sure they have a permit." I made my way to the front of the school, smiling when I saw the food truck ... and the crowd congregated around it. Grandpa and Mario must be making a killing. They've always got a line.

I ambled over to the truck, smiling when I saw the argument going on inside. My family is nothing if not consistent.

"You're making the patties too thick," Mario said.

"They're not too thick," Grandpa replied. "People like a thick hamburger."

"You're sending them out raw inside."

"Son, I've been making hamburgers since before you were born.

Hell, I've been making them since before your father was born, and I mean that literally."

"How many people did you kill with those hamburgers?" Mario asked.

"Two. That's barely anything."

"Are you serious?"

"Of course not," Grandpa said, thumping Mario on the top of the head. "Sometimes I think you were blessed with my sense of humor and sometimes I think you're just like your father."

"My father is your son."

"Don't remind me."

Mario caught sight of me out of the corner of his eye and turned swiftly. "Hey. What are you doing here?"

"Watching my soul die."

"You're still hating sports, huh?"

"I wish they would be outlawed."

Grandpa fixed me with a hard look. "Sports are part of the American dream," he said. "Don't crap all over America."

"That should be your truck slogan."

Grandpa pushed the thinning black hair, which had been slipping into his eyes, out of his face. "How are you, dolly?"

I shrugged. "In the middle of the worst two weeks of my life."

"You were once grounded for blowing up condoms and leaving them all over the front porch of the Baptist church across the street from your house," Grandpa pointed out. "Your mother was livid. She threatened to send you to a convent."

"I would have been the most popular person there," I said. "And, I didn't do that because it was a church. I did it because that pastor kept telling my parents I was going to hell for lying in the sun in a bikini. He said I was going to end up pregnant by the whole town. I figured he needed some shaking up."

Grandpa smiled. "And that's why you're one of my favorites."

"I thought I was off your list."

"You're never off my list," Grandpa said. "You just get bumped down from time to time, usually when you decide to act like your mother."

"I never act like my mother!" I'd never heard anything so hurtful in my entire life.

Grandpa chortled. "You might not like to admit it, but you have more of her in you than you think."

"And she has more of you in her than she'd like to think," I said. "And I'm way cooler than Mom."

"You're way wilder than your mother," Grandpa corrected. "You get that from me, and I'm proud. You still have her determination and you're just as stubborn as she is."

"You say that like it's a bad thing," I said. "Mom has scared my editor so badly I don't have to work Friday nights. How can that be bad?"

Grandpa's face softened. "You're miserable, aren't you?"

"I hate sports," I said, leaning my chin on top of the window counter. "I miss news."

"Quit."

"I've considered it," I said. "I've decided to take down my enemies instead."

"That's my girl," Grandpa said. "You've never met an enemy you didn't want to demolish, or start on fire. You get that from me."

"I'm not sure most people think that's a good personality trait."

"Do you ever lose?" Grandpa asked. "Over the long haul, I mean."

"No."

"Then how can it be wrong?"

I smiled. "Can I have a burger? I need something to eat. All the sweaty boys grabbing each other's junk is making me weak in the knees."

"You know what your other great quality is?"

"What?"

"You have a mouth like a sailor."

"Thanks, Grandpa."

"You're welcome," he said. "We'll have your burger done in a few minutes."

"It will just be raw in the middle," Mario grumbled.

"Your stock is dropping, son," Grandpa said, snapping a towel at Mario. "Cook your cousin a burger."

I turned back to look at the line, searching for a familiar face. I hadn't been able to push Jen's pale features out of my mind in days. I shifted my attention to the front door of the gym when I heard loud complaining. Since I knew my mouth was shut, I was mildly interested to hear where it was coming from. A wrestler – still in his little outfit – was pacing in front of the glass door.

"I can't believe that asshole disqualified me!"

"He obviously wants Richmond to win," another boy said.

"Of course he does, Marty," the first boy said. "Do you think I'm talking for my own health?"

"I'm sorry, Sam. I didn't mean anything by it."

I was interested, despite myself. "I'll be right back."

Grandpa grunted in acknowledgement.

I moved over to the two boys, deciding on a plan of action as I closed the distance. "Hey, what happened?"

Sam ripped his wrestling headgear off and fixed me with a dark look. "Who are you?"

"I'm covering the match for The Monitor," I said.

"You're doing a great job."

I tamped down my nasty retort. "I just wanted to get a burger. Did something happen in there?"

"Yeah, I was totally screwed over," Sam said, whipping his headgear forcefully into a nearby shrub. "That ref is just a dick."

"What happened?"

"I made a totally legal move and the ref disqualified me," Sam said. "Put that in your story."

"Did you kiss him or something?"

Sam's face was incredulous. "What?"

"Nothing," I said. "I just figured that would be frowned upon. So, what move did you make?"

Sam narrowed his eyes. "Are you one of those idiots who thinks wrestling is gay?"

"Of course not," I lied. "I think it's manly. Who doesn't think rubber is manly?"

Sam tilted his head. "Of course it's manly," he said. "Only a man can take down another man with nothing but brute force. Who wouldn't think it was manly?"

Only people with eyes. "So, you go to Catholic North, right?"

Sam straightened his shoulders. "I'm the top wrestler for Catholic North."

"Really? What's your name?"

"I thought you said you were with The Monitor?"

"I am," I replied hurriedly. "I'm new."

"I'm Sam Keaton," he said. "You're new at The Monitor? Did they make room for you under some chick affirmative action thing?"

I bit my tongue.

"I bet that's what it is," Marty said. "Still, she's a heck of a lot hotter than Dave Stewart."

"You've got that right," Sam said. "I bet she looks real nice with her shirt off."

"I bet she does, too," Marty said, ogling me.

I ignored the remark. "Did you guys know Kelsey Cooper?"

Sam made a face. "She's dead."

"I heard."

"She fell in a snow bank and froze to death," Sam said. "It was an accident."

"We don't have any snow banks yet," I said. "And the coroner says she was brutally raped and strangled."

"Like he would know."

I pursed my lips, considering. I decided to take a more subtle tactic. "So, are you guys on steroids?"

Sam took a step back. "What?"

I didn't like the look on his face. "I figured you'd have to be. I mean, you're so strong."

Sam relaxed, if only marginally. "I am strong."

"That's the word on the street." I seriously hate teenagers.

"He's the best wrestler on the team," Marty said. "He's a god."

I looked Marty up and down. He wasn't doing much to ward off my gay theory when it came to wrestlers. He might not be one, but he was clearly infatuated with one. "So, there's no gossip on the campus about steroids?"

"Steroids are illegal," Sam said.

"So is sex under the age of eighteen," I pointed out. "That doesn't mean it's not fun."

Sam ran his tongue over his teeth. "You look like you're a lot of fun."

Whoops. Apparently I'd just sent Sam the wrong message. I had to regroup. "I'm a nun."

"I thought you were a reporter."

"I have two jobs."

"I can live with that," Sam said, taking a step forward.

Crap. "I'm also gay."

"You're a gay nun who moonlights as a reporter?"

"I'm a busy girl."

"Do you want to be busier?" Sam asked.

"Not particularly."

Sam extended his index finger and ran it up the arm of my hoodie. "I bet I could change your mind."

"No, you can't," I said.

"Why do you say that?"

"I have a boyfriend."

"Nuns can have boyfriends?"

"How does a gay nun have a boyfriend?" Marty asked.

"You know what? I think my burger is probably ready," I said. "I should get going. Sorry you got booted from your match. I'll make sure the readers understand it was a terrible injustice."

Sam grabbed my arm when I tried to move away. "My truck is at the end of the parking lot. I can be quick."

"That's what all the girls here say," I said.

Sam frowned. "Is that supposed to be a joke?"

"Kid, if you don't take your hand off me, I'm going to end your wrestling career," I said.

"How?"

I didn't get a chance to respond. Grandpa had arrived, a burger in one hand and a spatula in the other, and he didn't look happy. "You'd best let her go, son."

"Who are you, grandpa?"

"I'm her grandpa."

Sam wrinkled his nose. "You brought your grandfather to a wrestling meet?"

"He's my chaperone," I said, trying to wrench my arm out of his grip. "Seriously. This is starting to hurt. Let me go."

"I'm not done talking to you yet," Sam said.

"Yes, you are," Grandpa said. "Let her go now."

"And what are you going to do to make me, old man?"

I sighed. This wouldn't be good. Grandpa smacked Sam on the head with his spatula. "Let her go."

"Ow."

"Let her go."

"Yeah, let me go," I said, yanking hard.

"You're not the boss of me," Sam said. "Neither one of you is the boss of me." His grip tightened.

Grandpa smacked him again. "Let her go."

"Ow!"

Sam's hand was still clenched around my arm, and Grandpa was at his wit's end. He lowered the spatula – just far enough to smack Sam in the nuts. Seriously, why wasn't he wearing a cup?

"Omigod!" Sam fell to the pavement, his hand moving from my arm to his most treasured possession.

Grandpa straightened. "You have the worst luck ever, I swear. You attract assholes every time you turn around."

"It's a gift," I said, rubbing my arm ruefully. "Thanks for saving me."

"That's what I'm here for," Grandpa said. "Here's your burger. That will be three bucks."

"Where are you?" Eliot asked.

I shifted my cellphone away from my ear, turning down the car radio as I considered how to answer. I wasn't thrilled with the thought of lying, but the truth would send him into a tailspin. "I'm at work."

It was Wednesday night, and instead of going to work I'd called in sick so I could stake out Sam Keaton's home. My run-in with the entitled brat had made me more convinced than ever that steroids were playing a big part in the dark underbelly of Catholic North's campus. I wanted to see if I was right.

"You're at work?"

"Yeah, I'm just answering phones tonight," I said.

"Really? You're sitting in your cubicle right now?"

I faltered. Something about his tone told me he knew I was lying. "I'm actually out picking up dinner right now," I said, changing tactics. "I will be answering phones shortly."

I could hear a voice in the background over the phone. "She's in the bathroom," Marvin said. "I can't go in there and get her. I'm not a girl. I'll tell her you stopped by when she comes out. I'm sure she's just having female problems."

Crap. "Where are you?"

"I'm standing next to your empty cubicle," Eliot said. "I decided to surprise you with dinner."

He really was sweet. "What did you bring?"

"Where are you?"

"Boston Market."

"Oh, that's funny, I'm holding Boston Market right now," Eliot said. "I got your favorite creamed spinach. I find it gross, but you seem to love it."

"I'll be back at the office in a few minutes," I said. "I'll just cancel my order."

"Avery?"

"Yeah?"

"Stanley says you called in sick."

"I ... ."

"Avery?"

I surrendered this round. "Yeah."

"Lying to me would be a really shitty way to reward me for going out of my way to spend time with you," Eliot said.

"I'm staking out one of the Catholic North wrestlers," I admitted.

I could practically see Eliot pulling himself together over the phone. "You're what?"

"I had a thing with one of the wrestlers last night," I explained. "He piqued my interest. I wanted to see if I could find anything out."

"Is that what a sports reporter would do?"

"It's what I do."

Eliot sighed. "How long are you going to be?"

"You're not going to argue with me?"

"Would it do any good?" Eliot asked.

"No."

"Then I'm not going to fight with you," he said. "When will you be home?"

"A couple hours," I said. "I promise not to be too late."

"If you're not back at your house in two hours – and I mean two hours – I'm going to strip naked and have sex with your neighbor."

It wasn't much of a threat. The woman living in the house on the right side of my home was married and pregnant and only men lived in the house on the left. "Are you mad at me?"

"Would that do any good?"

"Do you want me to come home right now?" I felt guilty.

Eliot made an exasperated sound. "No."

"You don't?" I couldn't rein in my surprise.

"I think you need it," Eliot said. "I'm going to overlook it. I'm also going to spank your bottom blue when you get home."

"Are you counting that as foreplay?"

"Avery, don't do anything that puts you in danger," Eliot said. "If you do, we're going to have a really big fight. I'm going to throw things and I'm going to take apart every one of those Lego *Star Wars* sets you have in your home office."

"Don't you dare!"

"I'm also going to burn those little manuals in your filing cabinet so you can't put them back together," Eliot warned. "You're just going to have a big pile of Legos ... and a cheating boyfriend ... to deal with."

"I'll be careful," I grumbled.

"Text me every half hour," he said.

"What?"

"That's your penance."

"Fine." I knew he was working hard to control his temper. "I ... I'll see you soon."

"You'd better be naked."

IN MOVIES, stakeouts look entertaining. Let me set you straight: They're not. I'd spent almost three hours on the street in front of Sam Keaton's house – and I was a half hour from Eliot's deadline – and nothing had happened.

The house was quiet. The main floor was dark, but there was an illuminated window on the second floor. Because the house was so large, I had a tough time guessing what room that window belonged to.

I was just about to call it quits for the night when a car pulled onto the street. Even though it was dark, the sporty two-door caught my attention. The car slowed in front of Sam's residence and the figure in the driver's seat appeared to be staring at the house. Instead of parking on the street in front of the Keaton house, the driver pulled to the end of the block.

The driver remained inside for a full two minutes before finally exiting and heading straight for the Keaton house. I couldn't make out much about the figure, but it was clearly male. I think the letterman's jacket was a dead giveaway.

Instead of walking to the front door, the dark shape entered the back yard through the driveway gate and disappeared. That was odd. If he lived there, he would have parked in the driveway or pulled into the garage. If he was visiting, why didn't he knock on the front door? Why did he try to hide his approach?

I watched the house for a few minutes, waiting for something to happen. It remained quiet. I punched the button to lower my driver's side window, warding off the cold by hunkering down in my hoodie. I still couldn't hear anything.

I weighed my options. I could sneak into the back yard and try to eavesdrop, which would put me in a vulnerable position – and totally piss off Eliot off – or I could wait for the figure to leave.

It was a hard choice.

I decided to keep my word. If it came down to it, I had no doubt that I could fight off Sam Keaton. But I had no idea who had just walked through that gate. It wouldn't be prudent to follow. Hey, wait, when did I become prudent?

After ten of the most excruciating minutes of my life – seriously, I think I'm getting old or something – the gate opened. The figure walked through and headed back to his car.

Prudence was gone. I had to see who it was. I had no idea why Kelsey Cooper's murder was driving me crazy. It just was.

I exited my car and followed the figure, pulling up short when I realized he'd heard my footsteps on the frozen pavement. When he swiveled, I recognized him right away.

"Marty?"

"Mrs. Keaton?"

Maybe I need to change my hairstyle. When kids start mistaking you for the mother of one of their friends, it's not good. "No. It's Avery Shaw."

"I wasn't doing anything wrong," Marty said. "I was just ... wait ... whose mom are you?"

"I'm not anyone's mom," I said, taking a step forward so the weak streetlight could reveal my identity. I was beyond caring about hiding.

"Hey, you're the reporter from last night," Marty said, straightening. I didn't miss the baggie he was trying to shove into his pocket.

"What's that?"

"What's what?"

"That baggie you're trying to hide," I said.

"I'm not trying to hide a baggie," Marty said. "This is my ... dry cleaning."

I arched an eyebrow. "Really?"

"What? Dry cleaning comes in bags." Marty was nervous.

"Not that fit in your pocket."

"It's underwear."

I pursed my lips, my mind going in a hundred different directions. "You had to come to your friend's house to pick up your underwear?"

"What? That's not unusual." Marty's voice was unnaturally high.

"Are they thongs?"

Marty shook his head, his shoulders straightening. "You know what? I don't have to answer you. You're not the police."

Marty was clearly stupid. It didn't take more than a split second to decide how to handle this situation. "Marty? That's your name, right?"

Marty nodded.

"Marty, let me tell you something," I said. "I'm registered with the Reporter's Guild of America."

"Oh, no!" Marty rubbed his hand over his forehead.

"As part of the RGA, that means I have the official right to question you," I said.

"Do I need a lawyer?"

"It doesn't matter," I said. "I'm not the police. I work outside of the police."

"Are you like the FBI?"

"Worse."

"Are you like the CIA?" Marty was ashen.

"Worse."

"Are you like the PTA?" Marty choked on the last letter.

"I'm exactly like the PTA," I said, taking a step forward. "I'm a tyrant."

"Please," Marty said, holding up his hands. "I'm so sorry. It was an aberration."

I extended my hand. "Give me the contraband."

"I don't have a rubber band," Marty said, his voice bordering on hysteria. "I promise. I didn't even know they were illegal."

I tamped my irritation down. "Give me the baggie."

Marty glanced around again, but since no one was present to save him he acquiesced.

I took the bag and ran my hands over it. That the bag contained pills was easy to determine, but I pulled my cellphone out of my pocket and used the screen light so I could study the tablets. When I was done, I fixed Marty with a hard look. "Is this what I think it is?"

"I'm sorry, ma'am," Marty said, his hands shaking. "Please don't tell my mom."

I was at a loss. "You're in high school."

"I know."

"You need a prescription for this," I said.

"I know."

I ran a hand through my hair to collect myself. "This is Viagra."

"I know."

"Marty, why are you sneaking around to get Viagra?"

"I need it," Marty whined.

"Why?"

"What do you mean why? I just need it."

"Marty, you're a teenage boy," I said. "Now, I know I look ancient to you, but it wasn't too long ago that I was a teenager. I've never known a teenage boy who needed Viagra. In fact, most teenage boys have the exact opposite problem."

"You need it if you're trying to be ... ."

Realization dawned on me. "You're gay."

"I am not," Marty protested. "I'm just confused."

"Are you taking Viagra so you can get it up for girls?" I asked.

"So? A lot of guys have trouble performing."

"Do you have problems getting it up for guys?"

"Who told you that?" Marty hissed, scanning the street for a third party. "That's a lie!"

I felt stupid. "Dude, if you can only get it up for guys, then you can only get it up for guys," I said. "It's nothing to be ashamed of. You were born that way."

"I'm not gay!"

"Why do you come here to get the Viagra?" I asked. "Is Sam gay, too?"

Marty made a face. "Have you seen his mother? She looks like that woman who won *American Idol* ten years ago. He needs it."

"So, wait, Sam's mother is ugly, and you buy Viagra pills from him – pills he stole from his father, I'm sure – to hide the fact that you're gay?"

"I'm not gay!"

"What about the steroids?"

Marty faltered. "What steroids? You're obsessed with steroids. No one has any steroids."

I narrowed my eyes. "Are you sure?"

"Steroids shrink your package," Marty said. "No one wants that."

He had a point. Still ... . "Hey, it's okay to be gay," I said.

"Not in a Catholic school."

I honestly felt bad for him. "It will get better."

"No, it won't."

I glanced down at the baggie in my hand. "Do you want your Viagra back?"

Marty paused by his car door. "Are you going to tell my mom?"

"Why would I?"

"The PTA is like the mafia," Marty said. "No one gets out alive."

I tossed the bag to him. "You're not going to get out of high school alive if you don't admit what's going on," I said.

"You're too old to understand."

I swallowed hard, ignoring his words. "It will get better, Marty. Just ... be yourself."

"That's easy to say, but it never works."

"You'd be surprised," I said. "Some people like you because you are different later in life. It just doesn't happen in high school."

Marty let my words sink in. "Do all old people go crazy in their twenties, or are you just randomly nuts?"

I narrowed my eyes. "Go home."

"Fine," Marty grumbled.

"And use a condom," I said. "Any girl who would have sex with you is clearly desperate."

"I'm not stupid."

"How do I look?"

Eliot lowered the newspaper and looked me up and down as I pivoted beneath the archway that separated my living room and dining room. "What's different? Is that a new *Star Wars* shirt?"

I made a face. "I'm wearing New Balance tennis shoes."

Eliot glanced at my feet, taking in the shocking pink shoes with bland disinterest. "They look comfortable."

I flicked his ear. "These are new."

"Baby, you have a new set of shoes showing up every week," Eliot said, returning his attention to the newspaper. "They're all tennis shoes."

"That's not true. I got those boots from Country Outfitter last week."

"You haven't worn them yet."

"They need good weather," I said. "They don't like it when it rains."

Eliot shifted his eyes to me. "Your shoes have feelings?"

"They're very sensitive."

He smiled. "You seem in a better mood today. Is that because you stalked high school boys last night?"

"I didn't stalk them," I protested. "I broke down on their street and I was waiting for a tow."

"I'm not the police or your boss," Eliot said. "You don't have to lie to me."

I'd forgotten. He has a lot in common with a prison warden. "Fine. I had a good time spying last night, although I missed you."

Eliot leaned forward so he could accept a quick kiss. "You're such a liar." He patted my rear affectionately. "How late are you going to be tonight?"

I scowled. "They're making me go to competitive cheer."

Eliot knit his eyebrows together. "What's that?"

"It's competitive cheerleading," I said.

"I figured that out myself, although I didn't know it was a real thing," Eliot admitted. "I thought high school cheerleaders just wore short skirts and jumped up and down screaming at basketball and football games."

I fixed him with a dark look. "How many cheerleaders did you date in high school?"

Eliot smiled. "All of them."

"We're breaking up."

He grabbed my hand. "Were you a cheerleader in high school? Because if you have one of those skirts left over I think I can come up with a new game for us to play tonight when you get home."

"I was not a cheerleader," I scoffed. "I beat up cheerleaders."

"Did you play any sports?"

"Is popularity a sport?"

"Are you saying you were promiscuous in high school?" Eliot asked. "I liked promiscuous girls when I was in high school."

"I was not promiscuous," I countered. "I was ... enthusiastic."

"You were easy."

"I was not easy," I argued. "I was ... accommodating."

Eliot smirked. "I love that you're not ashamed about being easy in high school."

"I hate that you dated cheerleaders."

"Well, blondie, if it's any consolation, I wish I'd dated you in high school," he said. "I think I would have had a lot more fun."

"Are you just saying that because you're hoping to get lucky tonight?"

"Nope," Eliot said, snapping the newspaper as he opened it again. "I'm saying it because I know I'm going to get lucky tonight. That's what happens when you date the school slut."

I cuffed him. "You're never getting lucky again."

"You say that now," Eliot said. "A true slut can never say no, though."

I hate men.

"SO, wait, what are they doing?"

"They're building a pyramid." The Richmond competitive cheer coach – she said her name was Sandy, which bugged me, because she looked like Sandy from *Grease* – was focused on the human triangle in front of her. "They need to get it right before they go out on that floor."

I nodded with faux enthusiasm. "Cool."

Sandy glanced at me. "You don't really think it's cool, do you?"

I wasn't sure how to answer. "It looks painful," I said finally.

"You weren't a cheerleader in high school, were you?" Sandy didn't look offended, merely resigned.

"I was a burnout in high school," I admitted. "We had a smoking corner."

"It's hard for girls like you to understand what's going on here," Sandy said. "It's not a slap at you, and it's certainly not a slap at them, it's just a breach."

"What do you mean?"

"I wasn't a cheerleader in high school either," Sandy said. "I hated them, in fact. I thought they were vacuous and stupid."

"Wow, what a great sport for you to coach," I enthused.

Sandy smiled. "You know coaches make a couple thousand dollars more a semester, right?"

Nope. I had no idea. "Oh, that's why you're doing it."

"At first," Sandy said. "When the job opened, I didn't think it was for me. I was like you. I hated cheerleaders."

"To be fair, I don't hate only cheerleaders," I said. "In fact, I'd much rather watch them than wrestlers."

Sandy giggled. "Yeah, wrestling is ... unique."

"I like to think of it as homoerotic."

"There are some interesting aspects to the sport," Sandy said. "Still, all wrestlers aren't one thing, and all cheerleaders aren't one thing. Just as all burnouts aren't one thing."

I considered the statement. "You're pretty rational for a high school coach," I said. "I've only met a few so far, but I can honestly say you're the only one I've liked."

"Who else have you met?"

"Just a bunch of douches."

Sandy smiled. "You're the news reporter who is being punished, aren't you?"

I faltered. How could she know that?

"The news about you has spread throughout all the schools," Sandy said. "Everyone knows that the famous Avery Shaw is on timeout."

"Most people I've come in contact with have no idea who I am," I said.

"Then they're not looking," Sandy replied. "You've broken some pretty big stories, and you've almost died a couple of times, if I'm not mistaken."

"That doesn't seem to matter to our new publisher."

"Why are you being punished? Girls, try the second pyramid

please." Sandy never moved her gaze from my face, even though she was doing two jobs at once.

"Because I pissed off a county commissioner."

"There has to be more to the story than that."

I shrugged. "I slept with him in college."

"And?"

"And I like to torture him," I admitted.

Sandy smiled. "You're a strong woman," she said. "You know what you want, and you don't give up. You're willing to be as tough as you have to be to get what you want. That's an inspiration."

"That's not what my boss says."

"What does your boss say?"

"He says I'm rude and stupid."

Sandy snickered. "How old is he?"

"About sixty."

"He's part of a different generation," Sandy said, raising her hands and instructing her girls to do something – I had no idea what – without words. "Men of that age think women should cook and clean. They think women are to be seen, and not heard."

"He's really not like that," I said. "He believes in me. He thinks I'm good at my job."

"Then why are you in sports?"

"Because the man in charge of him thinks I'm crazy."

Sandy snorted. "Are you crazy?"

"Sometimes."

"Are you good at your job?"

"Most of the time."

Sandy fixed her eyes on me, curious. "Are you sorry for being who you are?"

"Not in the least."

"I knew I liked you," Sandy said, turning back to her girls. "When I first was offered the job as coach I thought it was because I was a woman."

"That sucks."

"It was because I was a woman," Sandy said. "Competitive cheer is a small sport. The only reason we have it here is because a bunch of PTA mothers banded together to fight for what their daughters wanted."

"Yeah, I've heard the PTA is like the mafia," I said.

"It's worse," Sandy said. "They did good here, though."

"Why do you say that?"

"These girls aren't about getting in short skirts and turning on boys," Sandy said. "That's what cheerleading was for a long time. This is different."

"Is it like *Bring It On?*"

Sandy snorted. "Not in the slightest. Trust me, this sport isn't about transcending anything. It is about letting girls do what they want to do."

"And they want to cheer?"

"Don't look down on them," Sandy chided. "These girls are athletes."

"I'm not looking down on them," I said. "I'm trying to ... understand."

Sandy nodded her head, pursing her lips as she considered how to proceed. "Were you popular in high school?"

"That depends on who you ask," I said. "My boyfriend thinks I was very popular in high school."

"What does the boyfriend you had in high school think?" Sandy asked.

"I ... he knows I was different."

"Does your boyfriend now know you're different?"

"He likes that I'm different," I said.

"That's because age gives us strength," Sandy said. "Older men know that different women are a gift."

"He's not older," I cautioned. "He's just ... wiser."

"He'd have to be to snag you," Sandy said. "He's evolved, obviously."

I was confused.

"When I took this job, I thought I was just going to coach vapid teenagers," she said. "I was wrong. I have the chance to mold impressionable young women here. I don't care about the cheerleading. I don't care about the sport. I don't care about the petty arguments they get in when they're fighting about which boy likes which girl. "I care about teaching these girls that they don't have to conform," she continued. "I didn't realize that was what I was doing right away. I do now, though."

"How?"

"They come to me with their problems," Sandy said. "They come to me with their fears. They come to me when a boy is pressuring them into sex. They come to me when their friends are pressuring them to be thinner. I don't solve their problems, but I do serve as a sounding board."

"I forgot how obnoxious high school can be," I admitted. "My teachers were never helpful. A couple spent more time looking down my shirt than teaching. It sounds like you're doing it right."

"I want to do it right," Sandy said. "That's why I want you to come and talk to my class."

Oh, well crap. "I don't do well talking in front of people," I balked. "I'm really bad at it."

"You'll do fine," Sandy said, brushing off my concerns. "You'll show them that there's more to life than being someone's girlfriend. You'll show them that there's more to fight for."

"I'm a mess," I said. "I just got demoted."

"And why did you get demoted?"

"Because I make enemies wherever I go."

"Are you happy?"

"Right now? No."

"If you weren't in sports would you be happy?" Sandy asked again.

"Happiness is hard to define," I hedged.

"Yeah, you're perfect to talk to my class," Sandy said. "You're still figuring things out yourself. You're successful and you're driven, but you're not set in your ways."

"I'm totally set in my ways," I argued. "My boyfriend says I'm spoiled. Actually, everyone I know says I'm spoiled."

"Are you spoiled?"

"I just told you I was."

"Do you still work hard?" Sandy asked.

I sucked in a breath. "Yes."

"Then you're a role model."

"I'm not a role model." Someone must be taping me for a *Candid Camera*-type show, I swear.

"You're a role model because you don't give in," Sandy said. "You fight for what you want. I need these girls to know that they can be whatever they want to be. If they want to be a cheerleader, they can be a cheerleader. If they want to be a homemaker, they can be a homemaker."

Sandy turned to me. "If they want to be more, they can be you," she said. "No one has to do anything they don't want to do. I just want them to believe."

She was pretty convincing. "Where do I sign up?"

"**W**hy are you so dressed up?" Fish asked, his eyes suspicious as they landed on me Friday morning.

I glanced down at my black slacks and purple blouse and shrugged. "I have to go to Richmond to give a speech."

"About what?"

"What it's like to be a woman in a man's world."

"How would you know that?" Fish scoffed. "You think like a filthy longshoreman."

"That's why I was asked."

"Who asked you?"

"The Women's Studies teacher at Richmond High School," I said. "I think her name is Sandy Greason."

"Did she call you out of the blue and ask?" Fish asked.

"No, I met her when I was covering competitive cheer last night. She's the coach."

"What's competitive cheer?"

I shrugged. "Fancy cheerleading."

"I didn't even know that was a sport," Fish said. "Do they wear skirts and throw each other up in the air?"

"A little," I said. "It's more like they build extra-large pyramids."

"And why does this woman want you to talk to these kids?" Fish asked.

"Because I am a successful woman."

"Since when?"

I made a face. "Hey! I'm very successful."

"You wear tennis shoes with little aliens on them," Fish countered.

"They're not aliens," I said. "They're superheroes."

"Is that different?"

"Don't push me," I warned. "I'm crabby."

"I take it things aren't going well for you in sports," Fish said. "I had a feeling that would happen."

"They hate me."

"How do you feel about them?" Fish asked.

"I wish the big ball that drops on New Year's Eve would turn into a basketball and it would squish all of them."

"You have a way with words," Fish said. "Oh, crap, don't look up."

I looked up to find MacDonald striding into the newsroom. "There you are," he said.

"I'll leave you two alone," I said, starting to shuffle away.

"I was looking for you, Ms. Shaw," MacDonald said.

"Why?"

"What did you do?" Fish hissed.

"I understand you're talking to a group of girls in Richmond this afternoon," MacDonald said.

How could he know that? Past MacDonald's shoulder, I saw Duncan slinking into the newsroom, a triumphant look on his face. Of course. "I am."

"And how did this occur?"

I told him about my conversation with Sandy the night before, leaving out as many colorful embellishments as possible. MacDonald looked thoughtful when I was done.

"So, you're going to be talking about women in the workforce?"

I nodded.

"And you're not going to be doing anything ... weird, right?"

"Define weird."

"Well, it's come to my attention – from an anonymous source – that you have a penchant for saying crude things to young adults," MacDonald said.

I shot Duncan a scorching look. "I don't care what Duncan says," I replied. "I am perfectly capable of talking to a bunch of teenagers about their options in life without being crude."

"And that crude thing isn't just reserved for teenagers," Fish said. "She does it with adults, too."

"Thanks," I said.

"Don't mention it," Fish said.

"Well, I don't see the harm in it," MacDonald said.

"What?" Duncan took a step forward, his eyes blazing. "You can't let her warp an entire generation of teenage minds."

MacDonald glanced over his shoulder, which gave me the opportunity to flip Duncan off without being noticed. "I've always believed reporters should be involved in community outreach programs," MacDonald said. "That draws readers in because they become attached to the people writing the stories."

"But she's ... the Devil," Duncan sputtered.

I mimed horns over my head and did a little dance.

"She says she's going to behave," MacDonald said, swiveling back to me.

I straightened, pretending I hadn't been baiting Duncan. "I'm definitely going to behave."

MacDonald smiled. "I'm glad to see you're maturing."

"Me, too."

"WELL, I don't usually do stuff like this, so you're going to have to bear with me," I said, scanning the assembled teenage girls nervously. Usually, my mouth has no problem running away with me. This was different. These girls were looking for wisdom, not sarcasm. I was out of my depth. "What do you want to know?"

"You're a reporter, right?" The girl who asked the question looked as though she'd stepped off the pages of Seventeen magazine. Teenage girls weren't this put together when I was in school.

"I am."

"Do you make a lot of money?"

"No," I said. "Being a reporter is more of a ... calling. You're not going to get rich doing it."

"Katie Couric did."

I scowled. "Katie Couric is in television," I said. "Real reporters are never in television."

A couple of the girls exchanged dubious looks.

"So, did you always want to be a sports reporter?" Sandy asked.

"Absolutely not," I said. "I'm a news reporter. I'm just ... moonlighting in sports right now."

"How come?"

"Because men with small penises like to torture me." The words were already out of my mouth before I realized. Since the girls in the room were giggling appreciatively, I figured I was fine.

"Are you being punished?" Another girl asked the question.

"I am," I said.

"Why?"

I saw no sense in lying. "Because I ticked off one of the county commissioners and he filed a complaint with our new publisher," I said.

"Why doesn't this county commissioner like you?"

"We used to sleep together in college."

Sandy cleared her throat. "I think we're getting off topic here."

I pursed my lips. "Ms. Greason is right," I said. "Do you have any questions about my job?"

"Do you think this commissioner still has feelings for you?" The girls were much more interested in the gossipy tidbits from my life. I couldn't blame them.

"Just hate."

"Are you sure? Because there's this guy I know. We used to date, and now he's mean to me. I'm pretty sure it's because he wants to get back with me. He just doesn't know how to express his feelings."

"Tina, that's not what we're here to talk about," Sandy chided.

Tina ignored her. "Do you think that's why this commissioner is going after you? I know that's why Michael keeps going after me."

"Michael keeps going after you because you slept with his best friend," one of the other girls said.

"That's not true, Natalie," Tina said. "I'm still a virgin." She held up her left hand to display some sort of ring. "I'm waiting for marriage."

"Is that an engagement ring?" I asked.

"No. It's a purity ring."

"Who gave it to you?"

"My dad," Tina said. "We had a little ceremony, and I pledged to remain a virgin until marriage."

"Are you saying you're engaged to your dad until you get married?" I asked.

Tina wrinkled her nose. "Of course not."

That's how it sounded to me. "Okay."

"Are you waiting for marriage?" Tina asked.

"God no."

Sandy rubbed her forehead worriedly.

"I mean ... absolutely not," I said, shaking my head.

"How many guys have you slept with?" Natalie asked.

"I don't think that has anything to do with anything," Sandy interjected. "Ms. Shaw is here to talk about women in the workplace, not her social life."

"Do you have a boyfriend?" Tina asked.

"Yes."

"What's his name?"

"Eliot."

"Is he hot?" Tina pressed.

"He's very handsome," I said.

"But is he hot?"

"He certainly thinks so," I said.

"What do you think?"

I glanced at Sandy. She looked as if she was about to have a melt-down. "I think we should talk about your options as young women," I said. "Ms. Greason invited me here so you could question me about my job, not my boyfriend."

"Aren't you the reporter who was kidnapped by that guy who hacked up his wife and dumped her in the woods?" The girl who asked the question had purple streaks in her black hair. I kind of liked them.

"Yes," I said.

Sandy raised a surprised eyebrow. "That was you?"

"That was me," I said.

"Weren't you also shot at by that crazy woman who was killing people on the freeways?"

"That was me, too."

The girls started murmuring excitedly to one another.

"Are you the same reporter who was stalked at the newspaper office the night the sheriff was shot?"

I pursed my lips. "Yes."

"Wow," Sandy said. "How are you still alive?"

"Just lucky I guess."

"No, that's not it," Tina said. I noticed she had her cell phone out and she was staring at the screen intently. "The story in the Detroit Free Press says that you and Sheriff Farrell used to date."

A headache was starting to pulse between my ears. "It was a long time ago. We were in high school."

"But he got shot for you," Tina said. "Did he jump in front of the bullet to protect you? That's so romantic, by the way."

"He didn't jump in front of the bullet," I said. "He was shot from behind."

"Where were you?"

"I was ... ." My memory flashed to the night in question. "I was looking at him."

A crease formed between Sandy's eyebrows. "That's awful. You saw him get shot?"

"Yes."

"What did you do?" Tina asked.

"I tried to save him," I said quietly.

"Well, you obviously did," Tina said. "This story says you shot that guy in the chest to protect Sheriff Farrell. You killed him."

"I did."

"Wow," Natalie said. "Have you killed a lot of men? Do you have to be a reporter if you want to get away with killing a man?"

"Just the one."

"Do you regret it?"

I leveled my gaze at the classroom. "No. That guy was sick, and he was killing women and dumping them in the Clinton River. I don't regret what I did. Jake wouldn't have survived if I hadn't done what I did."

"You call the sheriff Jake?" Tina was intrigued. "Did you sleep with him when you dated in high school?"

"Yeah, how many guys have you slept with?" Natalie asked.

I frowned. "I don't think that's important," I said.

"Do you think you're a slut?" I had no idea who asked the question.

"No," I said. "I think that girls calling each other sluts is actually one of the worst things we do to one another as a gender."

Sandy smiled encouragingly. "Ms. Shaw has a point. You guys call each other sluts all the time. Does it make you feel better to tear someone else down?"

"Well, if you're a slut, you deserve it," Tina said, her tone haughty. "Just ask Erica."

Multiple sets of eyes shifted toward the shrinking girl in the back corner. Her hair was long and brown, wide waves offsetting a pair of terrified dark eyes. I felt sorry for her immediately. She was obviously the focal point of some serious wrath in this room.

"Don't do that," I warned.

"Don't tell me what to do," Tina sniffed.

"Then stop attacking that girl," I said.

"You don't even know her," Tina said. "They call her Easy Erica for a reason."

"I bet it's the same reason they call you Tina the Twat."

"Hey! You can't speak to me that way," Tina said.

"I just did."

"I think we should end this conversation here," Sandy said. "Everyone give Ms. Shaw a round of applause for agreeing to come and talk to us about ... well ... everything but her job."

I shot her a wan smile. She didn't return it.

"Great job, Erica," Tina said. "You ruined it for everyone. Again. You just can't do anything right, can you?"

Erica's lower lip quivered as she bolted for the door. I watched her go, helpless. The truth was, Erica wasn't the one who had let this situation get away from her. Per usual, that was me.

"Well, that was a great idea," Sandy said.

"I warned you," I replied, my gaze still on the door Erica had fled through. "I have no impulse control when it comes to my mouth."

"I thought you were exaggerating."

"Oh, my mouth needs no exaggeration."

"You realize that their parents are going to be calling the newspaper, right?" Sandy said.

"Don't worry. I'm used to it." I took a step toward the door, turning around long enough to fix Tina and her chortling minions with a hard look. "You're pretty proud of yourselves, aren't you?"

What? The day was already a disaster; I might as well drop a nuke on the little monsters before I left.

"I'm not the slut," Tina said.

"Why are you calling her a slut?" I asked.

"Because she slept with the whole Catholic North wrestling team."

I stilled. "Who told you that?"

Sandy looked as surprised by the claim as I was. "Yes, Tina, who told you that?"

Tina threw her hair back over her shoulder. "I'm friends with a girl over there," Tina said. "She told me that Erica went to one of their parties two weeks ago, and she made herself available to all of them. If that's not a slut, I don't know what is."

I knew something was wrong with those Catholic North asshats. "So, you think it's normal for a teenage girl to sleep with an entire wrestling team?"

"If she's a slut," Tina sad, crossing her legs at the ankles primly. "I'm obviously not one, but Erica is."

I wanted to smack the crap out of her. Instead, I crossed the room and stood in front of her desk. When she refused to look up, I kicked her desk leg for good measure. "Look at me."

Tina raised her eyes, practically daring me to say something to her. I'd never met a dare I didn't stupidly take. "You sit here on a make-believe throne and lord over all of your subjects," I said. "I see it. You think you're better than everyone at this school. It's written all over your face."

"I am better."

"Let me tell you how your life is going to go," I said, keeping my voice level. "You're going to go to a nice college. You're going to try to surround yourself with people just like you. A funny thing is going to happen, though. You're going to realize that the world isn't how you make it. In the real world, people don't have to fit in the box you create. In the real world, you have to make your own mold.

"A girl like you is incapable of that," I continued. "You get your power by trying to take it from others. That only works in high school."

I hunkered down so I was at eye-level with her. "You see, out in the real world you're nothing but the snotty girl who isn't any fun," I said. "The guys aren't going to want to hang out with you because you're too much work. When the girls realize this, they're not going to want to hang out with you because you can't get them access to guys, and that's the only reason they pretend to like you now.

"You're going to marry some suited moron who finally decides to settle for you because he thinks he can bring you home to his family and make them happy," I continued. "You're going to look at this as a win for a little while. You're going to think you've made it big. Then you're going to realize that the only kind of guy who would be interested in you is one who cares about appearances."

"You have no idea what you're talking about," Tina snapped.

I ignored her. "You're going to find that the guy you think you deserve is going elsewhere to get his fun," I said. "He'll let you bear his children, but he's never going to look at you as an equal. And, when your hips start to spread and he's really bored with you he's going to walk out one day. He's going to find his backbone and he's going to leave you all alone. You're going to go through life nothing but an empty, shiny little shell. And that's exactly what you deserve."

I straightened up and fixed Sandy with an apologetic look. "Go ahead and give the screaming parents my cell phone number. I can't wait to talk to a few of them."

Sandy's smile was small, but heartfelt. "I know this didn't go how I promised," she said. "In a weird way, I think you gave these girls exactly what I wanted you to give them."

"And what's that?"

"A harsh dose of reality."

I nodded. "Hey, so where is the bathroom? It's a long ride back to Mount Clemens."

I HEARD the sound of sniffling in one of the closed stalls as I moved to the sink to wash my hands. It wasn't hard to determine the source.

"Erica?"

She didn't answer, but the sniffling ceased. I crouched down and scanned for legs in the stalls. I found a pair in the last one. I knocked on the stall door.

"I know you're in there."

"I'm fine." Her voice was choked.

"You don't sound fine," I said. "Why don't you open the door? I'd like to talk to you."

"Why? Do you want to call me a slut, too?"

"I happen to like sluts," I said. "Some of them are my best friends."

Erica disengaged the lock, but she didn't get up from the toilet. "You don't have to do this," she said, wiping mascara-laden tears from her eyes. "I'm used to it."

I fixed the girl with a sympathetic look. "You shouldn't have to be used to it."

"You must not remember what high school was like," Erica said.

"Oh, I definitely remember high school."

"I bet you were popular."

I shook my head. "I had friends. I was very close with my cousins. I was at a really small school, and I decided I didn't like the popular kids at a pretty young age."

"Did they like you?"

"They were afraid of me," I admitted.

"Why?"

"I was a mouthy kid."

Erica waited.

"I'm a mouthy adult, too."

"I never would have guessed," Erica deadpanned.

I smiled. "All I can tell you is that this will get better," I said. "College girls are a lot more fun to hang out with than high school girls. You'll get to pick your friends there. You'll have a much bigger pool to choose from."

"I can't wait."

I debated how to ask the next question, and then I just went for it. "What happened with the Catholic North wrestling team?"

The limited color in Erica's cheeks drained. "Who told you that?"

"Take a guess."

"Tina?"

"Don't worry. That girl has 'bitter first wife' written all over her," I said. "She'll end up alone."

"How do you know that?"

"I've known a lot of girls like her."

"How did you handle them in high school?"

"I beat them up."

Erica's head jerked. "What?"

"I've been in a brawl or two."

"Did you always win?"

I shrugged. "I'm a biter. I also have a cousin who likes to fight, too, and she's vicious."

"At least you had someone to stand up for you."

I ran my tongue over my teeth, waiting a beat. Erica was being purposely evasive. She was hoping I would forget my line of questioning. "Tell me about the Catholic North kids."

Erica balked. "I don't want to talk about that."

Unfortunately, that wasn't an option. "Listen, I've had a few run-ins with those kids," I said. "They're all little shitheads. I haven't met one of them I like." Well, except for Jen, whose face was suddenly pushing to the forefront of my mind. "Were you invited to one of their wrestling parties?"

Erica nodded mutely.

I decided to take it a step at a time. "How many girls were there?"

"Just me."

I didn't like the sound of that. "How did you meet them?"

"I was at the wrestling quad here the Thursday before last," Erica said. "One of the students approached me and we got to talking. I thought he was nice, so when he invited me to the party I thought it would be fun."

"Did you know you'd be the only girl there?"

Erica bit her lip and shook her head.

"Did you ask about it when you got there?" I asked.

"Yes."

"What did he say?"

"He said the other girls were running late," Erica said. "Then he gave me a drink."

"What happened then?"

"I ... I started feeling sick to my stomach," Erica said. "I found a bathroom, and I threw up. I was going to rest there for a few minutes. I wanted to put myself together before I left for home."

"Did you drive there?"

"Yes."

I nodded. "What happened then?"

"I passed out," Erica said.

"Was something in the drink they gave you?"

"It was just supposed to be Diet Coke," Erica said.

"When you woke up, where were you?"

"I was on the floor in the living room."

"Were you ... dressed?" I almost didn't want to hear the answer.

"Yes." Erica's voice was barely above a whisper.

"Had something happened to you?"

"I'm not sure," Erica admitted. "I ... I was sore."

I pressed my eyes shut briefly. "Where?"

"All over," Erica said. "Everywhere."

I rubbed my forehead. "What do you think happened to you?"

"I didn't know for sure until I got home," Erica said. "I still felt weird, and I knew something wasn't right. When I took off my clothes, though, there was blood in my underwear."

I fought hard to control the rising bile in my throat. "Did you tell your mother?"

"I can't tell my mother," Erica said, her face fearful. "She'll blame me. She always warned me about things like this. She's going to be so disappointed in me."

"This isn't your fault," I said, resting my hand on her arm. "That's the most important thing you have to remember."

"It feels like my fault," Erica grumbled. "Especially since Sam told everyone that I had sex with all of them."

My heart stuttered. "Sam? Sam Keaton?"

Erica nodded.

"He's the boy who invited you?"

Erica nodded again.

"Erica, I need you to do something you're really not going to want to do," I said.

Erica's head was already moving. "No. I can't go to the police."

"You have to," I said. "If these boys keep getting away with this, other girls are going to be hurt. In fact, I think some already have."

"You do? You don't think it's just me?"

"Have you heard about Kelsey Cooper?" I asked.

"She's the girl who died at Catholic North, right?"

"Yes."

"I ... ." Erica paused. "You don't think ... ?"

"That's exactly what I think," I said, extending my hand in Erica's direction. "We need to go to the police."

"I'm too afraid to go the police. Cops freak me out."

"Well, luckily for you I happen to know a few police officers who are also good guys," I said.

"Like Sheriff Farrell?"

"And my cousin," I said. "Erica, you can't just let this go. You have to do what's right. I'll be with you every step of the way. I promise."

"What if everyone finds out?"

I shrugged. "What if someone else dies?"

Tears filled Erica's eyes. "Okay."

"What are we doing here?" Erica asked, glancing over from the passenger seat nervously. "You said we were going to the police. I thought that would be the Richmond police."

"Yes, but you were in Macomb Township when it happened," I said. "The sheriff's department handles Macomb Township, and I happen to know that they're investigating the Catholic North kids for a few things right now, including Kelsey Cooper's murder."

"What things?"

"Steroids, for one," I said. "They've received numerous tips about the wrestlers using steroids."

"Do you think they are?"

I tipped my head to the side. "It might explain some of their impulse control problems," I said. "It's hard to say."

"You said you'd had a few run-ins with them," Erica said. "Was Sam one of the kids you fought with?"

"My grandfather hit him in the nuts with a spatula the other night," I said.

Erica's eyes widened. "What?"

"He was trying to get me to go to his car with him," I said. "He said I was old, but doable."

"He's horrible," Erica said.

"Oh, don't worry, he's going to get what's coming to him," I said. "I promise you that."

"Are you sure I should do this?" Erica asked.

I could see the tension bringing her slight shoulders up. "I'm sure that we don't want anyone else to be hurt, or die."

Erica sucked in a breath. "Okay."

I opened the door, but Erica stilled me with a hand on my arm before I climbed out of the car. "You'll stay with me, right?"

"Don't worry," I said. "I won't leave you."

I LED Erica to the protective bubble that houses two sheriff's deputies in the main lobby. Unfortunately, I recognized them both. They weren't big fans of mine.

"Deputy Ferguson. Deputy Hanks."

"What are you doing here? I thought you were busted down to sports?" Ferguson asked.

"I need to see Derrick," I said. "I have someone who needs to talk to him."

Ferguson scanned the shaking girl behind me. "She looks messed up."

"You look messed up," I said. "Can you just buzz me back?"

"You're not allowed to just wander around back there. You know that."

"Then call Derrick and tell him to come get me," I argued.

"He's got a news conference in ten minutes."

I narrowed my eyes. "On Kelsey Cooper?"

"That has nothing to do with sports, does it?"

I shot the deputy a look. "You're really a dick, Ferguson."

"Right back at you, Shaw."

I pulled my cell phone from my pocket and gave Erica a reassuring look. "Don't worry. My cousin is nothing like these morons." I texted Derrick and waited for him to respond. After three minutes, I was about to give up, but the door that led to the inner sanctum of the department opened and I could see Derrick in the archway.

"What do you want?"

I ushered Erica forward. "It's nice to see you, too."

Derrick looked Erica up and down, his face softening as he took in her pale features. He might not know what was going on, but he could sense I was serious. "Let's go back to my office."

"Hey, she's not supposed to be doing news stuff," Ferguson said.

"Is that any of your business?" Derrick asked.

"No." Ferguson had the grace to look abashed.

"Then don't worry about it," Derrick said.

He led us to his office, and I kept my hand on Erica's back the entire trek. Once we were inside, I made sure she was settled in a chair before starting the discussion.

"This is Erica," I said, frowning when I realized I didn't know her last name. "I met her in Richmond this afternoon."

"What were you doing out there?"

"I was talking to a Women's Studies class about being a working woman in today's society," I said.

"Are you taking over a specific street corner?"

I ignored him. "Erica has a story for you to hear," I said carefully. "It involves some Catholic North wrestlers."

Derrick leaned forward, resting his elbows on his desk. "I'm listening."

Erica looked to me for reassurance. I nodded, and she haltingly told Derrick what she'd told me earlier. When she was done, Derrick was clearly shocked, but considerate. "Have you been to a doctor?"

"No," Erica said. "I didn't want anyone to know."

"I understand that," Derrick said. "We need to make sure you're okay, though. I can take you."

Erica clutched my hand, terror washing over her. "I can't go with you."

Derrick was calm. "Avery can go with you if that will make you feel better."

"What will the doctor do?"

Derrick looked at me, unsure.

"He needs to make sure you're not pregnant, for one thing," I said.

"I hadn't even considered that," Erica said.

"We also need to make sure they didn't pass any sexually transmitted diseases on to you," I added. "And, well, it was your first time. We need to make sure no permanent damage was done."

Derrick was uncomfortable with the turn in the conversation. "Yes, what Avery said."

"We could ... we could call your mother to come down to the hospital," I said. "If you want, that is."

"She's out of town until the middle of next week," Erica explained. "She went on a business trip with my dad to Las Vegas. She'd always wanted to go, and he surprised her."

"I'm sure they would come back," Derrick said.

"No," Erica said. "I'm not ready to tell them yet. It can wait until they come home. I just need some time to wrap my head around it."

"Okay," Derrick said. "We'll take you to the hospital. Avery and I will go together. After that, we'll take you home."

"She's not staying home alone this weekend," I said. "She can stay with me tonight."

Derrick looked surprised. "You're taking her to family dinner? Hasn't she been through enough?"

"She needs food and company," I said. "She shouldn't be alone. It will be fine."

Derrick nodded. "Okay. Well, I do need to get your official statement, Erica," he said. "It will take about a half hour, and I'm afraid Avery can't be here for that."

Erica straightened in her chair, terrified. "Where is she going to go?"

"I'll be right outside," I soothed. "I won't go far. You can trust Derrick. He would never hurt you."

Erica didn't look convinced.

"Hey, do you remember how I told you I used to beat up people in high school?"

Erica nodded.

"Derrick was one of the girls I used to beat up," I said.

Despite herself, Erica giggled. Derrick wasn't as thrilled. "You never beat me up."

"Did you or did you not have a black eye because of me?"

"That's because you tossed a broom handle down that pipe when I was looking through it," Derrick challenged. "And I don't care what you say, I know you did it on purpose."

"That was an accident," I said. "And that's not what I was referring to."

Erica looked more relaxed as she listened to the banter, so I kept it up.

"I was talking about the time you hid in the back of Dad's pickup truck because you were going to scare me by reaching through the back window while I was driving," I said.

Derrick made a face. "That wasn't funny. You hit the brakes so hard I almost flew over the cab."

"And then I beat the crap out of you," I said.

"I was practically unconscious from being thrown against the back of the cab," Derrick said. "I couldn't even focus."

"Hey, you had it coming," I said.

Derrick rolled his eyes. "You're unbelievable."

"I like her," Erica said, her voice small.

Derrick pursed his lips. "Well, if you promise not to tell anyone, I'll tell you a secret," he said.

Erica held three fingers up. "I promise."

"I like her some of the time, too," Derrick said. "Usually when she's asleep."

"She's tough," Erica said.

"She's a good ally for you," Derrick said. "She's a good ally for anyone to have. How about we get your statement, and then you can watch her in action at the hospital? Doctors hate her. She's great at torturing them."

Erica nodded. "Okay."

I got to my feet. "I'll be right outside," I promised.

"Hey, do me one favor," Derrick said. "I'm supposed to be down at that news conference. Find someone down there and tell them what I'm doing. Keep it quiet."

"Okay," I said. "Be nice to her," I warned.

"I'm not the mean one."

I waited.

"It will be fine," Derrick said. "You can beat me up if it's not."

I MADE my way down the narrow hallway that led to the conference room. I'd hovered outside of Derrick's office a full five minutes after leaving, just to make sure that Erica would be okay. When she didn't run screaming from the room, I left Derrick to his questioning. As much as I liked to mess with him, I knew he would be good to her.

I heard voices from the conference room, and slowed my approach to listen. I didn't recognize the voice, but I knew it didn't belong to Jake. I figured it was another investigator on the case.

"Do you have any leads yet?" I recognized the voice of the woman asking the question. It was Devon.

"We're looking at several different things right now," the voice said. "We can't go into any great detail when the investigation is ongoing. You know that. We're dealing with an unfortunate situation here. Kelsey Cooper died on private school grounds."

"Does that mean that the school isn't helping with the investigation?"

"That means that we have to approach this case in a different way," the voice said. "We're dealing with a suspect pool that involves minors. All of their parents have to agree to questioning, and that's been a difficult sell."

"Because they know their kids are guilty?" I didn't recognize the voice, but it was an interesting question.

"Because no parent wants their kid railroaded."

"Is that what you're doing, railroading the kids?" Devon asked.

"Do I even need to dignify that with a response?"

"You seem to be talking in circles here," Devon said. "You keep saying the same thing, and as far as I can tell you're not getting anywhere."

"I'm sorry you feel that way," the voice said. "We're doing the best that we can."

"This community is outraged," Devon said. "A teenage girl is dead."

"Thanks for the update."

"What are you going to do about it?" I couldn't help but be a little proud of Devon's tenacity. She was taking up my mantle.

"We're going to solve the case."

I turned away from the conference room and ran smack into a solid chest. The first thing I saw was the uniform. As I lifted my head, Jake's familiar features swam into view.

"Oh, hi," I said.

"Ms. Shaw," Jake said. "May I ask what you're doing here?"

"I ... I brought someone in to talk to Derrick," I said. "He's taking her statement now."

"I know," Jake said. "I went looking for him. He said you were supposed to tell me he couldn't make the conference."

"He didn't say to tell you," I said. "He said to tell someone, and it was already going on when I got down here."

"So, you decided to eavesdrop?"

"I decided to ... hey, I don't have to justify myself to you," I said, moving to head back to Derrick's office.

Jake snagged my arm. "Oh, you're going to talk to me, Avery," he said. "You're going to talk to me, and you're not leaving this place until we hash this out."

"I have no idea what you're talking about," I argued, averting my eyes.

Jake snorted. "We'll see about that."

J ake didn't let go of my arm until we were inside his office and the door was closed. He leaned against the door and crossed his arms over his chest as he regarded me.

"This is kidnapping," I announced.

"I'll let you file a report when we're done," Jake said.

"What are we even doing here?" I moved closer to his desk, overwhelmed by a desperate need to keep space between us.

"We're going to talk," Jake said.

"About what?"

Jake rubbed the back of his neck. "Why didn't you come and see me in the hospital?"

I was taken aback by the question. "I did."

"No, you didn't," Jake said. "There were flowers from you. I knew the second I saw blue roses that they were from you. You can't do anything like a normal person. That's one of the only constants in my life."

"I was there," I said. "We sat there all night to make sure you didn't … . Once we knew you were okay, we went home."

"And you didn't come back," Jake said. "I expected you to come back."

"W-why?"

"Because I was shot," Jake said. "You were there. You saved us both. I thought you'd want to talk about it."

I started pacing, nervous energy bolstering me. "What was there to talk about? It was touch and go there for hours, but you survived. I knew you would."

"You did? Because I seem to remember you crying and begging me not to die," Jake said.

"Well ... I didn't want you to die," I said.

"That's nice to hear," Jake said. "It would have been nicer to hear in person then."

I rubbed the heel of my hand against my forehead. "I was there. I came five different times. I even made it up to your room twice. I just couldn't go inside."

Jake's face was unreadable. "Why?"

"Why do you think?" I flapped my arms once. "I couldn't deal with what you said."

Jake's eyes clouded. "What did I say? I don't remember saying anything."

"You don't?"

Jake shook his head, and I searched his face for clues that he was lying. There were none there. Had I been putting distance between us for nothing?

"I remember telling you to leave me and run," Jake said. "Of course, you stupidly said 'no' and tried to load me in the car even though I was dead weight. If I had the strength to strangle you that night, I might have tried to do it myself."

"Hey, I got you in that car," I said.

"And that's when Zack showed up," Jake said.

"I remember."

"You were smart that night, Avery," Jake said. "You played him exactly right. I thought you were crazy when you accused him of wanting to have sex with his mother. It took me awhile, but when I figured out you were trying to enrage him I realized what a good idea it was. You did everything right that night."

"Everything?"

"Well, you should have stayed in the apartment like Eliot ordered you to do," Jake conceded. "Once you knew you were in trouble, though, you did everything right."

"Thank you."

Jake waited. "Are you going to tell me what I said that freaked you out?"

"No."

Jake looked down at the arms crossed over his chest. "It must have been pretty bad," he said. "You've been avoiding me for six weeks."

"I haven't been avoiding you."

"You have," Jake said. "I tried to talk to you at that basketball game and you couldn't get away from me fast enough. I want to know why."

"I had to cover the game," I lied.

"Has Eliot asked you to stay away from me? Is he the reason you don't want anything to do with me?"

"No," I said. "Cripes, Eliot doesn't even know I'm avoiding you."

"So, you are avoiding me?"

"I ... yes."

"Because of what I said?"

"Yes."

"I need to know what I said," Jake said. "I need to know why you've just ... cut me out of your life."

I licked my lips, considering. Either we got this out of the way now or I continue to hide like a coward. It was a tough choice. "You told me you loved me."

Jake straightened, his eyes searching mine for a second. I think I'd knocked the wind out of him. "I did?"

"Yes."

"What did you say?"

"I begged you not to die," I said. "Then you lost consciousness.

That's when Eliot showed up. He told me you were still alive, but I didn't believe him. Even after the doctor told us you were going to survive, I didn't believe him."

"I'm right here, Avery," Jake said. "I survived."

"I know, but you almost died because of me," I said. "You were there because of me."

"I would have been there for anyone in the same situation," Jake said.

"No, you would have let your deputies go to anyone else," I said. "You came because it was me, and if it hadn't been you, it would have been Eliot. I could have gotten both of you killed."

"I can tell this is bothering you," Jake said. "Is it because you regret killing Zack?"

"No," I said, shaking my head. "I don't feel bad about killing him. I just wish I could've done it before you got hurt."

"Avery, I don't regret going after you that night," Jake said. "If you think I have it in me to just sit around while you're in danger then you obviously don't know me. I'm not particularly thrilled with being shot, but I'd do it again to keep you safe."

"Because you love me?"

Jake shrugged. "I do love you."

My heart rolled painfully. "Jake ... ."

He held up his hand to still me. "I've always loved you," he said. "Some of the best times in my life were spent getting into trouble with you. That doesn't mean I can be with you."

I lifted my eyes, confused. "What?"

Jake moved closer to me. "You and I don't fit in the same world," he said. "Our worlds overlap. A lot. They don't mesh, though. I don't fit in your world, and you're incapable of fitting in mine.

"The truth is, as much as I'd like to convince myself that you could grow up and be what I need you to be, you can't," he continued. "And, if you managed to do it, you wouldn't be you."

"I don't know what to say."

"Then just listen," Jake said. "I'm always going to love you. I can't help myself. I'm not what you need, though. I need someone who can follow rules, and you've never met a rule you didn't want to break. You're like Eliot that way.

"The good news for you is that Eliot likes the crazy things you do," he said. "He finds ... delight in them. Sure, I think he wishes you would stay out of danger a little more, but he wouldn't change you."

"I wouldn't change you either," Jake said. "I wouldn't want a changed you. A changed you wouldn't be you. The real you cannot be with me, though, and the real me cannot be with you."

"Eliot said the same thing the other night," I admitted. "I thought he was jealous, but he appears to have gotten over that."

"I'm glad," Jake said. "He seems to make you happy. I definitely noticed that at the movies the other day. He gets you. He's happy to go to bad horror movies, and listen to you rant about utter nonsense. He not only puts up with your family, he seems to like them. He's good for you."

"Who's good for you?"

"I don't know yet," Jake said. "I think I've got to get myself together before I'm going to be ready for anything like that."

"Just don't let it be Celeste," I said. "I don't like her."

Jake smirked. "Thank you for saying that. It makes me feel better."

"I'm not going to like anyone you date, am I?"

Jake shrugged. "I don't know," he said. "I didn't think I'd ever like anyone you dated, but I'm having a hard time not liking what Eliot has done for you."

"Done for me? What has he done for me?"

"He's balanced you out," Jake said. "Oh, don't get me wrong, you're still loud and obnoxious, but you're also more thoughtful, and you're trying really hard to consider his needs when you make a decision these days. That's growth, whether you admit it or not."

"There's no reason to start insulting me," I grumbled.

Jake reached his hand out and tilted my chin up. "I still want you in my life. If that means we're just friends, then we're just friends. You have to stop hiding from me for that to happen, though."

I nodded.

Jake extended his arms. "Do you want to give your friend a hug?"

I stepped to him and wrapped my arms around his waist, resting my head against his chest. Jake tightened his arms around my back.

"Everything works out the way it's supposed to," he said. "That's what's happening here."

"I know."

"And, who knows? Things might change down the road," Jake said. "I might decide politics aren't my thing. I might decide I can't live without you and fight Eliot to the death for you."

I had my doubts, but I didn't voice them. "That's true."

Jake kissed the top of my head and exhaled heavily. "Everything is going to be okay. You're going to get your job back, and we're going to solve this Catholic North thing, and you're going to be ... happy."

"Let's not go overboard," I said. "I'm only happy when I'm irritating people. You know that."

"I do," Jake chuckled. "Let's just work on irritating Ludington, and leave me out of it, shall we?"

"Deal."

Jake held on for a few more seconds and then he let me go. "It's definitely a deal."

"Thanks for giving me a ride," Derrick said, looking out the passenger window as I sped toward Oakland County and family dinner. We were running late.

"Where is your car?"

"Devon has it," he said. "Her car is in the shop. She's going to meet me there, and we'll go home together. Try to keep it under eighty, will you? You're going to force me to write you a ticket."

I rolled my eyes and then glanced in the backseat of the car. "Are you feeling okay?"

Erica nodded. "I'm just thinking."

"The doctor tried to be as gentle as possible," I said. "I thought he was pretty good."

"He was fine," Erica said. "It was just embarrassing. Everyone knows what happened to me now."

"No one knows," I said.

"Tina knows."

"Tina is a bitch," I said.

"Who is Tina?" Derrick asked.

I told him about my afternoon with the class. His face twisted into a delighted smile when I was done. "I can't believe you said that to her in front of so many people."

"She's a bitch."

"You did good," Derrick said.

I eyed his profile, surprised. "Thanks."

"Don't let it go to your head," he said. "You're still an idiot most of the time."

"Thanks."

Derrick smirked. "So, what were you and Jake talking about?"

"The shooting."

"What did he say?"

"We had some things to hash out," I said.

"Did you?"

"Yes."

"Are you two ... all right?"

"We're fine," I said. "We're friends."

"Is that what both of you want?"

I shrugged. "It's the way it has to be," I said. "I'm with Eliot, and I'm happy with Eliot. Jake and I don't fit in each other's worlds."

"I know," Derrick said. "It still has to hurt. You guys spent a lot of time together when you were kids."

"We're not kids anymore."

"I was worried you two were going to elope right after graduation," Derrick said. "When Jake enlisted, I was surprised."

"I was surprised, too," I said.

"You were crushed," Derrick corrected. "Is that why you dumped him for Ludington?"

"No, I think that was temporary insanity," I said.

"Do you want to know what I think?"

"Not really."

"I do," Erica piped up from the backseat.

"I think you broke up with Jake because you realized there was no future for you two," Derrick said. "I think it hurt, but you did it anyway. I think he joined the military for the same reason.

"It's one thing to be young and dumb when you're a teenager," Derrick continued. "You both knew that holding on to each other was just going to hurt you more over the long haul. Distance made things easier for the two of you."

"It was never easy with us," I said.

"Is it easy with Eliot?"

I considered the question. "Yes."

"You know, when you first brought him around I thought you were doing it just to drive your mom crazy," Derrick said.

"Part of me was."

"Then I got to know him," Derrick said. "He just ... fits ... with you. You're both odd. You're both volatile. He seems crazy about you, and I'm not just saying that because I think someone would have to be crazy to stay with you for more than five minutes. You're good together."

"Thank you."

"Don't ever tell him I said that," Derrick warned. "I want him to live in fear of me."

I cocked an eyebrow. "Fear of you?"

"Hey, I'm a cop," Derrick said. "I'm terrifying."

"You're ... something," I said.

I PARKED in front of the restaurant and killed the engine. I turned to Erica and offered her a small smile. "My family is loud," I warned. "They're very friendly, though. You need to get some food in you, and there's no limit to the great food that we have to offer. Eat as much as you want, and save room for dessert."

"What are you going to tell them about me?" Erica asked, worried.

"That's a pretty good question," Derrick said. "What are you going to tell them?"

I furrowed my brow, thinking. "I'm going to tell them that Erica is interested in being a sports reporter and she's shadowing me for the day," I said. "I'll explain about her parents being out of town. Mom will be fawning all over her in thirty seconds flat."

"Do you think that will work?" Erica looked hopeful.

"Oh, don't worry, I've been lying to my mom for as long as I can remember," I said. "She never catches on."

Derrick rolled his eyes. "What about the time you told her the wine evaporated?"

"That was an aberration."

"What about the time you told her that Jake and you weren't having sex in the parked car and you were checking his tonsils to make sure they weren't infected?"

"She believed that."

"No, she just didn't want to deal with the truth," Derrick countered. "Hey, what about the time you told her the telephone pole moved and jumped in front of her car and that's why you crashed?"

"You're seriously starting to piss me off," I said.

Erica giggled. "You guys are like brother and sister."

"Don't remind me," Derrick said, opening the door. He pushed the seat forward and helped Erica out. "Avery is right, though, our family won't question you too much. If they make jokes about Avery's job, just go along with them. If you get caught, we'll help. It's going to be okay."

Erica nodded. "Thank you for all you've done."

"Thank you for being so brave." Derrick turned toward the restaurant. "Oh, man, what in the hell is that?"

I recognized Mario and Grandpa's food truck right away. "That's Mario's new business venture."

"Hey, thanks for telling him he could stay with me, by the way," Derrick said. "He's completely messed up my house."

"Make him clean."

"He says he doesn't know how," Derrick said.

"Who is Mario?" Erica asked.

I pointed to the round head bobbing behind the counter in the food truck. "He's our cousin."

"Why does he have a truck in the parking lot of a restaurant?"

"I'm assuming it's because he wants to give his dad a heart attack," I said.

"Does his dad own the restaurant?"

"No, our grandfather owns the restaurant," I said. "Our uncle manages it."

"What will your grandfather say? Won't he be mad?"

"He's the one cooking with Mario."

"Oh," Erica said, realization dawning. "Your family is weird, isn't it?"

"My family is batshit crazy," I corrected.

"I don't understand how they think a food truck in the parking lot is going to work in the middle of winter," Derrick said.

"I don't think they're worried about that," I replied. "I think they just want to drive Uncle Tim around the bend."

Derrick pointed to the angry figure stalking out of the back of the restaurant. "I think it's working."

"What the hell are you doing out here?" Uncle Tim bellowed.

"We're working," Grandpa said. "I know it's a foreign concept to you, but some of us work for a living."

"I work for a living," Tim said. "I do. You're just trying to pay me back because I told you to stop talking politics at the counter every morning."

"That's a vicious lie," Grandpa said.

"And you're paying me back because I told you I wasn't paying for any more fruity interpretive dance classes," Tim said, pointing his finger at Mario. "You both teamed up to pay me back. Admit it, you're trying to make me crazy."

"You're being paranoid," Grandpa said.

"I am not paranoid!"

"Your uncle's face looks really red," Erica said. "Do you think he's going to pass out?"

"Maybe," I said, shrugging. "It wouldn't be the first time. If it happens, don't be alarmed. He's one of those guys who can't handle the small things, so he overdoes it and then makes things worse."

"That's kind of a family trait," Derrick said.

"It is indeed," Eliot said, appearing from the far side of the parking lot and giving me a quick kiss. "How are you today, blondie?"

"I'm good," I said. "How was your day?"

"Long and boring," he said. "I'm looking forward to spending some quality time with you to make up for it."

I exchanged a quick look with Derrick. He caught on to my unsaid plea and led Erica toward the restaurant. "We might as well go inside. This could go on for hours."

Erica shot me a worried look. "Are you coming?"

"I'll be right in," I said. "Someone has to referee. I promise you'll be safe with Derrick."

Once she was gone, Eliot asked, "Who is that?"

I didn't have a lot of time, so I condensed the story. When I was done, he was angry. "I can't believe that happened to her."

"Her parents are out of town," I said. "She's kind of attached to me. I don't want to leave her alone. I know this is going to ruin our weekend, and I'm really sorry, because I know we need to spend some time together, but I don't know what else to do."

Eliot waved off my apology. "I think we'll survive," he said. "If it helps, I can stay at my place. She doesn't look comfortable around men right now, and I don't blame her."

"Let's play it by ear," I said. "She's a ball of nerves. She's barely let me out of her sight."

"That's because you're scary," Eliot said, giving me a longer kiss. "She knows you can protect her."

"She's been pretty good with Derrick," I said.

"How has he been with her?"

"Amazing," I said. "Sometimes I don't think I give him enough credit."

"Sometimes I don't think he gives you enough credit," Eliot countered.

"Well, we gave each other a lot of credit today."

"That's good." Eliot focused on the food truck. "What's going on over there?"

"Grandpa and Mario are trying to give Uncle Tim an aneurism."

"It looks fun. Do you want to eat from the truck?"

I shook my head. "I don't want to leave Erica, and it's cold out."

Eliot wrapped his arm around my waist. "You seem in a better mood today," he said.

"It's been an interesting day," I said.

"How did your speech go?"

I made a face. "I'll tell you about that some other time," I said.

"That bad, huh?"

"I was very good," I said. "I told them some things they'll never forget."

Eliot smirked. "I'll bet. Let's get some food. If I'm not going to get to spend the night with you I have to get my fill now."

"You're not mad, right?"

"Nope," Eliot said. "I'm a little disappointed, but I think Erica needs you a little more than I do."

"Thanks."

Eliot led me into the restaurant. I scanned the family table for Erica, and found her happily wedged near Lexie and Derrick. "Is everything okay?" I asked her pointedly.

"It's great," Erica said, giggling. "Lexie invited me over for a sleepover in her yoga studio tonight. I can go, right?"

How did I become the parental figure in this situation? "I ... um ... sure." I focused on Lexie. "Are you okay with this?"

"I like her," Lexie said. "I haven't had a sleepover in years."

Eliot slung an arm over my shoulder, a bright smile on his face. "Looks like my sleepover is back on."

I studied Erica for a few minutes, worried she would panic and change her mind. She didn't. Eliot and I settled at the middle table, and Erica didn't look to me once for reinforcement. It seemed I wasn't the one she needed after all. Lexie had her own brand of magic, and she was weaving it on Erica. Sometimes people surprise you, and Lexie was doing just that. I had no idea how she'd done it, but she'd managed to relax Erica and make her feel safe.

Jake was right. Things do have a way of working themselves out.

"Hey, there are a bunch of cops outside," one of the patrons said, pointing out the window. "It looks like they're loading people up in their cruiser."

I sighed. And sometimes my family just can't stop until law enforcement arrives to work things out for them.

"Are you sure you don't want to come inside with me?"

Eliot lifted an eyebrow. "Are you asking me to go in there and do yoga with you? Because, if you want to get sweaty I can think of better ways than turning yourself into a human pretzel."

Eliot was dropping me off for an afternoon of fun at Lexie's studio while he ran errands. I flicked his chin. "What happens if I don't want to stay?"

"I'm taking your car to get an oil change," Eliot said. "I'm not taking it to the moon. If you're bored, text me and I'll come and pick you up."

"What if I want to stay late?" I challenged.

"You can't stay past six," he said. "I made dinner reservations."

"What if something is wrong with Erica?"

"What if the sky suddenly explodes and aliens invade?" Eliot countered, his eyes bright. "What if you break a nail?"

"You're being awfully sarcastic," I said.

"I learned it from you," he said. "I won't be far. You haven't had the oil changed in this thing since I met you."

"So, you're basically running errands for me now?"

"I'm basically making sure this car isn't going to catch fire while you're driving it down the expressway," Eliot said.

I nodded sagely. "Because you're fond of me?"

Eliot smirked. "Yes."

"Okay," I said, pushing open the door. "Don't forget about me."

"I won't," Eliot said. "And, if something comes up with Erica, I'll understand. We can postpone dinner if we have to. She's the priority right now."

"What if something comes up with Lexie?"

"Then I'm not bailing her out," Eliot said, making a face. He has a tumultuous relationship with my cousin, one that usually culminates with him yelling at Lexie because she is so scattered. Since Lexie had made last night better for him, he seemed to be going with the flow today.

I gave him a quick kiss. "Thanks for taking my car for an oil change."

"Thanks for staying out of trouble for two weeks straight."

I paused before shutting the door. "That's kind of a backhanded compliment."

"Don't worry," he said. "I'm already regretting saying it."

"Why is that?"

"Now you're going to find trouble just to spite me," Eliot said.

I wanted to argue with him, but the niggling at the back of my brain was telling me he wasn't wrong.

"HEY, how are things?" I found Lexie and Erica in the studio portion of Yoga One That I Want. They were sitting on the floor stretching, and they both looked relaxed.

Erica smiled when she caught sight of me. "It's good," she said. "Lexie is so funny."

I forced a smile onto my face. Lexie was often funny. She was also tempestuous and irresponsible. Still, I didn't want to rain on Erica's parade. "She should have a standup routine. What did you guys do last night?"

I was trying to refrain from acting like a mother – especially my mother – but I was worried Lexie's propensity for pot had spoiled an otherwise innocent evening.

"We watched a movie," Erica said.

"What movie?"

Erica narrowed her eyes. "It was something I'd never heard of before. It was some old movie called *Mean Girls*."

I was definitely getting old if *Mean Girls* was considered old.

"It reminded me of Tina," Erica said.

"Let's just hope she gets hit by a bus," I said.

Erica clapped her hands over her mouth. "That's horrible."

"Not if it's true," I said. I turned to Lexie. " Show her *Heathers* tonight. That one is even more subversive."

"Good idea," Lexie said.

"Do you want me to spend the night again?" Erica asked, her eyes wide.

"Sure," Lexie said. "It will be fun. I haven't seen *Heathers* in forever."

"That's okay, right?" Erica asked, shifting her eyes to me.

I swallowed my sigh. She was treating me like the parent. Again. "You behaved yourself last night, right?" I asked Lexie pointedly.

Lexie's eyes narrowed. "What are you accusing me of?" She was going for faux outrage. I recognized it.

"There was no pot, right?"

"Of course not," Lexie said. "I would never corrupt a minor."

"Since when?"

"Since I know what poor Erica has been through," Lexie said.

I stilled. I was surprised Erica had told Lexie the truth. That must mean she's comfortable with her.

"I hope you're not angry that I told Lexie," Erica said, shyly lowering her eyes. "She didn't believe the story about me shadowing you."

"It's fine," I said. "It's your story to tell. You can tell anyone you want. She didn't give you alcohol or pot, though, did she?"

Erica shook her head emphatically. "Definitely not."

"When did you become the pot police?" Lexie asked. "You used to burn down with the best of them."

"I was a teenager," I said. "Now I'm the adult trying to rein the teenager in. There's a difference."

"Yeah, you're boring," Lexie said.

"I am not boring," I said. "There's a difference between boring and responsible."

"No, there's not," Lexie said. "They're the same thing."

"Stop talking to me," I said. "Your voice is giving me a headache."

"Oh, this is all my fault," Erica said, her eyes filling with tears.

"No, it's not," I said. "This is just how we communicate. Don't get all ... worked up."

Erica didn't look convinced.

"She's telling the truth," Lexie said. "This is how we communicate. It's fine. She's boring and she knows it. Acceptance is the first step on the road to recovery."

I cuffed Lexie on the back of the head. "Don't make me wrestle you down and spit on you."

"You don't have the strength," Lexie shot back. "Your old bones are too brittle."

I cocked an eyebrow in challenge. "Do you want to test that theory?"

Lexie thumped her chest. "Bring it."

I launched myself on top of her, hoping to take her by surprise, but she was ready.

"Let go of my hair," I snapped.

"You let go of my hair."

"I'm not pulling your hair," I countered. "You're pulling my hair."

"Get off me!" Lexie shoved with all her might. "You weigh a ton."

The bell over the front door jangled, and we lifted our heads to the archway between the lobby and the studio to see who was there. I wasn't surprised to see Carly pop her head inside. "Oh, good, you're here," she said.

"What are you doing here?" I asked. "Stop pinching me." I slapped Lexie's hand.

"You guys are doing that wrong," Carly said. "If you want to make money, you need an audience, and you should do it in the front window to draw men in."

"I was just showing Lexie that I can still beat her up," I said.

"Which she can't," Lexie shot back. "Ouch! You can't bite. Biting is outlawed."

"Since when?"

Carly shook her head, her gaze landing on Erica. "Who is this?"

"That's Erica. She was job shadowing me yesterday and then I took her to dinner at the restaurant. She and Lexie hit it off, so she spent the night here. Stop trying to snap my bra," I ordered Lexie. "That's so juvenile."

"This whole thing looks juvenile," Carly said. "It's nice to meet you, Erica. I'm Carly."

"Are you a cousin, too?" Erica asked.

"No. I'm Avery's best friend."

"I'm Avery's best friend," Lexie argued, her face red with exertion as she tried to buck me off. "Seriously, you need to go on a diet."

Carly rolled her eyes. "How long are you guys going to be doing that?"

"I haven't decided yet," I said. "At least until Lexie admits I'm stronger than she is."

"Never!"

"Why?" I asked.

"Because I've been watching Maria," Carly said, her eyes sparkling.

I had no idea who that was. "Who is Maria?"

"Tad Ludington's wife," Carly said, shooting me a "well, duh" look.

I froze for a moment. "Why have you been following her?"

"You said you needed dirt on Tad," Carly said. "I figured the best way to get that dirt was to follow his wife around. I mean, there has to

202 / AMANDA M. LEE
be something wrong with a woman who would willingly marry Tad
Ludington."

She had a point. Still, I didn't know a lot about Tad's wife. The
few times I'd run into her she'd seemed friendly ... and scared. Tad
obviously ran a tight ship at home, and since I'd lost track of how
many kids they had under the age of ten I also thought he had her on
a breeding schedule. "I think she's just shy."

"I've never understood why you stand up for her," Carly said.
"He started dating her right after he dumped you. He was obviously
cheating on you with her."

"So?"

"So, that makes her a tramp," Carly said.

"That woman did me a favor," I said. "Tad is a big tool – who
walks around with a tiny tool and overcompensates for it. I don't have
any malice for Maria. In fact, I think she's probably miserable. I feel
sorry for her."

"So, you don't want to know what she's been up to?" Carly asked.

"Well ... ."

"That's what I thought," Carly said. "I've followed her twice
now. Both times she drove to a house in Grosse Pointe Park."

Grosse Pointe Park was outside Macomb County, and even
though it was close to Detroit, it was one of the richest communities
in the state.

"Why would she be going there?" Lexie asked.

"How have you found the time to follow her?" I asked. "Doesn't
Kyle wonder where you're going at night?"

Carly was a newlywed, and while her life had revolved around
nothing but the wedding for almost a year, now that she was actually
married to her beloved Kyle she was finding her new life somewhat
constraining.

"I told him I joined a book club with you," Carly said.

Lexie snickered. "And he believed that?"

"What? We need a few nights apart," Carly said.

Living with Kyle was a new experience for Carly. It was a

learning experience. So far, Carly had learned that Kyle chewed too loudly, never picked up his clothes, refused to rinse the dishes before putting them in the dishwasher and mowed the lawn only after the city inspector stopped by with a warning citation.

In reality, they didn't have any big problems, other than Kyle's insistence on Skyping with his mother every day. They did have a hundred little problems, though, and married life was nowhere near as idyllic as Carly had imagined.

"So, you decided that the best way for you to deal with your problems was to follow my ex-boyfriend's wife around town?" I asked. That sounds totally reasonable.

"I don't have any problems," Carly said. "I am problem-free."

"Then how come you're always complaining?" Lexie asked.

"Shut up, Lexie," Carly snapped. "I'm going to help Avery wrestle you down and strip you naked so we can lock you outside if you don't shut up."

Lexie raised her hands in mock surrender.

"I still don't understand why you're following Maria around," I said. "Why not follow Tad?"

"I've been doing that, too," Carly said. "In fact, I thought I was following him the other night until I saw his wife get out of the car."

"In Grosse Pointe Park?"

Carly nodded.

"Did you see who she was visiting?" I asked.

"No."

"Then how are we sure that she's up to something? She could be visiting her mother, for all we know."

"A woman would never drive a vintage Corvette," Carly said. "That's a middle-aged penis- mobile, and that's what's parked in front of that house."

She had a point. "So, what do you think is going on?"

"She's obviously having an affair," Carly said.

"Obviously." I shifted my gaze to Lexie. "What do you think?"

"I think that she either has to be crazy or secretly evil to stay with

Tad," Lexie said. "He has all the appeal of a used tampon and yet she still keeps having kids with him. There has to be a reason."

"Maybe she loves him," Erica suggested.

"No, that's not it," I said. I slapped my hand down on my knees. "Okay, give me the address. I'll run it and see what I come up with."

"I have something better," Carly said. "Maria is over there right now. Let's go spy on her."

I froze. "She's there now? How do you know that?"

"Because I followed her," Carly said. "That's how I know she's having an affair, and she's probably pregnant with this man's baby. She looks rounder and she has a glow. Heck, maybe none of those kids are Tad's."

She'd jumped from penis-mobile to affair to kids pretty quickly. I could tell she'd given this a lot of thought. "So, you've convinced yourself none of those kids are Tad's?"

"Of course not," Carly said. "I've convinced myself that half of them aren't Tad's. What? That's totally a possibility."

"And you want to go there and spy on her now?" I asked.

"Yes."

"I'm not sure it's a good idea," I said. "Eliot is going to pick me up here at six."

"So? That's plenty of time," Carly said.

"I don't know ... ."

"I think we should do it," Lexie said. "We haven't had a good spying trip in ages."

"Now you want to go, too?" I was incredulous.

"Why not?" Lexie asked. "We have nothing better to do. We all know you're not actually going to work out."

She had a point. "I don't know," I said, risking a quick glance in Erica's direction to ascertain her mood. Her eyes were sparkling.

"Can I come, too?" She asked, excited by the prospect.

Heck, maybe this is exactly what she needs. I sighed, resigned. "Okay, we'll go," I said. "I'm in charge, though, and we have to be back here by six. Eliot is going to flip if he finds out we did this."

Erica mimed crossing her heart. "I'll never tell."

When I shifted my eyes to Lexie, her gaze was evil. "See, you're finding the fun again. Maybe you're not so old, after all."

I flicked her ear. "I'm going to lock you in the trunk if you don't stop it."

"I dare you to try."

Carly patted Erica on the shoulder reassuringly. "Don't worry. This is how they always get along. They'll be screaming at each other before the afternoon is through. Just you wait."

She was probably right.

"**T**his is a big house," Lexie said from the backseat of Carly's car, where she sat with Erica. "If Maria is sleeping with the guy here, why would she possibly need Tad?"

"We know it's not because the sex is good," I said, narrowing my eyes as I scanned the front of the house. "Are you sure this is the right house?"

"I followed her here twice," Carly said, pointing. "That's her car. I'm not stupid."

"No one thinks you're stupid," Lexie said.

"Thank you."

"We just think you're losing your mind because marriage is driving you insane."

Carly made a face. "I'll have you know, I happen to love marriage."

"Is that why you're lying to your husband about a book club?" Lexie asked.

"No. I'm lying about a book club to help Avery," Carly said. "Her career is hanging by a thread. She's depressed and despondent. It's a best friend's duty to help in situations like this."

"I'm her best friend," Lexie grumbled. "We're family. I've got dibs."

"Don't make me crawl back there and thump you, Lexie," Carly warned. "I'm her best friend. And I am happily married."

"Fine, you're happily married," Lexie said. "You just hate your husband."

"I don't hate my husband," Carly corrected. "I hate the way he chews. It's like I'm living with a cow."

"I like Kyle," I said. "I think he's good for you. He calms you."

"What is that supposed to mean?" Carly asked, suspicious.

"You tend to fly off the handle," I said, ignoring the warning flash in her eyes. "He reins you in. When you do crazy stuff, he's the one who talks you back from the ledge."

"I only do crazy stuff when I'm with you," Carly protested.

"And Kyle stops us both," I said. "He's quite invaluable to our operation."

Carly shrugged. "So, what do you want to do now?"

I stared at the house. "I need to see inside."

"How are you going to do that?"

"I'm going to sneak into the backyard and look inside. It's not rocket science."

Carly balked. "That's trespassing."

"Only if I get caught." I handed my cell phone to Lexie. "You stay here with Erica."

"But I want to come," Lexie protested.

"Someone has to stay here with Erica," I said.

"Why can't Carly do it?"

"Why can't I come?" Erica asked.

"You're still a minor," I replied.

"But I'm in the company of adults," Erica countered. "I can't be held accountable for my actions."

I'd used that argument myself from time to time as a teenager, including when I'd been caught paying the bum on the corner to buy a case of beer. I told my mother I was doing it as an experiment for class. When she'd asked what class and all I could blurt out was Home Economics, she grounded me for a month.

"You have to stay here," I said. "We shouldn't have brought you in the first place. We're teaching you bad habits."

"Yes," Carly said, pushing the driver's door open. "Everything we've done today is not only wrong, it's also illegal."

Erica nodded solemnly. "I understand."

"It's wrong to spy," I said. "It's also wrong to lie." I turned to Lexie. "If Eliot texts, pretend you're me and say we'll be done with yoga at six."

"I thought you said it was wrong to lie?" Erica asked.

"That's not a lie," I said. "It's an exaggeration. I plan to stretch as soon as I get out of the car. That can count as yoga."

"Oh, okay."

I felt good about spreading my wisdom to a younger generation. I was molding impressionable minds here, and it felt nice.

"And no smoking pot in the car," I said, focusing my attention on Lexie. "The cops here aren't going to believe you have glaucoma."

WHEN it comes to sneaking onto someone else's property, I'm nearly an expert. I've done it at least twenty times, and been caught only twice. That's a pretty solid ratio. Of course, it's easier when it's dark out, but that wasn't an option now.

"I think we should go around the back of the fence," Carly said. "Then I can boost you up and over."

"What about you?"

"I'll wait for you back at the car."

I wrinkled my nose. "You're scared to sneak on the property here, aren't you?"

"Of course not."

"Then why don't I lift you over the fence?"

"Hey, we're trying to save your job here," Carly said. "You have to be the one to go over the fence."

"Fine," I muttered. "Let's just get this over with."

We tracked the brick wall until we found ourselves along the back of the yard. The wall was six feet tall, and I wasn't sure Carly could boost me that high. "What do you think?"

"I think you need to lose some weight," Carly said. "I'm not sure I'm strong enough to lift you that high."

"We could get Lexie," I suggested. "She's stronger than she looks."

"She's also five feet tall," Carly said. "She's not tall enough. Erica is tall enough."

"Absolutely not," I said. "We're not corrupting a minor."

"She's sitting in the car while we trespass," Carly said. "We're not being very good role models."

"Hey, I told her it was wrong to spy and lie."

"And then you did the opposite."

"Yes, but I told her the right thing to do," I said. "That's all that counts."

"We're going to make really crappy parents someday," Carly said.

I glanced up at the wall. "Try to lift me up."

"Okay," Carly said, "but if I drop you, I don't want to hear a single complaint." She made a cradle of her hands and I stepped in it. "Oomph. You weigh a ton."

"Lift."

"I am lifting."

My fingers clawed the top of the wall. "Just a little more."

Carly heaved with all her might and I found myself toppling over the wall and careening toward the ground on the other side. I hit hard.

"Are you okay?" Carly hissed.

"I think I'm dead," I said.

"Are you a ghost?"

"Maybe."

"Are you a friendly ghost?"

"No."

Carly was silent.

"Just bruises," I whispered, rubbing my backside ruefully. "I landed on my ass."

"Well, you've got plenty of padding there," Carly said. "You should be fine."

"You know what?"

"What?"

"Lexie is my new best friend."

"Oh, whatever," Carly said. "I'll meet you back at the car. Try not to get caught, because if the cops show up I'm running. It's every woman for herself."

"Lexie would never leave me."

"Lexie would call the cops and narc on you," Carly countered.

She had a point. Once the shuffling of her feet faded I scanned the backyard. It was huge. My entire block could fit in this yard, although my white trash neighbors would fill it with garbage and chickens. I moved toward the house, taking refuge in the shadows of the gazebo, greenhouse, pool house and patio overhang as I moved closer. The grounds really were massive.

Once I got to the rear of house I moved along it until I was close to the French doors. They were beautiful, ornate and completely impractical. Who lived here? I crouched low to the ground and tried to peer inside. I couldn't see anything, but I heard voices.

"I've told you, I'm working on it." The voice was a woman's.

"You're not working hard enough," a male voice responded. "I'm sick of playing this game."

"I'm doing the best I can."

"I can handle it myself. I told you that. Why don't you let me just take care of this situation for you?"

"That's not going to work out," the woman said. "You know how he is. He'll have a heart attack or something."

If Maria was in the house I could only hope she was talking about Tad. What? I didn't say I wanted him to die. I just want to see if he really has a heart. A yearlong coma would be fine with me.

"Would that be so wrong? I'm sure he'll survive," the man said.

I was starting to like him.

"Stop saying things like that," the woman said. "You know I don't like it. It's not fair."

"Who cares about fair?"

"I do."

"Maria ... you're being unbelievable."

Maria? Holy crap, it was Tad's wife. Now, if only she would start having really loud sex.

"I'm not trying to be difficult," Maria said. "I just need more time."

The man made an exasperated sound in the back of his throat. "Fine," he said. "Just know that I won't put up with this for much longer."

"I understand," Maria said. "What are you doing?"

"Letting Killer outside. He's has to go outside."

Killer? Whoever Maria was sneaking around with has a dog, and its name is Killer.

I shuffled away from the door, freezing when I heard it open. I squeezed my eyes shut. I was about to be caught. Lies were flitting through my head. I was blind and wandered into the wrong yard. I'd been separated from my Girl Scouts troop. I was looking for a lost child. Thankfully for me, the door opened briefly and quickly closed.

A new fear took hold. I was now trapped in an enclosed space with Killer. He was probably one of those trained German Shepherds that rips people's heads off when they accidentally step off the side-walk. It could be a pit bull. Maybe this guy had gotten rich off of dogfights?

My eyes landed on a fancy rat. It had long hair, white teeth and a little pink bow tied in its long hair. It was hideous.

"Nice rat," I whispered.

Killer eyed me suspiciously.

"Listen, I like animals," I said. "I like them a lot. I even like rats – as long as they're in cages. So, let's make a deal. You stay there and I'll leave. How does that sound?"

Killer took a step forward, forcing me to tumble over onto my knees in my haste to get away from him. The sudden motion caused Killer to bark, or rather yip.

I pushed myself to my feet and started running. I imagined his little teeth gnawing my bones as I decomposed in the yard. The rat gave chase.

I made it to the front gate, panic overtaking me when I found it locked. I fumbled with the mechanism, but it was clearly designed to keep the brilliant rat inside. There could be no other explanation.

Killer yipped again.

"You stop that right now," I ordered. "I'll bring a block of cheese back tomorrow if you're quiet."

Killer tilted his head to the side.

"Thank you."

Killer growled. Holy crap, I had no idea a rat could growl. The gate sprang free and I rushed through, slamming it behind me and cutting the rat off before it could follow.

I jumped when a set of hands landed on my shoulders. I swiveled. "I got separated from my Girl Scout troop."

Eliot didn't look impressed when I met his gaze. "You're a Girl Scout?"

"What are you doing here?"

"I texted your phone," he said. "When you texted back that I should keep my pants on – unless I wanted to text back a photo of my junk – I figured something was up."

Uh-oh.

"When I called, Lexie answered," Eliot said. "She said you were in the bathroom. When I called back a few minutes later she said you were still in there. I asked if everything was okay and she said you were constipated."

I scowled. Carly was back on top of the best-friend list.

"So, I used the Track My Phone app I installed on your phone and found everyone else sitting in Carly's car there," Eliot said. "Do you want to tell me what you're doing here?"

I pointed to Killer. "That rat almost ate me."

"That's a dog."

"No, it's not. It's evil."

"It's wearing a pink bow."

"Its name is Killer."

Eliot grabbed my hand and started dragging me toward the street. "We're about to have a big fight."

"As long as the rat stays there, I'm fine with that."

Back in the car, Eliot exploded. "What are you doing sneaking into the backyard of this house?"

"Well ... ."

Eliot crossed his arms over his chest. "Don't you dare lie to me."

"Carly has been following Tad," I said. "One night, she realized she was following Maria, and she was coming here. Since she came here again, Carly thought it would be a good idea to follow her. She made me do it."

Eliot rolled his eyes. "Who is Maria?"

"Tad's wife."

Eliot furrowed his brow. "Tad's wife is in that house?"

"Yes."

"How can you be sure?"

"I eavesdropped on her and some guy," I said. "They said they had to keep whatever they were doing a secret for now, but Tad had to find out sooner or later."

Eliot ran his hand through his hair, pursing his lips. "Do you think they're having an affair?"

"Wait, I thought you were angry?"

"Oh, I'm more than angry," Eliot said. "We're just tabling the argument for a few minutes."

"Why?"

"Because when I realized you were in Grosse Pointe Park I ran the address you were parked at," Eliot said. "I had to know whether I'd need a gun."

"What did you find?"

"This house belongs to someone you know," he said.

"Who?" I was practically salivating.

"Your new publisher."

My breath whooshed out of me. This just got a heck of a lot more interesting.

"How long are you going to be angry?"

Eliot refused to look away from the television. "Until I'm not angry any longer."

"How long do you think that's going to be?"

"I have no idea," he said, leaning back against the couch and changing the channel to Sports Center. "I don't know, but I can tell you, the more you whine the angrier I get."

I threw myself on the couch next to him and crossed my arms. "I said I was sorry."

"You're only sorry because you got caught."

"That's not true. I'm sorry because ... I got caught."

I saw the muscles along his jaw tighten, but I could tell he was fighting the urge to smile.

"I was never in any danger," I said, hoping he would give in. "I had to know what Maria was doing."

"You were supposed to be doing yoga."

"I was stretching. That counts."

Eliot shook his head. "You are just ... so much work."

I wrinkled my forehead. "I'm not work."

"Oh, you're work," Eliot said.

"But ... ."

"You happen to be worth the work," Eliot said.

I smiled. "Thank you."

"You're still a pain in the ass," he said.

"My ass actually got hurt when I fell over the wall," I said. "You could rub it and make it feel better."

Eliot arched an eyebrow and fixed me with a look. "You want me to rub your ass?"

"Only if you want."

Eliot muted the television. "Do you understand why I'm angry?"

"Yes," I said. "You were worried the rat was going to eat me."

"That was a dog."

"That was not a dog," I said. "That was a rat with a bow."

"I asked you a question, Avery," Eliot said, ignoring my attempt at rat humor.

"I understand that you're angry," I said. "The important thing for you to realize is that I had no intention of going to that house when I went to the studio. It was unexpected, not planned. That has to count for something."

"I really want to be angry with you."

"We can have angry sex if you want," I offered.

"You're just far too happy to yell at," Eliot said. "It's like sneaking around and spying ended your depression."

"I wasn't depressed."

"You were depressed."

"I was not."

"Stop arguing with me," Eliot snapped. "I've watched you mope around here for two weeks. You were depressed. I know, because it was depressing me."

"I'm sorry," I grumbled.

"Don't be sorry," Eliot said. "The truth is, you weren't doing anything dangerous. You were trying to fix the situation. Don't get me wrong, you weren't doing anything smart, but it wasn't particularly dangerous, especially during daylight hours. I'm not angry because of what you did."

"Then why are you angry?"

"Because I figure I should be."

"I ... wait, what?"

"I'm so used to you doing something completely idiotic I'm conditioned to argue with you," he said. "I'm not sure there's anything to fight about here."

"We could still make up."

Eliot broke into a wide grin. "Do you promise to tell me the next time you decide to do something like this?"

I worried my bottom lip with my teeth, considering. "What would you have said if I told you what we were doing?"

Eliot thought it over. "I would have told you not to do it."

"Why?"

"Because I don't like the idea of you being in danger," he said, "even if it's only from a rat with a bow."

"See, I had no choice."

Eliot grinned. "I just need you to think before you do these things."

"I had backup."

"Lexie and Carly would have left you the second the cops showed up."

"Yes, but if someone had a gun they would have jumped in front of the bullet."

"You have a point," Eliot said, reaching for me so he could pull me onto his lap. "I want you to figure this out, and I want you to go back to being happy. I just don't want you dead."

"That rat was dangerous," I said.

Eliot groaned. "That was a dog."

"I don't believe you."

"It was a little dog."

"It was a rat," I said. "There can be no other explanation."

"Fine, it was a rat," he said. "Can we make up now?"

"Not when you're wearing so many clothes."

Eliot reached to take off his shirt, but stopped when my phone rang. "Don't stop," I said. "This will just take a second." I frowned when I recognized Lexie's phone number. "I hope something isn't wrong. Hello?"

"Get over here now."

"What's wrong?"

"The security alarm just went off downstairs," Lexie hissed. "There are people on the steps and they're trying to get into my apartment."

"Do you know who it is?"

"Now! Get here now!"

LEXIE'S studio was only a few blocks from my house, and Eliot's foot was heavy on the accelerator.

"Why didn't she call the police?"

"Because she knows we'll get there faster."

"And she probably knows the cops will arrest her for the pot."

"Is that important now?" I asked. "They're in trouble."

Eliot pulled out onto Gratiot without braking, ignoring the horns blaring behind him. "Do you think it's because of what you did today?"

"How would MacDonald track Carly's car to Lexie's studio?"

Eliot chewed the inside of his cheek. "That means they're either there because of something Lexie did or they're there for Erica."

My heart dropped. "How would anyone know where Erica is?"

"Maybe they followed you."

"I ... drive faster."

Eliot screeched to a halt in front of the studio, slamming his truck into park. "You stay here."

"No."

"Avery!"

I jumped from his truck and raced toward the studio. The stairs that led to Lexie's apartment had their own entrance, and I pushed through the door.

"Avery!"

I heard voices on the stairs. They were intermixed with the unmistakable sound of fists beating on a door.

"Open this door, you bitch!"

"If you try to get in here I'll start you on fire," Lexie warned.

"And then I'll kick your ass," I announced.

The two figures at the top of the stairs turned to me. They were wearing pullover knit ski masks to hide their features, but I could tell by the way they held themselves that they were young ... and male.

"Well, well, well," one of them said. "If it isn't Avery Shaw."

His voice sounded familiar. "Sam Keaton?"

The figure balked. "Of course not. I'm not Sam Keaton. He's too cool to be here. I'm a nerd. I can't be Sam Keaton."

I rolled my eyes and focused on the figure next to him. "Marty?"

"I ... I have to go." The second figure barreled down the stairs, blowing past me and then Eliot, and racing out to the sidewalk.

"Should I go after him?" Eliot asked.

I shook my head. "This is the one we want."

"You can't touch me. I'm a minor, and I'm certainly not Sam Keaton. He's a god. I'm a peon."

"Take your mask off," I ordered.

"Don't tell me what to do!"

Sam raced down the stairwell, his shoulder barreling into me as he knocked me backward. Eliot caught me, giving Sam a window to escape to the street.

"Are you okay?"

I nodded.

"Can I chase him?" Eliot asked.

"Kick his ass."

Eliot didn't need further encouragement. He was gone before I could give him further instructions. I climbed the remaining stairs and knocked on the door. "It's me."

"Are you being held against your will?" Lexie asked from the other side of the door. "Do they have a knife to your throat?"

"No."

"Would you tell me if they did?"

"Open up, Lexie."

When the door opened, Lexie stood on the other side. She was dressed in flannel sleep pants and a tank top, and her hair was in two braids. She clutched a butcher knife in her hand.

"Were you going to stab them?"

Erica appeared at her back, a rolling pin clutched tightly to her chest.

"And beat them?"

"We were ready," Lexie said, her tone grim. "Who do you think they were?"

"Sam Keaton and Marty," I said, fixing Erica with a worried look. "How do you think they knew you were here?"

Erica shrugged. "I don't know. I didn't tell anyone. I swear. I've been really careful. I just put it on Facebook."

I fought the urge to shake her. "What?"

Erica balked. "I ... I checked in at Lexie's studio yesterday before you got here. I didn't think it was a big deal."

I tucked a strand of hair behind my ear, exhaling heavily as I regarded Erica with as much compassion as I could muster. "Why?"

"I just ... this place is so cool," Erica said, fighting back tears. "I never go anyplace cool."

"It's okay," I said. "It's ... everything is okay."

"Where are the bastards?" Lexie asked.

"Eliot is chasing Sam," I said. "We let Marty go. He's a total follower. Sam is the threat."

"Do you think Eliot will kill him?"

"No."

"That's too bad," Lexie said, moving back into her apartment.

I followed her, watching as she slid the knife back into the block on the counter. "Did you call the police?"

"Of course not," Lexie said. "You know I hate cops."

"I hate them, too," I said. "We still have to call them."

"Absolutely not!"

I knew what worried her. "Where is the pot?"

"There's no pot here," Lexie hedged. "I graduated from rehab. You know I don't smoke pot anymore."

"I'm not stupid," I said. "We have to call the cops, and we have to do it right now. That means we have to hide the pot."

"Where are you going to hide it?" Lexie asked, narrowing her eyes.

"The toilet."

"No!" Lexie stomped her foot.

"We don't have a choice," I said. "This is a big deal, Lexie. Erica was attacked, and now the person who got her to the party and let everyone attack her tried to break into your apartment. The kid is from a school where a teenage girl was gang raped and murdered. Your pot habit is the least of our worries."

Lexie looked conflicted. "Can't you just hide it in Eliot's truck?"

"Not if I want to keep having sex with him."

"And how attached are you to that?"

"I'm calling the police right now, Lexie," I said, whipping my cell phone out of my pocket. "You have five minutes."

"Fine," Lexie grumbled, moving toward her bedroom. "I hate you. I hope you know that."

I sighed. "Don't forget the roaches in your ashtray."

"I'm not stupid."

BY THE time the police arrived, we'd flushed the toilet three times. I didn't bother to ask the question on my lips.

"What's going on?"

I was surprised to find Derrick on Lexie's welcome mat. "What are you doing here?"

"I got paged," he said. "I told the uniforms I would handle it. I was ... worried."

"It's all flushed."

Derrick didn't look convinced. "All of it?"

"I told her to get rid of it all," I said.

Derrick sighed. "Leave that out of your statement."

"You got it."

Derrick pulled out his notebook. "So, what happened here tonight, Ms. Shaw?"

I recounted my night.

"So, wait, why were you and Eliot fighting?"

I shot Derrick a look. "Is that really important?"

"I'm just curious," Derrick said, shrugging. "Where is he now?"

"He chased after one of the kids."

"And he's not back?"

"The kid had a head start."

"Is Eliot going to kill him?"

"Probably not."

We both jumped at the sound of scuffling, tilting our heads out the door to look down the stairwell. Eliot was grappling with a figure in dark clothing. "I found him hiding in a Dumpster. He has spaghetti sauce from that place around the corner all over his pants."

"Take the mask off," Derrick said.

"You can't do that," Sam protested. "I have a right to wear whatever I want."

"You don't have a right to attempt to break into my sister's apartment," Derrick countered.

"I did no such thing."

"Take the mask off," Derrick ordered.

Sam placed his hands on his hips and widened his stance. "I want to see your boss."

"Don't worry," Derrick said. "He's on his way."

My heart dropped. "Jake is coming?"

"Of course he is," Derrick said. "Whenever your name crosses our boards, he's alerted."

Eliot scowled. "Well, great."

"Eliot," I warned.

Eliot reached forward and yanked Sam's mask off, revealing the teen's smug face. "Is this who you thought it was?"

I nodded. "That's him."

Eliot's smile was tight. "Did you try to get my girlfriend to have sex with you in a car at a wrestling meet last week?"

Sam looked scandalized. "She's old. I wouldn't touch her."

"Hey!"

"Oh, give it up," Derrick said. "To him you are old. You should have grandchildren, as far as he's concerned."

I cuffed the back of his head. "I hate you."

"I'm going to have all of you thrown in jail," Sam said.

"Oh, really? How are you going to do that?" Derrick asked.

"Do you have any idea who my father is?"

I felt a bubble building in the pit of my stomach. "Who is your father?"

"Doug Keaton."

The bubble burst.

"Who is that?" Eliot asked, reading the worried look on my face.

"He's a county commissioner," Derrick said, exchanging a wary look with me. "Well, you've done it again."

"**W**hat's going on here?"

Jake, hair disheveled and dressed in jeans and a sweatshirt, ascended the stairs to Lexie's apartment.

"This is Sam Keaton," Derrick said, his tone clipped. "He's Doug Keaton's son."

Jake digested the information with a blank face. "What is he doing here?"

"He was trying to break into Lexie's apartment," Derrick said.

Jake scanned the assembled faces. "Why?"

"He's the boy who talked Erica into attending the Catholic North party," I said, my voice low.

Jake stilled. "And Erica is the girl you brought into the office on Friday?"

I nodded.

"Shit," he muttered, running his hand through his already scattered hair. "Has anyone called his father?"

"My father is going to make all of you pay," Sam said, his voice unnaturally high. "You're all going to wish you'd never been born."

"Isn't it enough that we wish you'd never been born?" I asked.

"Shut your mouth, bitch."

Eliot reached for Sam, but Jake stilled him with a hand on his forearm. "He's not worth it."

"I want to beat him," Eliot admitted.

"Join the club," Derrick said.

"He's not a threat," Jake said. "We can't beat him unless he's a threat."

"He was trying to beat his way into my sister's apartment," Derrick said.

"Speaking of that … ." Jake cast a worried look into Lexie's apartment. "Nothing … bad … is going to turn up when the crime scene team gets here, right?"

"I already handled that."

"Handled what?" Sam asked his eyes narrowing.

I fixed him with a look. "I made sure all the tampons were hidden away."

Sam made a face. "You're a sick bitch."

"That did it," Eliot said, reaching for him again.

"Stop it," Jake ordered. "You can't beat him up."

Sam shot a triumphant look in Eliot's direction.

"If anyone is going to beat him up, it should be Avery," Jake said. "It's still an uneven fight – Avery is a lot stronger than he is – but it would be fun to watch."

"He pushed her down the stairs," Eliot grumbled.

Jake's eyes widened. "What?"

"I caught her," Eliot said. "Still, he could have hurt her."

"Hey, I could have hurt him," I said. "I knew Eliot was standing there to catch me."

"You did not," Eliot protested.

"I did so."

"How could you possibly know that?"

"Because you're always there to catch me."

Eliot faltered.

"Oh, you two are so sweet I could just puke," Derrick said. "We need to get our ducks in a row before Keaton shows up."

226/ AMANDA M. LEE

"I'm already here," Sam said.

"Shut up," Jake snapped. "Derrick is right. Tell me what happened, and don't leave anything out."

I opened my mouth to respond, but Jake slapped his hand over it. "I was talking to Eliot."

"He wasn't here for everything," I mumbled around his hand.

"Yes, but he'll be much quicker and more concise than you," Jake said. "That's what I need right now."

I rolled my eyes as Eliot condensed two days of activity into two minutes. I was relieved he left out our trip to Grosse Pointe Park. When he was done, Jake's face was unreadable. "What do you think?"

"I think this kid is a sexual predator," Eliot said.

"Are you saying that because he asked Avery to get naked in his car with him?" Derrick asked.

Jake's shoulders rose. "What?"

"He kind of ... flirted ... with Avery at the wrestling meet the other night," Eliot said.

Jake swiveled to me and pulled his hand from my mouth. "Define flirted."

"He was rude and crude," I said. "He called me old, but still doable."

Jake tucked his upper lip beneath his lower one. "This has to be killing you."

"Grandpa hit him in the nuts with a spatula."

Derrick shifted. "This is the kid Grandpa smacked?"

I nodded.

"Why was your grandfather there?" Jake asked.

"He and Mario had the food truck out there."

"Why?"

I shrugged. "I can't decide if they really want to make money or if they just want to drive Uncle Tim insane."

"He's trying to drive Tim insane," Jake said.

"How do you know?"

"I've known your family as long as I've known my own," Jake said. "Trust me."

Eliot snickered.

"I think you should all be committed," Sam said.

"No one asked you," Jake said.

"You can't talk to me like that," Sam said. "I'm a very important person."

"You're a sexual deviant," I shot back.

"I'm a sexual god!"

"You can't be a god if someone needs a microscope to see your package," I said.

Sam's mouth dropped open. "You can't say things like that to me!"

"Huh, I just did."

Jake grabbed the back of my neck tightly. "Can you not throw kerosene on the fire?"

"I'm not sure if that's in my wheelhouse."

Jake sighed. "I know." He glanced at Eliot. "Do you think she's right?"

"I think there's something going on here," Eliot said. "I think this kid is clearly a ... heathen."

"You'll get no argument from me there," Jake said. "We're running out of time, though."

"What do you think his father is going to do?" I asked.

"I think he's going to chop you up and dump your body parts in the lake," Sam said. "Then a shark is going to eat you."

"It's a freshwater lake," I said.

"So?"

"There are no sharks in a freshwater lake."

"Haven't you seen *Jaws*?" Sam asked, puffing out his chest.

"That was an ocean, you idiot," Eliot chided.

"What's the difference?"

Jake rubbed his face with both hands. "I ... this ... I don't know what to say."

"Just cut me loose now," Sam said. "You have nothing on me."

"You tried to break into Lexie's apartment," Jake said.

"That wasn't me," Sam said. "That was some other guy."

"There was some other guy dressed in all black and a ski mask trying to break into this apartment?"

"I think it was Marty," Sam said.

He was turning on his friend. I shouldn't have been surprised. "You're a real prince."

"Do you want to see my crown?" Sam sneered.

"Son, if you say something like that again, I'm going to beat your ass," Eliot threatened.

"I'm not scared of you," Sam said. "I'm a wrestler."

"That just means you're gay," I said.

"Wrestlers aren't gay!"

I jumped. Sam wasn't the only one who said it. Jake and Eliot had chimed in, too. "Are you sure? Because you guys are awfully sensitive."

"Avery?" Jake tightened his grip on my neck.

"What?"

"Shut up."

WHERE is my son?"

Jake pressed his eyes shut briefly, and then got up from Lexie's couch. "Let me handle this."

"You got it," Derrick said.

"I wasn't talking to you."

"As long as you take that kid in custody, I'm fine," Eliot said.

Jake seemed flustered. "I wasn't talking to you either." He turned to me. "Keep your mouth shut."

"I'm offended."

"You are not," Jake shot back. "You have a thirty-second rebound rate. It goes in one ear and immediately out the other where you're concerned. This is a delicate situation."

"My dad is going to eat you all for lunch," Sam crowed.

"You shut up, too," Jake said, straightening his shoulders and facing Lexie's open doorway.

Doug Keaton is a small man. His eyes barely cleared Jake's strong shoulders, and yet the anger he carried into the room was big enough to accommodate several pissed-off larger men. Jake didn't shrink in the face of his rage.

"How dare you!"

Jake was calm. "Commissioner Keaton. I'm sorry you had to be called here for such a ... difficult situation."

"Difficult? Difficult! You're holding my son."

"Your son tried to break into this apartment."

"He did not." Doug turned to his son, whose countenance had quickly shifted from boastful to worried. "Tell them you didn't try to break into this apartment."

"I didn't try to break into this apartment."

"Pussy," I said.

Jake didn't acknowledge me, but I could see the nerve in his jaw ticking. "Commissioner Keaton, your son is a suspect in the attempted trespass at this apartment. He was found in the area with a ski mask over his face. He's also a suspect in a sexual assault."

Lexie and Erica were locked in the bedroom at Jake's behest. He'd ordered, in no uncertain terms, that they were to stay in there no matter what they heard in the living room. Lexie had been eager to acquiesce and Erica looked as though she wanted to find a hole to hide in. I wasn't worried about them coming out.

"That is ridiculous," Doug sputtered. "My son is a handsome boy. He wouldn't need to rape anyone."

"That's not really how rape works," I said. "Ted Bundy was handsome, too."

"Thank you, Ms. Shaw," Jake said, his voice terse.

"Ms. Shaw? Avery Shaw?" Doug shifted to face me. "Why are you here?"

"This is my cousin's apartment."

"So?"

"My cousin called me when your son and his friend tried to break in," I said. "I live only a few blocks away."

"Why didn't she call the police?"

I didn't blink. "She was flustered. It's not every day that someone tries to break into her apartment. She just wanted help."

"Why would my son try to break into your cousin's apartment?" Doug asked.

"Because the girl who filed a report against him happened to be staying here," I replied.

"And what girl is that?"

I narrowed my eyes. "That's none of your business."

Doug turned to Jake. "Do you want to tell me?"

Jake shook his head. "The victim is protected under rape shield laws."

"So you're saying that she can make up lies about my son and there's nothing he can do to protect himself?"

"They're not lies," I charged.

"Of course they're lies," Doug said. "My son is a popular boy. He wouldn't rape some mouse from Richmond."

I narrowed my eyes. "How do you know she's from Richmond?"

Jake fixed a hard look on the commissioner. "How do you know that?"

"I ... it was just a guess," Doug said, flustered. "It was just common sense."

"How?" Jake asked, refusing to let go of the line of questioning.

"I heard it somewhere."

"Where?"

"I ... my son is innocent!"

"Your son is guilty, and you know it," I said.

"Avery," Jake growled.

Doug scorched me with a hateful glare. "Listen, I know who you are. You're the reporter who sticks her nose where it doesn't belong.

You're the reporter who thinks she's above the law. You're the reporter who got our sheriff shot because she was so inept."

"Wait just a minute," Jake said, holding his hand up. "That is not what happened."

Doug ignored him. "You're the type of woman who gives your gender a bad name," he said. "You're a busybody and you're a slut. I heard how you were flirting with my son at the wrestling meet."

"I did no such thing!"

"Didn't you offer to have sex with him in his car?"

"I think you've got that the other way around," Eliot said.

"Why would my son want to have sex with her?" Doug asked. "She's old enough to be his mother."

"Hey!" Why do you people think I'm old? I'm in my prime, people.

"You're hot, baby," Eliot said. "Don't listen to them."

"Do you have to say stuff like that in front of me?" Derrick complained.

"She's obviously sick," Doug said. "She's a hateful person, and she's a sexual predator. Why is my son in cuffs when she's the deviant?"

"I think your son has been telling you some stories," Jake said through gritted teeth.

"My son is not a liar."

"You tell him, Dad," Sam encouraged.

"Shut up," Doug snapped.

"You don't have to be so mean," Sam whined. "I'm the victim here."

Doug ignored him. "I am not going to let my son get railroaded," he said, "especially by a slut like her. She's a tramp."

Eliot made a move, but he was too late. Jake's fist was already slamming into Doug's face.

"Omigod! You hit me!"

Eliot and Jake exchanged wary looks.

"That wasn't smart, man," Eliot said.

Jake closed his eyes. "I know."

"I could have done it myself."

"I know."

"I'll have your badge," Doug screeched. "You have no idea who you're dealing with. I am a county commissioner!"

"You tell him, Dad."

"I am going to kill you, Sam," Doug seethed, pinching his nose to stem the flow of blood. "Shut your mouth."

And I thought my family was messed up.

"What do you think is going to happen now?" I asked, leaning against Eliot's shoulder as I sipped from my tomato juice.

"I have no idea."

Jake sat across the table, Lexie and Erica sharing his extended booth seat. We'd decided to go to breakfast after Doug Keaton finally cleared out. He'd demanded to take his son with him, but Jake stood his ground. Sam was arrested and booked. His father wouldn't be able to bail him out until the next morning.

"Are you worried?" Derrick asked. I was sandwiched between him and Eliot.

"I hit a county commissioner," Jake said. "It's going to become public knowledge."

"You have witnesses," I said. "He had it coming."

Jake's smile was weak. "I'm not sure you're a reliable witness."

"Because I'm in sports?"

"Because you're you," Jake said. "Everyone in this county knows I was shot protecting you. They won't believe that Keaton had it coming. He's well-respected in the county. He's one of the commissioners who was reelected after the county administrator turnover. He has supporters -- a lot of them."

"But he's a dick," I said.

"He's definitely a dick," Eliot grunted. "You should have let me hit him."

"He would have sued you," Jake said. "He can't sue me without creating an uproar."

"He can try to get your badge," Eliot pointed out.

"I'm sure he'll try."

"You could have let the kid go," Derrick said. "You could have waited to press charges."

"No, I couldn't."

"Why not?"

"Because Sam is a rapist," I supplied. "Jake is worried there will be another victim."

Jake met my even gaze. "You can see what he is. It's written all over the kid's face. He's entitled and he thinks he's above the law. His father has raised him to be a sociopath."

"We could have put a tail on him," Derrick said. "We could have caught him in the act."

"And if we were too late?"

Derrick swallowed hard. "I ... I don't know."

"I did the right thing," Jake said. "That kid is a menace."

"You did the right thing," Eliot agreed. "Keaton is going to come at you like a tornado, though."

"I'm ready for him."

"No, you're not," I said. "We need to go after him. That's the only way you'll be protected."

Jake arched an eyebrow. "What did you have in mind?"

"He's a politician," I said. "They all do nefarious stuff. We just have to find his weakness."

"His weakness is his kid," Eliot said, leaning back and slinging an arm over my shoulders. "He knows the kid has been doing heinous things. We just have to find out how far he's gone to protect the kid."

"He's right," I said. "Sam doesn't hide his attitude. He's done this more than once, and he's not shy about it."

Erica shifted in her seat. "You don't think I was the first?"

"No," I said, opting for honesty. "I don't think you were the first, and I definitely don't think you'll be the last. We have to find the other victims."

"Any idea where to start?" Derrick asked.

Funnily enough, I did. "Jen."

Eliot furrowed his brow. "Isn't that the girl you saved in the parking lot?"

I nodded.

Jake steepled his fingers and rested his elbows on the table. "Remind me what happened there."

I told him the story again.

"How can you be sure she was a victim?" Derrick asked.

"There was something about her," I said. "She was ... broken."

"Like me," Erica said, her voice hollow.

"She was vulnerable," I said, refusing to give in to Erica's despondency. She needed to find some courage. "She was afraid of those boys. There has to be a reason."

"And the kids were obnoxious," Jake said. "They were threatening."

"And they're on the same team as Sam," I said.

"Do you think they're all doing it together?" Derrick asked, shooting a worried look in Erica's direction. "Do you think they're all ... working together?"

I pursed my lips and met Erica's gaze levelly. "I think that a lot of them are doing it," I said. "I think that others might not be doing it, but they clearly know what's happening."

"You think they all had sex with me, don't you?" Erica looked crushed.

Lexie rubbed her shoulders in a soothing manner. "You didn't do anything wrong. You can't blame yourself. It's not your fault."

"It's not," I agreed. "They're the ones in the wrong."

"We need to track down this Jen," Jake said. "She's our best option."

"What if you can't find her?"

"There can only be so many girls with that name at the school," Jake said. "I've seen her. I'll recognize her. I'll question them myself. I'll go out there on Monday, Tuesday at the latest."

"A girl might not trust you," I said. "Maybe I should go?"

"You can't," Jake said. "This has to be official. You're not an option."

"I ...."

"No," Jake said, shaking his head vehemently. "We have to do this right. There's no room for mistakes."

"I wouldn't make a mistake," I protested.

"Avery, you've already sniffed more out than anyone else could," Jake said. "This has to be by the book. You know that."

"I ... she was really scared," I said.

"That's why you went after her," Jake said. "You sensed it. That's what you do."

"I do not," I said. "I just didn't like the looks of the boys following her."

"You said the boys didn't show up until you were already talking to her," Eliot said. "You went after her because she was in pain."

"That's insulting." I crossed my arms over my chest.

Eliot tightened his arm around my shoulders. "You're a good person," he said. "You don't like to admit it, but you are. You sensed she needed help, and you gave it."

"I threatened to kick the kid in the balls."

"And you protected her," Jake said.

"You guys protected her," I argued. "You're the ones who ended everything."

"And you're the one who made sure we could end it," Jake said. "You're also the one who stood up for Erica."

"Erica stood up for herself."

"Only because you told me I had the strength to do it," Erica said, squaring her shoulders. "You took those girls on. You took Tina on. I didn't know anyone could do that until you did it. Even the teachers in our school are afraid of those girls."

"They're just bullies."

"And you bullied them right back," Erica said. "You made them feel stupid. You did it because of me."

"You were only part of the reason," I corrected. "I went after them because they needed it. They're never going to be complete people if they don't learn."

Jake smirked. "You never were one to put up with a snob."

"No," Derrick agreed. "You were the girl who beat up the snobs."

"Did she really get in fights with girls in high school?" Erica asked. "She told me that, but I'm not sure I believed it until now."

"She did," Derrick said. "She's an exceptional hair puller."

"And she taught me to do the same," Lexie said.

"I want to do the same," Erica said. "I want to ... be like Avery."

"Think it over," Derrick teased. "People try to shoot her."

"And stab her," Jake added.

"And kidnap her," Eliot said.

"They also respect her," Erica said. "I ... I think I'm ready to call my parents."

The conversation stilled a moment. "I thought you didn't want to interrupt their vacation," I said.

"I don't," Erica said. "But I need them now. They're my parents. They should know."

"I agree."

"I'm going to go home," she said. "I'm going to call them. I want to be there when they get home."

"Do you want me to come with you?"

Erica shook her head, unsure. "I think I should probably do it myself."

"I'm not sure you should be alone," Jake cautioned.

"I'll go with her," Lexie said. "I'll stay at the house until her parents come back."

"You will?" I was surprised. Lexie was growing by leaps and bounds in my estimation these days, her choice in men notwithstanding.

"I will," Lexie said. "I want to be with her, and I promise not to take over the conversation."

Jake was confused. "Since when do you do something for others?"

"Since Avery taught me that it was the right thing to do," Lexie said. "She's the one who gave me purpose. She's the one who gave me drive. She's the one who taught me that black and blue should never be worn together because it's an eyesore. She's also the one who believed in me and gave me the money to follow my dreams."

I bit my lip.

"Thank you all for what you've done for me," Erica said. "It's time I stood on my own two feet, though. Well, four feet. I want Lexie with me."

"If you need anything, you can always call," I said.

"I'll keep that in mind," Erica said. "Once breakfast is over, I'm going to call my parents."

Jake met my gaze over the table, a small smile playing at his lips. "And Avery Shaw strikes again." For once, I knew it wasn't an insult.

"I'M proud of you," Eliot said, stripping out of his shirt and discarding it on my bedroom floor.

"Don't be ridiculous," I said, mimicking his actions. "I didn't do anything." It was almost three in the morning and we were exhausted. Sleep somehow seemed elusive, though.

"You gave Erica the strength to face her demons," he said, dropping his pants. "That's not nothing in my book."

My cheeks flushed. "I think you're exaggerating."

Eliot climbed under the covers and regarded me with an enigmatic look. "I think you don't like taking credit for things."

"I always take credit," I argued. "I'd carry around a trophy if I could."

"You take credit on articles," he said. "You take credit when you make a grown man cry. You take credit when you knock Ludington down three pegs. You don't take credit for stuff like this."

I removed my jeans. "I take credit when I do everything."

Eliot shook his head. "No, you don't."

I rolled my eyes and turned away from him.

"When I first met you, I thought you were just a mouthy reporter with a sense of entitlement," Eliot said. "You were hot, don't get me wrong. I knew I wanted to sleep with you the second I saw you.

"Then I heard where you were going," he continued. "I knew there had to be something more to you. What hot blonde goes to hear the *Star Wars* symphony? I was intrigued.

"The more time I spend with you, the more amazing I think you are," Eliot added. "I'm really proud of you."

My tongue felt too thick to speak around.

"Don't get me wrong," Eliot said. "You're still a pain in the ass, and a lot of work. But you're a great person, too."

I forced myself to turn and meet his eyes. "Are you trying to get me to have sex with you? You don't have to manipulate me to do that."

Eliot frowned. "I'm trying to get you to admit how strong you are."

"I know I'm strong."

"You're not strong only because you like to fight and take people down," Eliot said. "You're strong because you ... care."

"I don't care," I protested. "I'm shallow."

Eliot rolled his eyes. "Turn off the lights."

I did as I was told.

"Now come here," he said.

I climbed into the bed next to him, sighing as he drew me into his arms. "I'm proud of you."

"Thank you," I murmured, resting my head on his chest.

240 / AMANDA M. LEE

"I'm really fond of you, too."

"Right back at you."

Eliot sighed. "You're my hero, Trouble."

Tears flooded my eyes. "I ... I don't know what to say."

"Then go to sleep," he said. "You'll find the words in the morning."

I had no doubt he was right.

Eliot wrapped his arm around my back as I nestled next to him.

"Something tells me you'll find enough words to fill ten mornings. You're nothing if not chatty."

"Eliot?"

"Yeah."

"Go to sleep."

"I don't understand why you insisted on coming here." Dave Stewart looked me up and down, his face dubious as he regarded me during the Monday night meet. "You hate wrestling."

"I love wrestling," I argued, focusing on the gym floor below us. "It's a great sport. It's just like watching gay porn, and who doesn't love that?"

"You have to stop saying things like that," Dave said. "You're going to alienate our readers."

"If our readers like this sport, they're already aliens," I said.

"Then why did you insist on coming?" Dave challenged.

"I ... want to learn more about the sport," I said.

"Why?"

"Because knowledge is power."

"Why did you wear that outfit?" Dave asked.

I glanced down at my shirt. "I thought it fit the setting."

"It says 'Looking for love in Alderaan places.'"

"So?"

"It seems to hint at incest."

"So?"

"So, it's inappropriate," Dave said.

I pointed to the two boys on the floor. One of them had his face pressed against the inner thigh of the other, while the second was gripping the first boy's rear end, and they were grunting. "How can my shirt be inappropriate when that's going on in public?"

"That's a sport," Dave said, his eyebrows leaping up his forehead.

"Well, then I'm going to start petitioning for sex to be an Olympic event," I said.

"You're just ... sick," Dave said.

"Thanks for the news flash," I said. "I'll be sure to include that in my Christmas cards this year."

"You send out Christmas cards? Let me guess, are they *Star Wars*?"

"No," I scoffed. "They're also *Lord of the Rings*, *Harry Potter* and the Hulk."

"Why the Hulk?"

"Because you wouldn't like me when I'm angry," I said. I kept my eyes on the floor, my attention drawn to the man pacing the edge of the mat. His face was red as he yelled instructions at the Catholic North wrestler.

"Get on top and pound him!"

I shifted a questioning look in Dave's direction. "That doesn't sound gay to you?"

"Shut up," Dave snapped.

"Grab him! Yank on it!" The man was animated.

"Don't say a word," Dave said.

"Slide in there and really give it to him!"

"You've completely ruined this sport for me," Dave complained.

"Who is the guy doing the yelling?" I asked.

"That's Luke Haden," Dave replied. "He's the Catholic North coach."

"How long has he been with the team?"

"About two years."

"He looks relatively young," I said.

"He was a big wrestler here in the county about a decade ago," Dave said. "He even wrestled in college. An injury ended his career, and then he decided to come back to the area and coach. He's really turned this team around."

"What do you mean? They weren't always good in wrestling?"

Dave shook his head. "They were pretty bad a few years ago. They didn't even have enough wrestlers to fill all the weight classes."

"And Haden coming to the school changed all that?"

"Yeah," Dave said. "He's a real inspiration. It's a great story."

"Will you just pound his ass?" Haden screamed at his wrestler.

"He seems a peach," I said, getting to my feet.

"Where are you going?"

"I want to get a better look at the action," I said.

"Since when?"

"Since I decided to embrace my new career in sports," I lied.

"Just don't do anything annoying," Dave said. "Whatever you do reflects on us, and let me tell you something, the stuff you say makes us look like we've been on a three-day bender."

"You say the sweetest things."

I climbed down the bleachers and edged my way across the floor until I was behind Haden. I'd never really considered him, but now that I knew just how messed up the Catholic North kids were I was looking for the thread that tied their misbehavior together. Haden, and his nonstop screeching, seemed a good place to start.

I was so caught up watching Haden I didn't realize – until too late – that I'd drawn the attention of the idle wrestlers on the sidelines.

"Hey, lady, you're blocking the action."

I glanced over my shoulder to find my old friend Alex watching me. The apology died on my lips. "You'll live."

"Oh, it's you," he sneered. "What are you doing here?"

"I'm covering the meet."

"I can give you something else to cover," he said, pointing to his crotch. "I'm probably too big for you, but I'm sure we can figure something out."

I rolled my eyes. "I've graduated from the twigs-and-berries crowd."

Alex scowled. "You have a mouth on you."

"Someone should teach her how to use it," one of his cohorts chimed in.

"Kid, you wouldn't know what to do with a girl who didn't cry when you took your clothes off," I shot back.

"Would you applaud?"

"I probably wouldn't be able to stop myself," I said.

The kid beamed.

"From pointing and laughing," I added.

Alex got to his feet. "I'm sick of you."

"Then stop talking to me," I suggested.

"I will, as soon as you get out of my face." Alex took a threatening step toward me.

"Sit your ass down," I said.

"You're not the boss of me," Alex said. "You're nothing but a lowly sports reporter. The only thing you're good for is ... something you're too old to do."

"Sit down," I repeated. "I've had enough of you."

"Listen, bitch ... ." Alex reached for my forearm but I wasn't in the mood for his antics. I shifted my arm, made a fist and punched him in his special place as hard as I could. The good thing about fighting with your cousins – even as adults – is you know exactly how to hit, and you don't pull your punches.

The look that crossed Alex's face was comical. He cupped his hands over his crotch and sank to the floor, his face red, foam forming at the corner of his mouth. He tried to speak, but no words would form.

"Now sit down and shut up," I said, turning back to the action on the floor. Unfortunately, the altercation had caught Haden's attention.

"What's going on?"

I shrugged. "I think one of your wrestlers fell down."

Haden peered around me, his gaze landing on the floor where Alex was moaning. "What happened to him?"

"He slipped."

Haden arched an eyebrow. "And who are you?"

"I'm Avery Shaw," I said. "I'm ... ."

"You're a reporter for The Monitor," Haden finished.

"I see my reputation precedes me."

"Well, actually, I was on the phone with Doug Keaton at the crack of dawn this morning," he countered. "You see, I had to do without one of my best wrestlers today because he missed school."

"That's what happens when you're arrested," I said.

"I understand you're the reason he was arrested," Haden pressed.

"I'm pretty sure that Sam was the reason he was arrested," I said. "He tried to break into my cousin's apartment."

"I have trouble believing that."

"Try harder."

Haden opened his mouth and then shut it before exhaling heavily through his nose. He was trying to collect himself. "You know, you have quite the reputation in this area."

"I know," I said, refusing to back down.

"People say you're a hothead," Haden said. "People say you put your nose into things you have no business putting your nose in. People say that you have a death wish."

"People say a lot of things."

"People also say you've been harassing my boys," Haden said. "I didn't believe it." He gestured to Alex, his regular color was slowly returning to his face. "I'm starting to believe it now."

"Your boys are sick little bastards," I said. "The only reason I'm going after them is because they're a bunch of brutal rapists."

Haden's face was ashen. "Why would you say something like that?"

"Because I've seen them in action," I said. "I also happen to know at least one girl who was drugged and taken advantage of at one of their little parties."

"You're going to take the word of one girl over my whole team?"

"Yes."

"That doesn't seem like a very smart way to go about being a reporter," Haden said.

"I never said I was smart."

"I'll have you know, this is the finest bunch of boys I've ever known," Haden said. "They would never do anything like you're suggesting. It's not their fault that girls throw themselves at them. It comes with the package when you're an elite athlete."

"They roll around on the floor with other boys," I said. "How elite can they be?"

Haden clenched his jaw.

"They're really just one step away from the Village People," I added.

"Now listen ... ."

Dave appeared at my elbow, clearly nervous. "Is something wrong?"

"I don't like your new co-worker," Haden said.

"No one does," Dave said. "Trust me. She's not popular."

"That must be why she's going after my boys," Haden said. "She's jealous of their success."

"Yes, that's it," I said. "I'm jealous of the wrestlers. There can't possibly be another reason, like they're gang rapists."

Dave balked. "Who told you that?"

"One of their victims."

Dave shifted his gaze to Haden. "That's not true, is it?"

"Of course not," Haden said. "She's making things up. She's trying to make a name for herself by taking my team down."

Dave was unsure. "I think you should probably go," he said finally.

"Doesn't he have to coach the team?" I asked.

"I was talking to you," Dave said.

I made a face. "You can't kick me out."

"I can, though," Haden said. He snapped his fingers to get the attention of the two security guards loitering by the gym door and then pointed to me. "Can you show Ms. Shaw out? She's overstayed her welcome."

I WAS still fuming in the parking lot fifteen minutes later. I'd considered making a scene, because that's what I do, but ultimately decided against it. That wasn't going to help anyone, no matter how good it made me feel. I needed to think.

I texted Eliot what happened. Instead of texting back, he called. "Why did they kick you out?"

I told him the story. When I was done, he was silent on the other end of the phone.

"Are you still there?"

"I'm just looking up the symptoms of an aneurism on WebMD."

"What? I didn't do anything. That kid was going after me."

"And you should have walked away," Eliot said. "You never should have gone down there."

"I wanted to get a better look at the coach," I said. "Let's face it, these kids have to be getting their ideas from someone."

"And you think it's their coach?"

"He's as good of a suspect as anyone," I said.

"You still don't know he's guilty," Eliot said. "It could be one of the parents."

"Do you think that those rumors about the steroids have anything to do with what's happening to these girls?"

"I think it would be one heck of a coincidence for one small school to have a group of rapists and a huge drug trade on the campus at the same time," he said.

"Is there any way to force drug tests on these kids?"

"That's out of my area of expertise," Eliot said.

"I don't know what to do next," I admitted. "I feel I'm close, but I'm missing something."

"There's nothing more you can do tonight," Eliot said. "I'm missing something, too. Why don't you come home and do your brainstorming here?"

"What are you going to be doing?"

"Hopefully you," Eliot said.

"I haven't eaten dinner yet," I said.

"We'll order some pizza."

"I'm probably supposed to go back to the office and answer phones," I said.

"It's your choice," Eliot said. "Pizza and nudity with me or answering calls. I know it's a hard choice."

"I'll see you in a half hour," I said.

"I'll be waiting."

I sent Fish an email telling him what happened and that I was going home (I was trying to cover my bases) and then pulled out of the parking lot. A set of headlights flashing in the rearview mirror caught my attention. The meet couldn't be over already, could it?

I pulled onto the main road and headed south. Traffic was light. As far as I could tell, the only vehicles on the road were mine and the one my shadow was driving. Instead of taking my normal route home, I turned down 21 Mile Road and headed toward the freeway. The distance was greater, but it would save me time.

The trailing car made the same turn.

I'm not one to be paranoid – most of the time – but something about this situation was bugging me. I purposely slowed my car so I wouldn't make the upcoming traffic signal. Since the streetlights were brighter at the crossroads, I took the opportunity to study the vehicle behind me.

It was large, and if I had to guess, was a Ford Expedition. It was dark, either blue or black, and the driver was clearly male – and alone. That's all I could make out under the streetlights.

Once the signal turned, I continued toward the freeway. I tried to push the Expedition out of my mind, but it was still on my tail when I merged with traffic on Interstate-94. I reduced my speed again, setting the cruise control below the speed limit. I wanted to test a theory.

The roads were dry and bare, so there was no reason to drive slowly. Instead of passing me, though, the Expedition driver matched my speed. I was liking this less and less. I reached over to the passenger seat and grabbed my cell phone.

Eliot picked up on the second ring. "Please don't tell me you're going back to the office."

"I think someone is following me."

Eliot paused. "Be more specific?"

"When I left the parking lot at the school, an Expedition pulled out after me," I said. "I've made a couple of turns, and it's still following me."

"Where are you?"

"On the freeway."

"Get off at the next exit," Eliot ordered. "Pull over at the first well-lit place you can find. I'll stay on the phone until you get there, and then I'll come to you."

"I ... I'm sure I'm overreacting," I said.

"I don't care," Eliot said. "Do it anyway. How far are you from an exit?"

"About a half mile."

"Good. Just stay calm."

"I was calm until I called you," I said. "Now I'm freaking out."

Eliot drew in a steadying breath. "I'm sorry. Just keep your eyes on the road in front of you. Don't get distracted by the vehicle behind you."

"Okay."

"Avery, it's going to be okay."

I flicked my turn signal. "I'm getting off now."

"Good."

I shifted my eyes to the rearview mirror. The Expedition was following me. Crap. "He's still there."

"Just stay focused on the task."

The Expedition accelerated, jerking forward and aiming in the direction of my rear bumper.

"Shit!"

"What?"

I tugged on the wheel to avoid the collision I was sure was coming. Careening off the road because of the exit curve, I overcorrected. Too late. I couldn't regain control of the car, and I was heading toward a grove of trees down the embankment.

Well, this wasn't good.

"Can you describe the other vehicle?"

"It was dark," I said.

"I know it's dark," the sheriff's deputy said. "I was asking about the other vehicle."

I rubbed my forehead irritably. "The vehicle was dark," I said.

"What kind of vehicle was it?"

"I think it was a Ford Expedition."

"You think?"

"Are you trying to piss me off?"

Derrick appeared at the deputy's elbow. "I'll take it from here."

"It's just a traffic mishap, sir," the deputy said. "It's beneath you."

"She's my cousin."

The deputy looked me up and down. "I'm sorry."

I blew an unladylike raspberry in his direction.

"We're all sorry," Derrick told the deputy. He eyed me carefully. "Are you okay?"

"I'm fine," I said. "I didn't hit anything. I managed to stop before I hit the trees. I guess I'm going to have to thank Eliot for having my brakes checked when he had the oil changed."

"Eliot is doing your car maintenance now?"

"So what?"

"It's just cute," Derrick said. "I didn't realize he was so ... domestic."

"You should see him in an apron," I said.

A truck pulled off to the side of the exit and I recognized it as Eliot's right away. "Speaking of Eliot."

"Did you call him?" Derrick asked.

"I was on the phone with him when it happened."

"You know it's illegal to drive while talking on your cell phone, right?"

"Write me a ticket."

Eliot exited his truck and rushed toward me. He pulled me in for a quick hug and then looked me over. "Are you all right?"

"I'm awesome," I said.

He cupped the back of my head and forced my face up so he could study it. "Did you hit your head?"

"How would you tell the difference?" Derrick asked.

"Now probably isn't the time for your family ... crap," Eliot snapped, giving me another hug. "You gave me a heart attack."

"The car isn't even damaged," I said, pointing. "Although, someone is going to have to tow it out of there."

"I'll take care of it," Derrick said. "I'll have them bring it straight to your house. I figure Eliot is going to want to take care of your driving needs for the rest of the night."

"Try the rest of her life," Eliot grumbled.

Another vehicle joined the small fleet on the side of the road, causing the three of us to turn in tandem.

"What is he doing here?" Derrick asked.

"Who is it?"

"Jake."

Eliot frowned. "I'm sure he's here because of Avery. Whenever she's in trouble he comes running."

Jake jumped out of his truck and strode toward us. He slowed when he caught sight of me. "Are you okay?"

"I'm fine," I said.

"What happened?"

I told him the story. When I was done, his frustration was evident. "You just can't stay out of trouble, can you?"

"How is this my fault?"

"It's always your fault," Jake snapped. "You purposely antagonized that kid, and his coach, and then you wonder why someone tried to run you off the road."

"I didn't do it on purpose!"

"Oh, just don't," Jake said, running his hand through his hair, frustrated.

I crossed my arms over my chest, pouting.

"For once, I'm going to take Avery's side," Derrick said.

Three sets of eyebrows shot up.

"I know. I'm surprised, too," Derrick said. "The thing is, she might be on to something with the coach. She's the perfect person to knock him off his game."

"I know," Jake said. "I only wish she hadn't made herself a target in the process."

Something about this conversation bugged me. "What do you know about this coach?"

Jake and Derrick exchanged looks. "He's on our radar. That's all I can say."

"You'd better say more than that," I warned. "You know I won't rest until I find out the truth, and if that means I have to start stalking Haden, I'll do it."

"No, you won't," Eliot said.

"Don't tell me what to do," I huffed.

"Don't make me tell you what to do."

"Don't make me make you ... wait, what was I saying?"

"You're going to have to tell her," Derrick said, his voice low.

"I know," Jake grumbled.

"Tell me what?"

Jake shook his head. "Not tonight. I have plans tonight."

I looked him over and saw the hints I missed on first inspection. Instead of his uniform, he wore black slacks and a white shirt. His coat was leather instead of the polyester blend that matched his uniform. And his hair was perfectly coiffed. "Are you going on a date?"

Jake seemed surprised by the question. "Why do you ask that?"

That was an aversion. "Because you're dressed up."

"Maybe I have a charity function," Jake said.

"Do you have a charity function?"

"No."

I tilted my head to the side and peered closer at his vehicle. Someone sat in the passenger seat, and the silhouette shouted female.

"Is that Celeste?"

Jake wrinkled his nose. "I told you I wasn't going to date her anymore."

"Who is it?"

"Mind your own business," Jake said.

"Tell me what's going on with Haden and I will," I countered.

"I ... I don't have time for that," Jake said. "We have reservations."

I narrowed my eyes. "Where?"

"Why do you care?" Eliot asked.

"I'm hungry," I said. "I haven't eaten dinner yet."

"Buy her a pizza," Jake said.

"That was the plan before she almost died," Eliot replied.

"I didn't almost die," I said. "I had a traffic mishap."

"Then you can wait until tomorrow for your update," Jake said, turning back in the direction of the road.

"Hey, I'm starving, and I almost died," I said.

"I'm going on a date, Avery," Jake shouted over his shoulder.

"Is everything okay?" The woman from Jake's truck was moving, and it seemed her destination was the four of us. She wore a flared skirt and a low-cut blouse, and her heels were so high I couldn't figure out how she was still standing on them as she made her way down the grassy embankment.

"It's fine," Jake said. "Ms. Shaw wasn't injured."

"Oh, that's good," the woman said. "I was really worried."

"Cara, this is Avery," Jake said. "Avery, be nice."

I extended my hand. "It's nice to meet you."

"You, too," Cara said, grasping my hand tightly. "I've heard so much about you. It's like you're famous."

"Most crazy people are," Derrick said.

"Do you know who tried to run you off the road?" Cara asked.

"I have a few suspects," I said, smoothing my T-shirt in the face of Cara's confident countenance. "Unfortunately, Jake won't tell me whether I'm right."

"Why not?" Cara asked, her eyes wide.

"Because we have reservations," Jake said. "I don't have time to deal with Avery's … issues."

"But she seems so upset," Cara said.

"I am."

Eliot pursed his lips to keep from laughing.

"We're supposed to be going to dinner," Jake said.

Cara turned to me. "Have you eaten?"

I shook my head. "No, and I'm starving."

"I know," Cara said, "let's all go to dinner together!"

Jake shot me a look. "I don't think Avery is dressed for … ."

"It will be fine," Cara said, cutting him off. "You're the sheriff. They'll never say no to you. Then, over dinner, you can tell Avery what she needs to know."

"I don't think it's a good idea," Jake hedged.

"Oh, come on," Cara pleaded. "This will give Avery and me a chance to get to know each other. What are you afraid of?"

I lifted an eyebrow at Jake, daring him to say no.

"I'm afraid you'll pick up her bad habits," Jake said.

"Please?"

Jake's defense collapsed. "Sure. Let's all go to dinner. What could possibly go wrong?"

· · ·

"SO, it must be exciting to be a reporter," Cara said, her brown eyes sparkling as she eyed me from across the table. "What's it like?"

"There's never a dull day," I said. While I was anxious to hear Jake's update, Cara's rampant enthusiasm made me leery. She seemed so ... eager. I wasn't used to Jake's dates trying to befriend me. Usually they tried to blind me and rip my hair out. I encouraged that behavior.

"That's so cool," Cara said. She turned to Eliot. "And what do you do?"

"I own a pawnshop," Eliot said, leaning back in his chair.

"He's also a private investigator," Jake said. "He's diversifying."

"Oh, do you two know each other?" Cara asked.

"We served in the military together," Jake said carefully.

"So you're friends?"

"We're ... friendly," Jake replied.

"He's just being coy," I said. "They go on man dates all the time."

Cara looked interested. "Man dates?"

"Oh, you know, they go to bars and play pool," I said. "Then they beat their chests and scream like Tarzan."

Cara's eyes clouded. "Are you joking?"

"She's joking," Jake said.

"Yes, Avery is a laugh a minute," Eliot said.

"I think she's neat."

"Did you hear that? I'm neat."

"Eat your dinner," Eliot instructed. "I don't want to hear you complaining about being hungry when we get home."

"So, how did you two meet?" Cara asked.

"Avery came into my store to buy a gun," Eliot said. "Someone was stalking her."

"That's horrible." Cara pressed her hand to her heart.

"Give it time," Jake said. "You'll want to hurt her, too."

Cara ignored him. "Was it love at first sight?"

Eliot shifted uncomfortably. "Honestly? I thought she was crazy."

Jake snickered.

"When did you change your mind?"

"Well, it wasn't at the *Star Wars* symphony concert later that night," Eliot said.

"Ah, yes, that was a fun night," Jake said.

"You were there?" Cara was enthralled.

"I was called there because the rebel alliance and dark side got into a fight," Jake said.

"I don't know what that means," Cara said. "I've never seen *Star Wars*."

My mouth dropped open.

"You've rendered her speechless," Eliot teased. "I didn't know it was possible."

"It's like seeing a unicorn," Jake said.

I rolled my eyes and decided to change the subject. "So, what aren't you telling me about Luke Haden?"

"Who is Luke Haden?" Cara asked.

"He's the wrestling coach at Catholic North."

Jake ran his hand over his jaw. "Tell me again about your run-in with him tonight."

I did as instructed, even though I knew Jake was only buying time with his request.

"Did he seem ... interested in you?" Jake asked.

"He seemed to hate me," I said. "Does that count?"

"He didn't seem sexually interested in you, though, right?"

"Yeah, I'm guessing he wouldn't want to be near me if I was the last woman on Earth," I said. "I have that effect on men."

"Oh, if only that were true," Eliot mused.

I pinched his leg under the table. "You're hurting my feelings."

Eliot rolled his eyes. "Fine. You're the prettiest and most amazing woman in the world."

"Thank you."

Jake's face was serious. "I need you to stay away from Haden," he said.

"Why?"

"He's not a nice guy," Jake said. "Can we just leave it at that?"

He was acting as though he'd just met me. "Um, no."

Jake made an exasperated sound in the back of his throat. "This is a mistake."

"Oh, just tell me. You know you want to."

"I don't want to."

"If you don't tell her she's going to get in even more trouble," Eliot said.

"I know," Jake said. "That's why I'm going to tell her."

"Yay." I clapped my hands together.

"What do you know about him?" Jake asked.

"Just what Dave told me tonight," I said. "He said he was some big wrestler, and he wrestled in college until an injury ended his career."

"An injury didn't end his career," Jake said.

"What did?"

"During Haden's senior year at Michigan State there was a string of brutal rapes on campus," Jake said.

I froze.

"Haden was a suspect, but the rapist wore a condom," Jake continued. "There was no forensic evidence. One of the women identified Haden as her attacker, though."

"So how is he walking around?" Eliot asked.

"The day before the trial the woman disappeared," Jake said. "They had no other evidence and her body never turned up. They had no choice but to drop the charges."

"But ... how could Catholic North hire him after that?"

Jake shrugged. "Haden left Michigan State under a cloud of suspicion," he said. "His file was sealed by a judge. Catholic North officials probably don't know."

"So tell them," I said.

"I can't," Jake said. "That's against the law."

That didn't mean I couldn't tell them. Jake must have read my mind. "Don't even think about it."

"What?"

"I know what you're thinking," Jake said. "Stay out of this."

"Fine," I said, lowering my gaze.

"Fine?"

"I said fine."

"I don't believe you," Jake said.

"That's because you're suspicious by nature," I said. "It's one of your worst qualities."

Jake growled.

"So, this dinner is great," I said, shoveling a forkful of pasta into my mouth as I turned to Cara. "How did you two meet?"

"Oh, it's a great story," Cara said. "Let me tell you about it."

I tuned Cara's story out as I formulated a plan. I knew whom to consider now. I only needed to find out all of his secrets so I could splash them on the front page of the newspaper and avenge all the girls he'd wronged. If it also happened to get me out of sports and back into news, so be it.

What? There's no harm in wanting a little something for myself. I'm growing as a person, but I'm still emotionally stunted.

Technically I wasn't working, so visiting the county courthouse on my own time Tuesday afternoon wasn't against the rules. I wasn't sure how that distinction would fly back in the office, but I was beyond caring.

I made my way straight to the clerk's office and searched the faces for one in particular. Elyse Sampson was one of the few workers at the county level who didn't make me want to scream. She's friendly and has a great sense of humor. She reminds me of myself. Her co-workers hate her for some reason.

"Hey, Avery," she said when I caught her eye. "What are you doing here?"

I moved over to her desk. "I need some help."

"With what?"

"I need to find some information on a sealed court file," I said.

Elyse's eyes widened. "That's against the rules."

"Barely."

"No, it's totally against the rules," Elyse countered.

"Come on," I prodded. "It's for a good cause."

"I thought you were in sports now."

"It's a sports story," I said.

"You're researching a sports story at the circuit courthouse?"

"What? That's possible."

Elyse sent me a withering look. "Tell me what's going on."

"I need to find a file on Luke Haden."

"Why does that name sound familiar?" Elyse asked.

"He's the wrestling coach at Catholic North."

"Oh, that's right," Elyse said. "I read his name in the article Marvin wrote about that girl dying. He was going on and on about what a tragedy it was and how the school was rallying together to deal with it."

I hadn't yet read Marvin's piece so I had to take Elyse's word for it. "Her name was Kelsey Cooper."

"Do the cops have any new leads on who killed her?"

I raised an eyebrow.

"Oh, no way," Elyse said. "The coach can't be a suspect. He was so nice in the article."

"Yeah, well, he's a total douche in real life."

Elyse sighed. "This case isn't in our system?"

"No," I said. "He was at Michigan State."

"That's going to take me at least an hour to track down," Elyse said.

"I can wait."

"You're going to get me fired one of these days," Elyse said. "I just know it."

"Yes, but just think of the good you're doing," I pressed.

She blew out a sigh. "Fine. Sit there, and don't touch anything."

"OKAY, I've got it."

I snapped out of my reverie and focused on Elyse. "Great."

"I printed it out," Elyse said. "I knew you would want a copy as soon as I read through it."

"You read it?"

262 / AMANDA M. LEE

"Of course I read it," Elyse said. "I'm as nosy as you are. I just don't have a newspaper to spread my gossip."

"It's not as much fun as it sounds," I said, taking the folder from her. "You have to back the gossip up with pesky facts. It's a pain."

"Listen, I printed that out on the auxiliary printer," Elyse said. "That means there's no way for anyone to prove where you got it."

"Thanks."

"I knew you'd like that."

"I do."

"It also protects me when this inevitably blows up in your face," Elyse said.

I scanned the first few pages of the file. "This guy is a real dick."

"That file says they could tie him to only the one rape," Elyse said.

"The file also says that the other seven rapes – that sick bastard – were all done in the exact same manner," I said. "The assailant crawled in through an open window after cutting the screen out. He then raped the woman and beat her senseless. Most of the other women couldn't even remember the assault. The only one who could was Lauren Miller."

"And Lauren Miller has been missing for years," Elyse said.

"Since right before the trial," I confirmed.

"Was he a suspect in her disappearance?"

"Of course," I said. "He seems to be the only suspect. His alibi was non-existent. He said he was home watching television when she disappeared. They could never prove he was guilty, though."

"Was he out on bail before the trial?"

"Yeah."

"I can't believe they would let a guy suspected of multiple rapes out on personal bond," Elyse said. "You would think they'd have him on a tether."

"He was only up on charges in the Miller rape," I said.

"Still ... ."

"I know," I said. "Rapists are scum."

"Do you think Haden raped Kelsey Cooper?"

"Kelsey Cooper was gang raped," I said.

"None of the news stories say that," Elyse pointed out. "They say she was sexually assaulted and strangled."

"It's not public knowledge yet."

"Do you think he has a partner?"

I was worried he had a whole team of them. "I think he might be grooming his partners," I admitted.

"What are you going to do?" Elyse asked.

"Stop him."

WHEN I got to the newspaper, I was surprised to find a familiar figure walking out of the front office. The Monitor's executive offices are at the front of the building. The rest of the staff – you know, the people who do the real work – are housed in open cubicles and wide rooms. All of the executives have bay windows and leather furniture. They also have an executive refrigerator full of items they don't have to purchase from a vending machine. What? I'm not bitter.

"Ms. Shaw," Tad said, slowing as he caught sight of me.

"Mr. Ludington."

"Commissioner Ludington," Tad corrected.

"Only for a few more weeks," I said.

"Life is change."

"Especially when the voters refuse to reelect you," I shot back.

Tad scowled. "You're impossible."

"That's my official middle name."

"I thought it was 'bitch.'"

"Is something going on out here?" MacDonald ambled out of the front office, his gaze bouncing between the two of us.

"Tad was just telling me what a bitch I am."

"I said no such thing," Tad protested, causing my eyes to widen. "Do you see how she makes up things?"

"I heard you say it," MacDonald said.

"No, you didn't," Tad said. "You must be hearing things."

"Like annoying little politicians nattering on and on," I said.

MacDonald's face was unreadable, but I could almost swear amusement momentarily flashed across his eyes. "You're here early today, Ms. Shaw."

"I was running an errand downtown," I lied. "It didn't make sense to go home for forty-five minutes and then turn around and come back."

"And how is sports treating you?" Tad asked. "I'll just bet it's killing you to be forced out of everyone else's business."

"I like sports," I said. "I've learned a lot." I knew Tad was baiting me. He wanted me to blow my stack in front of MacDonald. Two could play that game.

"I'm glad you're embracing your new assignment," MacDonald said. "I enjoyed your competitive cheer article the other day."

I cringed. I'd forgotten about my speech at the school. I knew a few of the parents had called him. The nasty voice mail messages they left for me promised just that.

"I also heard about your speech," MacDonald said, ending my misery. "It sounds like it was something to behold."

I met his gaze worriedly. "Things got a little out of hand."

"I talked to the teacher," MacDonald said. "She said you handled things exactly right, even going so far as to stand up for a student who was being mistreated by others. She says you told off half of the class."

"That sounds like Avery," Tad said. "She's always been a bossy little thing."

"I was only bossy with you because you had no idea what you were doing in bed," I shot back, immediately regretting my words. Well, I'd already made things worse. Why not go all the way? "That's what happens when the equipment is too small to register."

"Stop telling people that," Tad seethed.

MacDonald ignored my outburst. "I understand you told some of the girls how life was going to change for them once they were out of high school," he said.

"I might have ... expanded their world views," I hedged.

"I raised three daughters," MacDonald said. "Their teenage years were like living in quicksand. One of them was a snob, one of them was a nerd and the third was a member of the school band. They all had ... issues."

"Most girls at that age do."

"I wish someone had told them what you told those Richmond girls," MacDonald said. "You were very wise, and you didn't pull any punches. Girls that age need a reality check. Life is not proms, quarterbacks and cliques. I like your message."

This was news to me.

"Don't encourage her," Tad said. "Women should be taught that their place is at home."

MacDonald frowned. "I think taking care of children and a home is a very important job," he said.

Tad shot me a triumphant smile.

"I also think a woman can do anything she wants to do."

"That's what I said," Tad whined.

"Since you're a fan of mine now, do you think you can transfer me out of sports?" I asked. What? He's never been this nice to me before.

"I still think you're learning your lesson," MacDonald said.

"No, I've graduated."

MacDonald extended his index finger. "Don't press your luck," he said.

"Fine," I grumbled, turning back toward the newsroom.

"And Ms. Shaw?"

I stopped.

"Please try to refrain from punching any more wrestlers in the family jewels at meets."

"That's assault," Tad said. "You should be arrested."

"Not when the wrestler is making suggestive comments,"

MacDonald said. "I don't agree with what the kid said to you, and two parents did call in your defense. They said they watched the whole thing and the kid had it coming."

I waited. I knew he wasn't done.

"One of the first things we learn as children, Ms. Shaw, is that we're supposed to keep our hands to ourselves," MacDonald said.

"I do that fifty percent of the time," I replied.

"Let's make it a hundred and see where we go from there."

"Yes, sir."

I was halfway down the hallway when I heard Tad's final complaint. "That's it? I thought you said you were going to fire her."

"I make the decisions about my staff, Commissioner Ludington," MacDonald said. "If you don't like that, you can take it up with ... I really don't care who you take it up with. Just get out of this office."

Crap. I was starting to like MacDonald. My whole world was upending. Again.

"**D**o you ever miss going on an actual date?" Eliot asked, tilting his popcorn to the side so I could grab a handful of it.

"We never went on dates," I scoffed. "We watched television on the couch and then had sex."

"Those are the best kinds of dates."

We were watching a basketball game. Stanley had assigned me to cover it, making me promise before I left the office that I wouldn't hit any of the players in the nuts if they got mouthy. Eliot decided to join me. I think he worried that someone would follow me again, even though I was nowhere near Catholic North.

"So, what's the deal with these teams?" Eliot asked.

"I think they're trying to put the ball in the basket," I said.

He flicked my ear. "Thank you, smartass," he said. "Are either of them any good?"

"They're in the MAC Bronze," I said.

"What's that mean?"

"It means they're the smallest teams in the county."

"Does that mean they're bad?"

"I guess."

Eliot smiled. "Have you actually learned about the different divisions?"

"I'm a dedicated employee," I sniffed.

"You're too smart for your own good," Eliot said, leaning back and extending his legs to stretch. "I don't remember bleachers being this uncomfortable when I was in school."

"Did you go to a lot of the games?"

"I played in a lot of the games," Eliot said. "I only sat on the bleachers when I was catching a breather at dances."

I rolled my eyes. "I bet you always had a different date for these dances."

"Of course," he said. "Sticking with one woman is creepy."

"You're a prince."

"Didn't you go to dances in high school?" Eliot asked.

"Sure," I said. "I just never danced."

"What did you do?"

"Jake usually snuck in a flask, and then we'd hide under the bleachers and ... talk about world events."

Eliot scowled. "Don't tell me about your high school antics with Jake. It bugs me."

"It shouldn't," I said. "I don't see him watching a high school basketball game with me."

"I'll bet he would if you asked."

I pinched his cheek. "Is someone jealous?"

Eliot jerked his face away. "I'm not jealous."

"Okay," I said, focusing back on the game.

"I'm not."

"I know."

"I'm not!"

"Chill out and eat your popcorn," I said. "This is supposed to be a date. You don't yell when you're on a date."

"I do when I'm on a date with you," Eliot said.

I ignored him. This was my second basketball game and it was as boring as the first. I decided to multitask. "What did you think of the file I left on the table? Did you read it?"

"I read it," Eliot said. "I think someone needs to lock Haden up. He's obviously an animal."

"We have to find proof first," I said.

"You don't have to do anything," Eliot said. "You have to watch your little game and answer phones."

"Yes, Dad."

Eliot sighed. "Listen, I don't like what we've found on this guy," he said. "I especially don't like that he knows who you are and that you're going after his wrestlers. I made sure all your windows were locked, by the way."

I smiled. "I don't think I'm in the age group he finds attractive."

"Rape isn't about sexual attraction," Eliot said. "It's about power. Rapists want to dominate women. They especially want to dominate women they think are too big for their britches. That describes you to a tee."

"I thought you liked my britches," I teased.

"I like them when they're on the floor," Eliot said, smiling as a cheerleader jumped up and down in front of him. The girl met his gaze and grinned as she kicked her leg above her head.

"Oh, good grief," I said. "Stop flirting with the teenagers."

"I'm not flirting," Eliot said. "I'm encouraging them. They're working hard. They deserve positive reinforcement for a job well done."

"Yes, waving their pom-poms around is clearly taxing them," I said. "That one looks like she wants to faint in your lap."

Eliot pinched my cheek. "Is someone jealous?"

I slapped his hand away. "I'm not jealous."

"I'd understand if you were," he said. "I'm very desirable. These girls clearly see it."

Three of them were now staring directly at Eliot as they chanted some nonsense about not messing around and getting down.

"You know they're picturing you naked, right?"

"I hope I look good."

I stuck my tongue out. "They're all hoping you have an old letter-man's jacket hanging around for them to wear."

"If I did I'd make you wear it," Eliot said.

"Over my dead body."

"I was hoping you wouldn't be wearing anything else."

"I'll consider it," I said, the idea starting to intrigue me.

"I'll buy a jacket."

"Make sure it's not red," I said, wrinkling my nose. "You know I hate red."

"I do. I don't understand why, but I've learned to live with it."

"Yes, I'm sure it's been a tremendous hardship for you."

Eliot rubbed my thigh. "Have you talked to Erica?"

"I talked to Lexie," I said.

"How did everything go with that?"

"Her parents were upset," I said. "Lexie said they handled it well, though. They're getting her some counseling."

"That's probably a good idea," Eliot said. "It's going to take her a long time to get over this."

"Do you think she will?"

"I think she's strong," he said. "I think she's stronger than she has any business being at that age. I also think she's picked a great role model."

"Lexie?"

"No, not Lexie," Eliot said, making a face. "She considers Lexie as a peer. She looks at you as a role model."

"I am not a role model," I protested. "That's the meanest thing you've ever said to me."

Eliot grinned. "Face it," he said. "Avery Shaw is a role model. She's what all teenage girls should aspire to be."

"Fashionably unique?"

"Well, except for that," Eliot conceded.

"I thought you liked how I dressed?"

"I'm used to how you dress," he said. "An occasional skirt would be nice, though."

"Why do you want me to wear a skirt?"

"Because they're easy to reach under," Eliot said, waggling his eyebrows in a bad imitation of Groucho Marx.

"I'll consider it."

"By the way, I bought you a new shirt while I was out today."

"You did?"

"Don't get too excited," he said. "It's a lot like the last shirt I got you."

I loved that shirt. The second Mom had read "Jedi on the streets, Sith between the sheets" she'd almost had an aneurism. "What does it say?"

"You like *Star Trek*, too, right?"

"I do."

"Let's just say you're going to be happy."

"Can I wear it to dinner on Friday?"

"Only if you don't want me to go," Eliot said.

"Oh, come on," I said. "You love it when my mom freaks out."

"I like it when your mom freaks out on you," he corrected. "I don't like it when she freaks out on me. When you told her I bought the last shirt she had a fit. She didn't talk to me for an entire meal."

"That's a win, babe."

He smirked. "You're cute sometimes."

"I'm cute all the time."

"If you say so."

We turned our attention back to the game. After a few minutes I saw two of the cheerleaders moving in Eliot's direction. "Don't look now, but your fan club wants some autographs."

Eliot smiled lazily. "At least they're wearing skirts."

"Don't make me slap you."

"Excuse me," one of the girls said.

"Do you need something?" Eliot asked.

"We just have a question."

Eliot waited.

"Are you a model?" The perky blondes dissolved into hysterical giggles.

"I'm a pawnshop owner," Eliot said.

"Do you model in your own ads?"

"No."

"Have you ever considered modeling?" The taller girl was rubbing her hands together in anticipation.

"Because you totally could." The shorter girl seemed more cautious, but equally enthralled.

"Yeah, Eliot," I said. "You should be a model. We can take you to the spa and shave all your body hair tomorrow."

Eliot frowned.

"Oh, you have body hair? How old are you?"

"Not old," Eliot said.

"If you have body hair, you're old."

I smirked. "He's even got hair on his back," I said. "The AARP has started sending him magazines."

"Eww."

"Gross."

"I do not have hair on my back," Eliot said.

"Can we see?"

Eliot sent me a challenging look.

"Hey, if you want to take your shirt off, go nuts," I said. "It will be much more amusing than watching this game."

One of the girls shifted her attention to me. "Are you his sister?"

Eliot pursed his lips.

"No," I said.

"Cousin?"

"No."

"Mother?"

"Seriously, how old do I look?"

Eliot barked out a laugh. "You don't look old," he said. "You look ... seasoned."

"You're sleeping alone tonight."

"Speaking of sleeping alone, I have to run," he said, grabbing his coat.

"Are you really going to make me sleep alone tonight? You know I was just joking about the back hair thing, right?"

He shook his head. "I have to close the store. Don't worry, I'll be waiting for you when you get home."

I was relieved, despite myself. When did I become so needy?

Eliot got to his feet and gave me a quick kiss. "I'll see you in a few hours. Try not to get in any trouble without me."

A quick look at the two cheerleaders told me they were crushed. Once he was gone, the taller girl fixed me with a scorching look. "You shouldn't kiss your son that way."

I really do hate teenage girls.

"Thanks for coming in early," Fish said.

It was Wednesday, and he'd pulled me into a conference room so we could speak without prying ears.

"It's no problem," I said. "I'm bored most afternoons anyway. I've almost aced Lego Marvel, though. If only I could fly."

Fish knit his eyebrows together. "You're not a normal woman."

"Thank you."

He shook his head. "I looked through the copy of the file you left for me. It made for some interesting reading."

"That's putting it mildly."

"Do you think Haden has something to do with Kelsey Cooper's murder?"

"I think it's a definite possibility," I said.

"What's your next step?"

"I thought I was supposed to be a sports reporter," I challenged.

"Don't be cute," Fish said.

"I'll try," I deadpanned.

"So, what are you going to do?"

"I need to talk to some of the students," I said. "I need to find out whether Kelsey Cooper had any ties to the wrestling team."

"Do you think she was a guest at one of their parties?" Fish practically choked on the final word.

"She was gang raped," I said. "Erica was gang raped, too. That can't be a coincidence."

"Erica is a Richmond student, though," Fish said. "Kelsey was a Catholic North student."

"Maybe they're branching out to other schools because they don't want their party guests to compare notes," I suggested.

"That would be smart," Fish mused. "Do you think they're that smart?"

"They are if they've got an adult telling them what to do."

"Haden must realize that people will find out about his past."

"Maybe not," I said. "He thinks the file is sealed."

"Still, there had to be news stories about the case," Fish said.

"I don't understand how he was even hired," I said. "I thought schools performed background checks on their employees. A simple Google search would have told Catholic North that they were hiring a predator."

"Maybe they didn't care."

"Why would you think that?"

"He's a big name," Fish said. "Before he came to the school the only thing Catholic North was known for was losing. They wanted a winning team. Haden was their best shot."

"Would they seriously overlook the possibility of him being a rapist just to win?"

"I think you underestimate the power of prep sports," Fish said. "People take high school sports very seriously."

"Why?"

"Why do you take *Star Wars* so seriously?"

"Because it's awesome."

Fish cocked an eyebrow. "It's awesome to you," he said. "Most other people -- most normal people -- find it juvenile."

"Tell that to George Lucas and his piles of money."

"We have to focus on three important things," Fish said. "First, we have to find out whether the school knew that Haden was a rapist when he was hired. The second is what you suggested: We need to know whether Kelsey Cooper had ties to the wrestling team."

"What's the third?" I asked.

"We have to find out whether there were other victims," Fish said. "Once this story breaks, I think they're going to be coming out of the woodwork."

"That means I need to go to the Catholic North basketball game tonight," I said. "I need to get into that school."

"So, what's the problem?"

"Dave told Stanley that Haden doesn't like me," I said. "Stanley has barred me from events at Catholic North."

Fish pinched the bridge of his nose. "Don't worry. I'll take care of Stanley."

I brightened. "Can I watch?"

"Don't be cute."

ABSOLUTELY not," Stanley said, placing his hands on his hips obstinately. "She is not allowed at Catholic North."

"She's going," Fish said.

"I said no, and I'm the boss."

"You're the boss of sports," Fish corrected. "I'm the boss of the newsroom."

"Are you saying that you're overruling me?" Stanley voice began to rise to a female octave.

"I'm saying that she's going," Fish said.

"She can't go," Stanley said. "She's been banned from the property."

"Says who?"

"Says ... Haden."

"The wrestling coach does not have the power to ban her from the property," Fish said. "If she goes and they won't let her in we'll deal with it then."

"I don't want her to go," Stanley said.

"I don't care what you want."

"She's a menace," Stanley said. "She punched one of the Catholic North wrestlers in the nuts."

"I heard he had it coming," Fish said.

"He's a teenager."

"That doesn't mean he can manhandle a woman," Fish argued.

"She's not a woman," Stanley said. "She's a tyrant. Have you seen her boyfriend? He's big and ... mean."

Fish narrowed his eyes. "When did you meet her boyfriend?"

"He brought her ice cream one night last week."

"He sounds terrifying."

"He threatened to beat up Brick."

"Are we sure Brick didn't bait him?"

"Of course not," Stanley said. "Brick is even-tempered and easygoing."

"In what world?" I had been quiet for the bulk of the argument, enjoying the show while resting against the counter that housed the newsroom printer and police scanner, but I couldn't hold my tongue any longer.

"You just antagonize Brick," Stanley said. "You get off on it."

"That's a vulgar lie."

Fish shot me a look.

"Okay, it's a tiny lie," I corrected.

"She can't be a part of this department any longer," Stanley said.

"We made a deal," Fish said.

"I've faxed you fifty indiscretions," Stanley said. "You've found fault with each one."

"She did not cause global warming," Fish said.

"Her mouth sucks up all the oxygen in the room."

Fish sighed. "She's going."

"She's not going."

"She's going."

Stanley screwed his by now plum-purple face into an incredulous look. "I guess I'm just going to have to go above your head."

"Oh, and how are you going to do that?"

"I'M SICK to death of all the arguing in this department." MacDonald was irritated. Stanley had made a beeline for his office. Fish and I had been summoned a few minutes later.

"I handled the situation," Fish said. "I told Stanley that Avery is a part of sports and she is going to the Catholic North basketball game tonight."

"And I told Fred that Avery should be committed," Stanley said.

MacDonald focused on me. "Do you have anything to add to this conversation?"

"I really like your suit," I said, forcing a bright smile.

"She can't stay in sports," Stanley said. "Either fire her or send her back to news. She's not smart enough to be a sports reporter."

"Yes, all those little score boxes are just too much for me to add up," I said.

MacDonald's sigh was weary. "Does anyone want to tell me what's really going on?"

"What makes you think something is going on?" Fish asked.

"I've been watching Ms. Shaw's progression in sports," MacDonald said. "I've found it to be ... interesting."

"What did you like best, the time she punched the kid in the nuts or the time she interviewed the city councilman about his tax position at the basketball game?" Stanley asked.

"That was one quote," I protested.

"I liked the time she punched the kid in the nuts best," MacDonald said. "That's what tipped me off that Avery has spent a lot of time at Catholic North games."

Uh-oh. He was on to me.

"She's been to several wrestling meets and two basketball games," MacDonald continued. "That's pretty interesting, especially since Avery hasn't even been in sports for three full weeks yet."

"Do you believe in coincidences?" I asked.

"No," MacDonald said.

Fish ran his tongue over his teeth. I could see his mind working. He was going to tell MacDonald the truth. What a wuss. I couldn't let that happen.

"I'm just really interested in Catholic schools," I said. "I've been considering becoming a nun."

"Nuns can't swear," Stanley said.

"I can live with that."

"Nuns can't have sex," Stanley said.

"I'll quit cold turkey."

"Nuns can't wear *Star Wars* shirts," Stanley said. "Or shoes. Or hoodies. Or socks."

"It was just a whim," I said. "I'm not married to the idea." I shot Stanley a look. "I have underwear, too."

"See, she's incorrigible," Stanley said.

MacDonald slammed his hands on the table, ending the bickering. "Are you investigating Kelsey Cooper's death?"

Stanley was confused. "Who's Kelsey Cooper?"

"Read more than the sports section," MacDonald ordered.

"Of course I'm not investigating Kelsey Cooper's death," I lied. "I'm a sports reporter. I'm investigating sports."

MacDonald sighed as he sank down into his chair. "What have you found out?"

I exchanged a nervous look with Fish.

"Tell him," Fish said.

"Tell him what?" Stanley asked.

"Shut up, Stanley," MacDonald said. "I want to hear from Ms. Shaw now."

I swallowed hard, and then laid everything out for MacDonald. I held nothing back, and when I finished I waited for him to fire me.

"You managed to do all of this and cover games?"

"I really haven't covered that many games," I said.

"Still ... it's impressive."

"Avery is a good reporter," Fish said. "I told you that when you wanted to send her to sports. She's wasted there."

"What are you going to do at Catholic North tonight?" MacDonald asked.

This had to be a trick. "I'm going to cover a basketball game."

MacDonald steepled his fingers, staring intently at me. "What are you really going to be doing?"

"I'm going to be questioning students," I said. "I need to know whether Kelsey Cooper had ties to the wrestling team and I need to know whether anyone at the school knows about Haden's past."

"See, she can't go," Stanley said. "She's a terrible employee."

MacDonald made his decision swiftly. "She's going."

"What?"

"Yeah, what?" Now I was confused.

"Go to the game," MacDonald said. "Try not to draw attention to yourself. I know it will be hard, but try. Whatever information you find we'll use to our advantage. We'll have a meeting tomorrow and go over what you have."

"How is this happening?" Stanley asked nobody in particular.

"For now, you're still a sports reporter," MacDonald said.

"What happens if I break this story?" What? I have my eye on the prize.

"Then we'll talk," MacDonald said.

That was enough for me.

"I can't believe Stanley sent you," said Dave, who sat next to me in the bleachers, notebook in hand and disgruntled look on his face.

"Join the club," I said. "Did he tell you why he wanted you to come?"

"He said you would screw it up on your own."

He wasn't wrong. "Okay," I said, pushing up and moving around him. "You cover the game."

Dave tilted his head to the side. "What are you going to do?"

"I'm going to interview some of the students for color."

"Why?"

"Because ... it will make the story better," I said.

"What do you think they're going to tell you?"

"I think they're going to tell me that they wish the ball would go into the basket more."

"And you have to interview them to find that out?" Dave was suspicious.

"I like to be thorough."

I made my way to the concession area and bought a bottle of

water, ultimately leaning against the wall so I could watch the students interact without drawing too much attention to myself.

You can learn a lot watching teenagers talk to one another. The girls in the corner, for example, taught me that when you want a boy to notice you it's best to pretend they're not on even on the same planet. The boys they stared at when they thought no one was looking were giving me an education on male bonding. They were trying to one-up each other with ever-increasing boasts that couldn't be true.

"So, I was at the arcade in the mall the other day, and there was this girl who totally wanted to do it with me," one of them said.

"What did you do?" He had his buddies on the hook now.

"I told her we could do it in my car," the boy said. "Then she wanted her twin sister to join in."

"You dog! Did you do it?"

"Of course," the boy said, reeling them in. "I gave them both the rides of their lives. I was unstoppable. Now they're stalking me. I can never see them again."

"That's too bad. You could have totally taken them to the winter formal."

"Those are the breaks," he shrugged a little too nonchalantly.

I had to bite my lip to keep from laughing. Some things never change. The female conversations were worse.

"I can't believe that my dad actually wanted to drop me off in front of the school," a tall brunette said.

"Omigod! That's so embarrassing!"

"I told him that he had to drop me off at the corner like the other dads. He just doesn't get it. I'm popular for a reason, and that's because I don't have parents."

"It could be worse," a petite blonde in a letterman's jacket said. "You could be like Jen over there. She's slept with half the school and she's still tragically unpopular."

I jerked my head in the direction the girls were staring. I didn't like the predatory glint in their eyes. Another thing that never

changes is that teenage girls get off on torturing the weaker members
of the herd. I cut them off before they could close the distance and
box Jen in.

Jen was surprised to see me. "What are you doing here?"

"I'm covering the basketball game," I said. "I'm glad you're here. I
want to talk to you."

"I didn't do anything," Jen said. "I swear."

"I'm not accusing you of anything."

"So, Jen, who's your friend?" The girl in the letterman's jacket
eyed me with derision.

Jen lowered her head as the gaggle of gossips approached. "She's
not my friend, Shawna. She's just a woman looking for directions to
the bathroom."

"It's right there," Shawna said, pointing.

I fixed her with a look. "Thanks for the update."

"You can go now," Shawna said.

"I think I'll stay."

"You don't want your bladder to explode or something," Shawna
said. "Right, Tammy?"

"Right," one of the other girls chimed in. "That happened to a
friend of mine, and she died."

"What's her name?" I asked.

Tammy blanched. "Whose name?"

"The girl whose bladder exploded and died," I said. "I think that
would make a good story."

"Who are you?" Shawna asked.

"I'm Avery Shaw," I said. "I'm a reporter with The Monitor."

"Ooh, can I be in the paper?" Tammy asked.

"Have you done something to get in the paper?"

"I got a B on my history paper last week," Tammy said. "Oh, and
I got the last pair of Steve Madden boots at DSW. They were even on
sale."

That was impressive. "I'll have my secretary call you," I said.

"Great," Tammy said, her eyes bright.

I turned back to Jen. "Why don't we go outside and talk?"

"What do you have to talk to Jen about?" Shawna asked.

"None of your business," I said.

"Everything that goes on at this school is my business."

"Really? I heard that some of the cheerleaders were trying to change the school colors," I said. "They're leaning toward orange and pink."

Shawna's mouth dropped open. "Those colors clash."

"Well, you'd better go and take that up with the cheerleaders."

Shawna and Tammy exchanged panicked looks. "We have to nip this in the bud right now!"

Once they were gone, I focused on Jen. "Are you okay?"

"I'm fine," she said. "Why would you think I wasn't okay?"

The concession area was too busy, so I gestured to the hallway that led to the classroom section of the school. "Let's go down here. I want to talk to you."

"I didn't do anything," Jen repeated.

"You're not in trouble," I said. "I promise. I only want to talk to you in private."

Jen didn't look convinced, but followed me anyway. Once we were alone, I searched my mind for the best way to broach a sensitive topic. It had to be firm but unthreatening. "Did the wrestling team attack you?" That probably wasn't the best way to go.

The color drained from Jen's face. "Who told you that?"

"No one told me," I said carefully. "I just ... I know they've attacked someone else, and I saw the way some of the boys treated you the other night. It made me wonder whether something had happened to you."

She was panicked. "Are you the one who sent the sheriff here?"

I froze. Jake had said he was going to question students, but I'd forgotten to press him for an update. "He's concerned about the situation here."

"You did send him." Jen ran her hand through her hair. "Do you have any idea how embarrassing that was?"

"You shouldn't be embarrassed," I said. "Whatever happened, it wasn't your fault."

"How do you know anything happened?" Jen's lower lip was trembling.

"Because you look like a person with a lot on your mind," I said.

"I ... I can't talk about this," she said. "I promised myself I was going to pretend it never happened."

"I'm not sure that's possible," I said. "I don't know a lot about things like this, but I do know you can't move past it until you tell someone. You can tell me, and I can get you some help."

"I don't need help," Jen spat. "I need to be able to go back in time. Have you ever wanted to do that?"

"Sure," I replied. "For example, when George Lucas made the *Star Wars* prequels, I wanted to go back in time and show him the originals so he would remember what a good movie looked like."

Jen made an exasperated face.

"Or, when I was a teenager, there was a time when I got caught having sex with my boyfriend in the dugout on the baseball field," I said.

Jen's eyes widened. "What did you do?"

"I told my parents that my I'd accidentally slipped and the wind ripped off my clothes," I said. "I was grounded for a month."

"It's not the same thing," Jen wailed.

"I know," I said. "I just don't know when to stop talking sometimes. I often wish I could go back in time and muzzle myself."

A small smile tugged at the corners of Jen's mouth. "You're really bad at this, aren't you?"

"Horrible," I admitted. "I'll tell you what I am good at, though. I'm good at listening, and I'm good at getting payback. Why don't you tell me what happened?"

Jen was still wary, but she told me a story. It was long, and it was heartbreaking. When she was finished, I knew exactly what I had to do.

. . .

286 / AMANDA M. LEE

"ARE you sure you don't want me to come with you when you tell your parents?" I asked.

We were in the bathroom. Jen was splashing cold water on her face. She'd cried so hard her eyes were almost swollen shut. "I think I should do this on my own," she said.

"I think you've made the right decision," I said.

"I'm going to have to leave this school," Jen said.

"Why?"

"Once people know, there's no way I'll be able to hold my head up and walk down these hallways," Jen said. "You saw Shawna and Tammy. It's going to be even worse when the wrestling team is arrested. Right now I'm a slut. Tomorrow I'm going to be the tramp who took the only good thing this school has and ruined it."

"Jen, you can hold up your head wherever you go," I said. "You're the one who did the right thing."

"I only wish I could have confirmed that Coach Haden was there," Jen said. "I just can't remember."

"It's okay," I said. "If Haden is involved, his precious wrestlers will roll over on him when they try to cut a deal."

"Do you think they'll get away with it?" Jen looked terrified.

"I know the sheriff in these here parts," I said, going for levity. "He won't let that happen."

Jen smiled. It was weak, but it was there.

"I won't let it happen either," I said. "Trust me, I know a little something about drumming up public outrage. They're going to elect you county executive by the time I'm done."

"I still wish I could go back in time."

"You can't," I said, pulling open the bathroom door. "You have to keep moving forward."

Jen stepped into the hallway in front of me, pulling up short when three figures moved toward her. I pushed her to the side swiftly, taking her place and coming face to face with Alex.

"Well, well, well," he said. "Look who it is."

There were only three of them, and I wasn't sure that Alex's mute friends would fight if it came down to it. I knew I would.

"You really need to pick better friends, Jen," Alex said. "This one is going to get you hurt."

I didn't like his tone. "We're leaving," I said, grasping Jen's arm securely. "Get out of my way."

"I don't think you're going anywhere," Alex said. "There's someone who wants to talk to you."

"Well, I'm not in the mood to talk to Coach Haden," I said, giving Jen a little push to get her legs moving. "I'll give him a call tomorrow."

"I said you weren't going anywhere," Alex hissed. "And neither is Jen. It seems she's been talking out of turn. We need to shut her up."

I made my decision quickly. I pushed Jen. Hard. "Run!"

Jen did as she was told, sprinting down the hallway without a backward glance. As long as she made it back to a public area she'd be safe. That's all that mattered right now. When one of Alex's cohorts made a move to follow her I lifted my leg and smashed it into his knee as hard as I could. He was a big guy, but he screamed like a girl. He fell to the ground and rolled on his back, holding his knee as he caterwauled like a wounded animal. I was sad there was no one to put him out of his misery.

"Why did you do that?" Alex asked.

"Because I felt like it."

He grabbed my shoulders roughly. I moved to pull away, but Alex was too strong – and too determined. "You stupid bitch!" He slammed me into the wall, snapping my head into the painted cinder block. The pain was intense, but flared only for a second before the lights went out.

I have no idea how long I was out, but it was long enough for Alex and his friends to move me. When consciousness poked at the black expanse behind my eyelids, I realized I was lying on a hard floor. Cold was seeping into my body from the cement below, and it was painful. I wanted to sit up, but fought the urge.

I kept my eyes closed and listened. I heard voices, but they didn't sound as though they were in the same room. I took a peek and found myself alone in a gym locker room. I shifted my body in an attempt to alleviate the pressure on my hip, but the movement caused my head to throb with pain.

I swallowed the bubbling groan.

Think, I told myself. There were voices, but whomever they belonged to weren't watching me. I had to find a way out of the room. I glanced around, the invasion of light exacerbating the pounding at the back of my head. I gingerly ran my hand over the tender spot and felt a blue ribbon knot that wasn't finished growing. Great. I probably had a concussion. I hate these kids.

I focused on the room. A quick scan told me I was in trouble. The only way out was in the same direction from which the voices were emanating. Even without knowing how many people were out there, trying to escape that way wasn't an option. I was slow and fuzzy. I wouldn't be able to put up much of a fight.

I ran my hands over my jeans, sighing with relief when my fingers detected the telltale form of my cell phone. I dug it out and stared, focusing, at the screen for a moment. My brain didn't seem to be working as fast as it should. I knew I had brain damage.

My fingers worked slowly, but I managed to tap out a message to Eliot. I sent it, and then flicked the button that muted all incoming sounds. I shoved the phone back in my pocket as the voices grew louder.

"Wakey, wakey," said Alex, stepping into the room and clapping his hands several times. "I'm so glad you decided to join us. It will be a lot more fun if you know what's happening to you."

I kept my face impassive ... mostly because it hurt to make an expression. "You have no idea what you've done, do you?"

"I know exactly what I've done," Alex said. "I've solved a problem." He knelt next to me. "You were the problem."

"I'm going to be even more of a problem now," I said.

"How do you figure that?"

"Because people know I'm here."

Alex, still kneeling, leaned back a bit. "What people? Dave Stewart? Will he even miss you?"

"Not just Dave," I said.

"Jen? People are out looking for her right now," Alex said. "She won't get far."

"Don't you dare even think about touching her," I snapped, rubbing my head when my voice kicked my headache into overdrive. Now I know how Eliot feels when I go on a diatribe during Sports Center.

"Oh, I'm going to touch her," Alex said. "I'm going to touch her until she can't stop screaming."

I lashed out to kick him, but he expected it and shifted away. "I'm wise to your bag of tricks, girlie," he said. "You won't catch me off guard again."

I smacked him across the face, taking delight in his surprise. "Yeah, your reflexes are great."

Alex made a move toward me, but he stopped with the arrival of another figure. I knew an adult was leading the kids; the one standing there staring at me came as a surprise, though.

"Fred Springer," I said, my voice catching as I tried to put the pieces of a shifting puzzle together.

"Ms. Shaw," Springer said, stepping into the room. "I'm so happy to see you again."

"I wish I could say the same," I said. "Shouldn't you be coaching the game?"

"I told you already, I don't need to be there for everything," Springer said. "Unfortunately, the assistant coaches had to take over tonight when an urgent family situation came up."

"That's the lie he came up with when I told him that I caught you and Jen together," Alex said, bursting with pride.

"Well, it's a great one," I said. "As long as the cameras in the parking lot don't catch him leaving the school between now and when classes resume tomorrow morning, there shouldn't be a problem."

Alex frowned. "Coach Springer is a genius," he said. "I'm sure he's already thought about that."

A quick look at Springer told me he hadn't. "Yeah, he's a real brain trust."

"That will be quite enough of that, Ms. Shaw," Springer said. "I know you're used to being in charge, but you're in an ... awkward ... situation here."

"Awkward? I was thinking it was more criminal than awkward," I said.

"Criminal? We found your body in the locker room," Springer said. "Unfortunately, you were already dead. It was really quite the tragedy. It's too bad that the cameras didn't capture the act itself, but they've been down for maintenance for the past month. Someone vandalized them, and the school doesn't have the money to repair them. In any case, I'm sure you'll be remembered as a hero in certain circles. I can see the headlines now."

"Except Jen was with me when your little minions slammed me into a wall," I said. "That's cheating, by the way."

"Jen won't be a problem after tonight," Springer said. "My boys are on it."

"Your boys? Aren't your boys the basketball players?"

"The basketball team sucks," Springer replied. "Even a coach with my obvious talent can do nothing for them."

"And you needed boys who could convince girls to go to private parties," I said. "The losing basketball team wasn't capable, but a winning wrestling team was."

"You're smarter than you look."

That wasn't the first time I'd heard that. I was hoping it wouldn't be the last. "How did you approach them? Was your opening line, 'Anyone want to gang rape somebody?'"

Springer smirked. "Most of the girls at these parties don't even know anything has happened," he said. "How can there be a crime if nobody knows anything occurred?"

"They all know something happened," I said. "They just don't know what. They also know they were alone, and they think no one would believe them. You picked vulnerable girls on purpose. There's a reason you didn't pick the popular girls. You knew they would scream until someone listened. You went for the shy girls on purpose."

"You do have a wild imagination, Ms. Shaw," Springer said. "Just what is it that you think you know?"

"I know quite a bit," I said. "I know, for example, that the Richmond girl you raped and brutalized has already filed a complaint with the sheriff's department."

Springer's eyes shifted to Alex. "And how do you know that?"

"I was with her when she did it," I said. "I also know that Jen is going to tell someone what happened in the hallway tonight. If you haven't caught her yet, you're not going to. She's smarter than you give her credit for."

"We'll deal with Jen," Springer said. "The whole school knows she's a slut."

"Because your wrestlers spread the rumor after they raped her," I said.

"Tell a story often enough and it becomes the truth," Springer said.

"You're sick," I said.

"I guess you'll find out, won't you?"

"I'll pass."

"Oh, that's not an option for you," Springer said. "You have to be found in exactly the same condition that Kelsey Cooper was found in."

My blood ran cold. "Why did you kill her?"

"Kelsey was a mistake from the beginning," Springer explained. "We never should have invited her. She was absolutely no fun."

"She was a wet rag," Alex agreed.

I narrowed my eyes. "You're going to be really popular in prison, Alex," I said. "You've got prison bitch written all over you, and your cellmate is going to love it when he finds out you were a wrestler. I bet he gets you in some really interesting positions."

"Shut up!"

"Stop antagonizing him, Ms. Shaw," Springer said. "We need you in one piece until the school empties out. If Alex kills you now he'll ruin the night for the rest of us."

"Oh, and we don't want that," I said.

"Of course we don't," Springer said. "You're in for quite the party."

I fought the dryness in my mouth and throat. "You still didn't explain to me why you killed Kelsey Cooper."

"She woke up during the party," Springer said. "I really blame myself. We were experimenting with dosages. It's not very exhilarating when they just lay there. I was hoping to get some sort of reaction from her. I didn't expect her to wake up.

"Then she started screaming," he continued. "Everyone was so surprised they scattered. When she ran, I had to give chase. I hoped we could convince her that she'd imagined everything, but it wasn't really an option.

"She tried to escape onto the football field," he said. "That was her first mistake. She should have stayed in the residential area. She thought she would find salvation at the school. Unfortunately, it was empty and locked."

"So we killed her," Alex said, grinning. "It was fun."

"We didn't kill her," Springer corrected. "We solved a problem."

"Right," Alex said, nodding. "I forgot."

Something wasn't adding up. I had been convinced Haden was involved. "What about Haden?"

"What about him?" Alex asked. "He's a great coach."

"He was a suspect in a string of rapes when he was at Michigan State," I said. "I was certain he was involved in this."

"That's what you're supposed to think," Springer said, jabbing a forefinger in the air. "I went to great pains to make sure that Haden would be the prime suspect. When he started winning and getting all those accolades it really rubbed me the wrong way. When I did a little searching, though, I found out some interesting things about our Coach Haden, things I could use to my advantage."

"How did you go to great pains?"

"If any of the girls did talk Haden would be the obvious prime suspect, given his past," Springer said. "Well, that and the steroids he's been supplying to his team."

I cocked my head to the side. "Haden is supplying his team with steroids?"

"Why do you think they suddenly started winning?" Springer asked. "It's not because they're great athletes."

Click! I was finally seeing the whole picture. "You found out Haden was supplying the kids with steroids," I said. "You decided to use that to your advantage. You knew the kids didn't want to start losing again, and that's why you approached them. They all had something to lose.

"When you started to worry about only inviting girls from Catholic North to the parties, you branched out," I continued. "That's how you found Erica. By then the kids were already in too deep. Killing Kelsey was probably a rude awakening for some of them, but they didn't have any options. You didn't give them any options.

"People have been calling in tips to the sheriff's department about the steroids," I said. "Some have even tipped off the newspaper. You're the one tipping everyone off. You like to start rumors, and you used the rumor machine at this school to further your agenda."

"That's not true," Alex shouted, looking to Springer. "Why would he do that?"

"Because he knows he's going to have to close up shop," I said. "He knows the parties can't continue, so he's serving Haden up on a silver platter. Once Haden is arrested, you're going to find that your brotherhood of boy rapists is closed for good."

Alex turned to Springer, pleading. "That's not true! Tell her that's not true!"

"Of course it's not true," Springer said, but his eyes said something else.

"The noose is tightening, Alex," I said. "And your precious coach isn't going to think twice about sacrificing you right along with Haden."

"You have no idea what you're talking about," Alex spat.

"She's just delaying," Springer said, his tone soothing. "Don't let her get to you."

"I want to get to her," Alex said. "I want to ... ." He mimed a sexual act.

"You want to make me do interpretive dance?"

"Shut your mouth!" Alex was enraged, his fists clenched.

The sound of sirens caused both Alex and Springer to startle.

"What's that?" Alex asked.

Springer fixed me with a look. "What did you do?"

I pulled my phone from my pocket. "Did I forget to mention I texted for help? You'd better start running now."

"**M**ove!"

Alex and Springer handled my information well. They screamed at each other for thirty seconds, and then called for Alex's cohorts in the other room. Now the four of them were trying to navigate me through the dark hallways of the school.

I knew Jake and Eliot were on the way. I hoped that Springer wouldn't sacrifice me for the hell of it along the way.

"What are we going to do?" Alex asked.

"We're going to go out the back exit," Springer said. "We're going to load Ms. Shaw into your truck, and then we're going to regroup at my house. The windows of your Expedition are tinted. Why do you think I wanted to borrow your vehicle when I tried to run her off the road? We can still get out of this."

"He's lying to you, Alex," I said. "He borrowed your Expedition so you would be blamed if someone managed to read the license plate. He's using you."

"Shut up!" Springer grabbed the back of my hoodie and shook me. My head still hurt, but watching Springer unravel was contributing to a rapid recovery.

"What are you going to do, Fred? Jake has this place surrounded. You'd be better off surrendering. If my boyfriend catches you, he's going to kill you."

"Boyfriend? What man could put up with you?"

"This one." Eliot stepped around the corner we approached and slammed his fist into one of the teen's faces. The kid hit the ground hard, and he didn't so much as twitch.

The other boy, the one who limped from my kick, seemed unsure as he looked Eliot up and down. "I'm not afraid of you," he said, the words bolder than his tone.

Eliot didn't miss a beat as he punched the boy, knocking him to the side. That left only Alex and Springer.

"I'd like you to unhand my girlfriend," Eliot said, his voice calm. Springer still had a firm hold on me, so Eliot didn't make any sudden moves.

"How can you date her? She's mouthy and mean." Alex was flummoxed, and terrified.

"That's how I like my women," Eliot said. "Now hand her over to me."

"I don't think so," Springer said, tightening his grip on my neck and making me yelp.

Eliot's voice went much lower. "If you hurt her, I will kill you."

"I don't have a lot of options here, Mr. ... ?"

"Kane," I supplied helpfully.

"Mr. Kane, as you can see, you're blocking our escape," Springer said. "How about we make a deal?"

Eliot said nothing.

"If you let us go, I promise to release Ms. Shaw once we get to safety," Springer offered.

"How about you just hand her over to me right now and I promise not to beat you to death," Eliot countered.

"Mr. Kane," Springer said, trying a different tactic. "You're outnumbered here. There are two of us and only one of you."

Eliot shot out his arm, punching Alex in the face. The teen didn't lose consciousness, but he stumbled into the nearby lockers as he covered his nose and screamed.

"Now there are just the two of us," Eliot said.

Springer yanked my hair viciously. "I can still kill her, Mr. Kane."

"If you don't take your hands off her right now, I'm going to lose my temper."

"You don't want to see that," I said. "He turns into the Hulk."

"Shut your mouth," Springer screamed, shaking me again. "Why can't you just shut your mouth for five seconds?"

"Because it's not in her nature."

I recognized the new voice before Springer turned. Judging from the direction of his voice, Jake was in the darkened hallway somewhere behind us.

"Where did you come from?" Springer was unraveling, and fast.

"We got a call from a student," Jake said. "It seems half the wrestling team was chasing her. When we calmed her down, she told me an interesting story about a blond reporter holding off three assholes so she could get away. I had a feeling I knew the reporter."

"And, let me guess, you want her, too?"

"I want you to hand her over to Eliot very slowly," Jake said.

"And if I don't?"

"Then I'm going to look the other way while he beats you to death," Jake said. "It's too bad it's so dark in here."

Springer's fingernails dug tighter into my neck. "I want to make a deal."

"What deal?" Jake asked.

"I want to trade information," he said. "I happen to know that Luke Haden is supplying the wrestlers with steroids."

"And you used that information to form your own little gang-raping tribunal," I snapped.

Springer shook me again.

"Stop talking, Avery," Jake said.

"Don't expect a miracle," came Derrick's voice from somewhere near Jake, but moving. "She can't keep quiet. It's physically impossible for her."

"Way to kick me when I'm down," I sputtered.

"I'm going to kick you in the teeth if you don't shut up," Derrick said. I could see his shape now as he knelt near the first boy Eliot had hit. "He seems like he's out."

"That one over there is still awake," I said, pointing to Alex. "And I want him put in a cell with a really big rapist."

"I'll see what I can do," Jake said, his tone even.

"I'm innocent! That bitch is a liar!"

"Don't make me hit you again," Eliot warned.

"Can we all focus on me?" Springer seethed. "I'm the one in charge here."

I'd had enough. I was starting to get bored, and my head hurt. I leaned to my left, just enough to catch Springer off guard, and when he tried to overcompensate and draw me back I swiveled – and did the one thing that came naturally.

Springer grabbed his crotch, screaming as he dropped to his knees.

"That really never gets old," I said.

Eliot was on me, his arms pulling me tight to his chest as Jake and Derrick rushed forward to take Springer into custody.

"Are you okay?"

"They threw me into a wall and I was knocked out for a while," I said.

Eliot ran his hand tenderly over the back of my head. "You've got a big bump. Do you have a concussion?"

"I don't think so," I said. "I think I might have brain damage, though."

"I probably won't be able to tell the difference," Eliot said, giving me another hug.

"You definitely won't," Derrick said, yanking Alex to his feet and pushing him toward one of the other deputies now crowding the hall, beams from their flashlights bouncing off the walls of lockers. "Book him." He glanced at me. "And put him in a cell with Big Burt."

"Oh, no!" Alex screamed as the deputies dragged him down the hallway.

"There's not really a Big Burt, is there?"

"No," Derrick conceded. "Alex doesn't know that, though. It will be fun to watch him squirm."

Jake had Springer on his feet and cuffed, but the coach was having trouble staying upright.

"Wait," I said, pulling away from Eliot. "There's one more thing I want to do."

"You can't kick him in the nuts again," Jake said.

"Please? He admitted to killing Kelsey Cooper. He admitted to raping other girls. His only complaint is that they weren't fun."

Jake cocked an eyebrow.

"He admitted to running me off the road, and he was going to let his team rape me. Then he was going to kill me and dump me where he dumped Kelsey Cooper," I said.

Jake sighed. "Fine. Everyone turn around." He paused long enough to point at me. "Consider this your Christmas gift, missy."

"WELL, you don't have a concussion."

The paramedic flashed the light in my eyes once more for good measure.

"Do I have brain damage?"

"No more than you had before," Eliot said, rubbing my shoulders. He hadn't left my side, even when I'd insisted that ice cream would make me feel better. He was hovering, and it was kind of cute.

Jake had been busy for the past hour, although he'd stopped by several times to update us. All of the Catholic North wrestlers were accounted for, and they'd been taken into custody. Luke Haden had been found at home. He'd admitted to supplying his wrestlers with steroids – although he denied any knowledge of the rapes. Jake was still holding him for questioning. He was hoping to get him to admit to murdering Lauren Miller but that seemed a long shot.

Jen had been reunited with her parents, and Jake had given them a quiet room inside of the school to talk. I hadn't seen her since we split up when Alex and his goons cornered us, but I hoped she was okay. Eliot said we could check on her before we left.

The crowd outside the school was rapidly growing, and included reporters from various news outlets and television stations. Jake insisted they stay back at the road. I had a feeling that was to save me from becoming the news instead of reporting it -- again.

"You have to file your story tonight," Derrick said. "Jake agreed to hold them off only until tomorrow."

"Thanks."

"You're filing a story tonight?" Eliot was incensed.

"You bet she is." MacDonald appeared out of the gloom. "That's what a news reporter does."

I shifted my gaze to the approaching man. He looked out of place in his expensive suit. "What are you doing here?"

"Fish called me with an update," MacDonald said. "I figured I should probably come here and deal with the fallout."

"What fallout?"

"You've stepped in it again," MacDonald said.

"Hey, wait just a minute," Eliot said. "She protected a young girl and unearthed a huge story tonight. What more do you want from her?"

MacDonald looked Eliot up and down dubiously. "Who are you?"

"I'm her boyfriend."

"My condolences," MacDonald said, smiling. "Ms. Shaw, I have an apology to make. When Commissioner Ludington told me you were rude, crude and obnoxious I shouldn't have listened to him."

"I told you he lies," I said.

"Oh, no, you're all of those things," MacDonald said. "You're also a good reporter. I think taking you away from the job you excel at was a mistake, and I'm not saying that just because Stanley has threatened to kill himself if you return to sports."

I smirked. "So, I'm a news reporter again?"

"You are," MacDonald said.

A memory tugged at my mind. "Wait a second," I said. I knew I was jeopardizing my future at The Monitor, but I had to know one more thing. "Are you having an affair with Maria Ludington?"

MacDonald's shoulders stiffened. "Excuse me?"

"I know she's been going to your house," I said. "I heard you and Maria talking about keeping a secret from Tad."

"You were spying on me?"

"No," I said. "I just got lost while I was selling Girl Scout cookies."

MacDonald sighed. "Not that you deserve an explanation, but Maria is my daughter."

"What?"

"Maria is my daughter," MacDonald said.

"That means ... eww ... Tad is your son-in-law."

"Not for long," MacDonald said. "In fact, Maria is filing paper-work to end her marriage tomorrow morning. That's what you heard us discussing."

"Oh," I said. I was inexplicably disappointed.

"Yes, 'oh,'" MacDonald said. "I can't believe you spied on me."

"I didn't spy," I said. "I am terrified of your pet rat, though."

"I don't have a pet rat."

"I told you that was a dog," Eliot said.

"Ms. Shaw, in the future, I would appreciate it if you stayed off of my property," MacDonald said.

"I will," I promised.

"If you don't, I'm going to put you in the features department," he said.

I felt the color draining from my face at the thought of being forced to write articles about the latest trend in bridal dresses.

"There will be nothing but hundredth birthday parties and

touch-feely human interest stories in your future if you try anything like this again," MacDonald said. "And if that doesn't work, I'll put you on the religion beat. I hear you're very popular with the nuns in this county."

"Oh, make her do that," Derrick said. "Avery has a way with nuns. They all like to hit her."

"Shut up," I grumbled.

MacDonald started to move away, but he paused before he'd gone too far. "Oh, and Ms. Shaw?"

"Yeah?"

"If you were to refocus your attentions on my former son-in-law once this story dies down, you wouldn't hear any complaints from me."

I rested my head against Eliot's shoulder and gave MacDonald a wide smile. "Consider it done."

"**P**ut your legs down. I can't see the television."

I rolled my eyes, but I did as Eliot demanded. After a late night at the newspaper – while he'd sat in a chair behind me and watched me work for hours so I had no chance of escaping and finding more trouble – we were spending the day in bed.

Marvin was handling the follow-up, even though it was killing me to hand the story off. Eliot hadn't given me a choice. Either I willingly handed the story over to Marvin or he tied me to the bed. Those were my only options.

"I thought you hated soap operas," I said.

"I do," Eliot said. "I think they're stupid."

"So why are we watching *General Hospital*?"

"Because if we watch Sports Center you'll drive me crazy," Eliot said. "Plus, I just have to know if that guy ever finds his shirt."

"That's Nathan," I said. "He doesn't need a shirt. He's the rare cop who can solve crimes shirtless."

"I've never seen him solve a crime."

"That's because he's too busy getting busy," I said.

"Soaps make absolutely no sense," Eliot grumbled.

"And yet you watch them with me. What does that say about you?"

"That I'm ... really fond of you," Eliot said.

"That's good to know," I said, snuggling in closer to him. While a day in bed wouldn't have been my personal choice, it did offer some nice perks.

My cell phone, which was resting on the nightstand, dinged with an incoming text message. I reached for it before Eliot could stop me.

"You're not supposed to be working," Eliot said. "You're off until Monday. You need to recuperate."

"It's not work," I said, wrinkling my nose.

"What is it?" Eliot looked over my shoulder.

"It's a photo of Lexie and her new employee," I said, grinning.

"Is that Erica?"

I nodded.

"I hope Erica is a good influence on Lexie," Eliot said.

"Lexie might be a good influence on Erica," I countered.

"Not unless Erica needs to learn how to weigh pot."

I smacked his arm. "Lexie is working hard," I said. "You should give her some credit."

"As long as she doesn't drag you into her crap I'm willing to give her tons of credit," Eliot said.

I shifted to my side so I could look him over more closely. His hair was tousled and his jaw was speckled with stubble. He looked even more appealing than usual.

"You know, I really ... like you." That wasn't what I initially envisioned myself saying, but for some reason I couldn't find the right words.

Eliot glanced down at me. "I really like you, too."

"Does that mean you're going to cook for me tonight?"

"It does."

"What are you going to make?"

Eliot rolled on top of me. "Whatever you want." He gave me a kiss. "The hero gets whatever she wants today."

"I want to go to work."

Eliot narrowed his eyes. "Fine. The hero gets whatever I want today."

"And what do you want?"

"I want to see if I can give shirtless Nathan a run for his money."

"Okay," I said. "He doesn't have a hairy back, though."

"Stop saying that," Eliot said. "It's not funny, and completely untrue."

"Hey, I have to scare these young whippersnappers away any way I can," I said. "One of them may turn your head and then I'll be out on my ass."

Eliot tickled my ribs. "Oh, I can't deal with the young ones," he said. "I prefer my women old and mouthy."

"I am not old."

Eliot covered my open mouth with his. Instead of putting up a fight, I gave in. There were still words to say, plans to make and a job to settle back into – but those were all problems for another day. Today I was just going to lay in bed and ... play ... because all was right in my world.

"Let's watch *Star Wars*," I suggested once Eliot and I had separated.

"Fine," he said. "Just know, I'm not pretending to be Han Solo later. If you want me to role play, then I'm going to be Aragorn."

"That's fine," I said. "Just be prepared to show me your sword."

"I'm always prepared to show you my sword."

Yup, everything in my world was perfect today. Next week, though? Tad Ludington should probably start running now.

Made in the USA
Coppell, TX
12 March 2025

47003542R00184